yer

Paul Doherty was born in Middlesbrough in 1946. He was admitted to Liverpool University where he gained a First Class Honours Degree in History and won a state scholarship to Exeter College, Oxford. While there he his wife, Carla.

aul worked in Ascot, Newark and Crawley, before be g appointed as Headmaster to Trinity Catholic High hool, Essex, in 1981. The school has been described one of the leading comprehensives in the U.K. and s been awarded 'Outstanding' in four consecutive OFS TED inspections. All seven of Paul and Carla's children e been educated at Trinity.

 l has written over 100 books and has published a series utstanding historical mysteries set in the Middle Ages, ssical Greece, Ancient Egypt and elsewhere. His books h e been translated into more than twenty languages.

Also by Paul Doherty

The Brother Athelstan Mysteries

PAUL DOHERTY

The House of the Red Slayer

CANELO

First published in Great Britain in 1992 by Headline Book Publishing, a division of Hodder Headline PLC

This edition published in the United Kingdom in 2021 by

Canelo
31 Helen Road
Oxford OX2 0DF
United Kingdom

A CIP catalogue record for this book is available from the British Library.

Print ISBN 978 1 80032 564 7
Ebook ISBN 978 1 78863 889 0

First published in 1992 under the pseudonym of Paul Harding.

Look for more great books at www.canelo.co

Printed and bound in Great Britain by Clays Ltd, Elcograf S.p.A.

1

To Jeffrey Norwood of Tower Books, Chico, California, USA.
A good and loyal friend.

Prologue

June 1362

Murder had been planned, foul and bloody, by a soul as dark as midnight. Only the searing sun and the glassy, wind-free waves of the Middle Sea would bear silent witness to Murder's impending approach.

The day had started hot and by noon the heat hung like a blanket around the three-master-carrack out of Famagusta in Cyprus. The sails drooped limp, the pitch and tar melted between the mildewed planks. On board, the passengers – pilgrims, merchants, travellers and tinkers – sheltered in whatever shade they could find. Some told their rosary beads; others, their red-rimmed eyes shaded against the sunlight, searched the skies for the faintest whisper of wind. The decks of the *Saint Mark* were hot to the touch; even the crew hid from the glare and heat of the sun. A look-out dozed high in the cross yard. Above his head a silver St Christopher medal nailed to the mast caught the dazzling sunlight and sent it back like a prayer for shade and a strong, cooling breeze.

Beneath the look-out, at the foot of the mast, dozed a knight clad in a white linen shirt and sweat-stained hose pushed into leather boots, which he moved restlessly. The knight wiped the sweat from his brow and scratched his black beard which ran from ear to ear. He looked towards a young boy, sheltering in the shadows of the bulwarks, who gazed in round-eyed wonderment at the armour piled there: mailed shirt, gauntlets, breastplate and hauberk. What caught the boy's attention was the livery of white cotton surcoat with a crude but huge red cross painted in the middle. The boy peered at the knight, his hands going out to touch the wire-coiled handle of the great, two-edged sword.

'Touch it, boy,' the knight murmured, white teeth flashing in his sunburned face. 'Go on, touch it if you want.'

The boy did so, his face wreathed in smiles.

'You want to be a knight, boy?'

'Yes, sir, a crusader though I am an orphan now,' the child replied seriously.

The knight grinned but his face grew sombre when he glanced at the poop. He had seen the helmsman call the captain; now both were staring out to sea. The captain looked anxious. Doffing his great, broad-brimmed hat, he stamped the deck and the knight heard his murmured curses. Above him the look-out suddenly yelled: 'I see ships, no sails, fast approaching!'

His cry roused the vessel. Boats with no sails skimming across the sea could only be a Moorish corsair. The people on the deck stirred, children cried, men and women shouted. There was a patter of hardened feet on ladders as both soldiers and sailors roused themselves. The chorus of groans grew louder.

'No sails!' a soldier cried. 'They must be galleys!'

The clamour stilled as fear of death replaced resentment against the hot searing rays of the sun. The day would die, darkness would come and the air would cool, but the green-bannered, rakish-oared galleys of the corsairs would not disappear. They slunk round the Greek Islands like ravenous wolves and, if they closed, there would be no escape.

Genoese crossbowmen began to appear, heads covered in white woollen scarves, their huge arbalests bobbing on their backs; behind them ran boys with quivers full of jagged-edged bolts.

'One galley!' the look-out screamed. 'No, two! No, four! Bearing north by north-east!'

Sailors, passengers and soldiers ran to the rails, making the ship dip like a hawk.

'Back to your posts!' The puce-faced captain scampered down the ladder of the poop. 'Boson!' he roared. 'Armaments out! Crossbowmen to the poop!'

Again there was a rush; huge buckets of seawater were quickly placed round the deck alongside barrels of hard grey sand. Sailors and soldiers roared oaths at the frightened passengers, ordering them down into the stinking, fetid darkness below decks. The knight stirred as the captain approached.

'Galleys,' the seaman murmured. 'Lord help us – so many!' He looked up at the blue sky. 'We cannot escape. One might not attack, but four...'

'Will you fight?' the knight asked.

The captain spread his hands. 'They may not challenge us,' he replied despairingly. 'They could stand off and just take a levy.'

The knight nodded. He knew the sailor was lying. He turned to the small boy now sidling up beside him.

'A good day to die,' the knight whispered. 'Help me arm.'

The lad ran to the bulwarks and staggered back under the load of the heavy mailed shirt. The knight looked around as he dressed for battle. The crew had done everything they could. Now there was a deathly hush, broken only by the slap of water against the ship's sides and the growing murmur from the approaching, dark-shaped galleys.

'Bearers of death,' the knight murmured.

The captain heard him and spun round. 'Why so many?' he asked, perplexed. 'It's as if they knew we were here.'

The knight struggled into the mailed shirt and clasped the leather sword belt around his waist. 'Your cargo?'

The captain shrugged. 'Passengers,' he replied. 'Barrels of fruit, some pipes of wine, a few ells of cloth.'

'No treasure?'

The captain sneered and went back to search the sky for a breath of wind but the golden dazzle of the sun only mocked his anxious scrutiny. The knight studied the galleys, long, black and hawkish. On their decks he glimpsed the massed troops in their yellow cotton robes and white turbans. He stiffened and narrowed his eyes.

'Janissaries!'

The boy looked up. 'What, Master?'

'By the Bones!' the knight replied. 'What are elite troops, the cream of the Muslim Horde, doing packed in galleys hunting a ship which bears nothing but wine and fruit?'

The boy looked up mutely and the knight patted his head.

'Stay with me, lad,' he whispered. 'Stay beside me, and if I fall, show no fear. It's your best chance of life.'

The galleys swept in and the knight smelt the foul stench from the hundreds of sweating slaves who manned the oars. He heard the Moorish captain's commands, the

4

harsh Arabic syllables carrying clear across the water. The oars flashed up, white and dripping, like hundreds of spears as the galleys surrounded the becalmed ship. One took up position on the stem, another on the prow, with a third and fourth huge galley to either side. The captain of the *Saint Mark* wiped his sweating face with the cuff of his jerkin.

'They might not attack,' he whispered. He turned and the knight saw the relief in his eyes. 'They wish to talk.'

Agile as a monkey, the captain scrambled back on to the poop. The galley to starboard moved closer and the knight saw the brilliant liveries of a group of Moorish officers. One of these climbed on to the side of the galley.

'You are the *Saint Mark* from Famagusta?' he shouted.

'Yes,' the captain answered. 'We carry nothing but passengers and dried fruit. There is a truce,' he pleaded. 'Your Caliph has sworn oaths.'

The Moorish officer clasped two of the upraised oars to steady himself.

'You lie!' he screamed back. 'You carry treasure – treasure plundered from our Caliph! Hand it over, and let us search your ship for the culprit who stole it.'

'We have no treasure,' the captain whined back.

The Moorish officer jumped down. One beringed hand sliced the air, a guttural order was issued. The captain of the *Saint Mark* turned and looked despairingly at the knight and, as he did so, both he and the helmsman dropped under the hail of arrows which poured in from the galleys. The knight smiled, closed the visor of his helmet and pulled the young boy closer beside him. He grasped his great two-edged sword and placed his back against the mast.

'Yes,' he whispered, 'it's a good day to die.'

The kettledrums in the galleys beat out the glamour of war, cymbals clashed, gongs sounded. The Genoese archers on the merchantman did their best but the galleys closed in and the yellow-robed, drug-emboldened Janissaries poured across the decks of the *Saint Mark*. Here and there, pilgrims and merchants fought and died in small groups. Individuals tried to escape into the darkness below; the Janissaries followed and the blood poured like water through the tar-edged planks of the ship. But the real struggle swirled around the mast where the knight stood, feet planted slightly apart. His great sword scythed the air until the gore swilled ankle-deep, causing further assailants to slip and slide as they tried to close for the kill. Beside the knight, the young boy, his face alive with the excitement of battle, screamed encouragement but no man could resist such a force forever. Soon the fighting died and the galleys drew off, their sterns packed with prisoners and plunder. The *Saint Mark*, fire licking at its timbers, drifted gently on a strengthening breeze until it became one blazing funeral pyre. When darkness fell, it had sunk. Here and there a body still bobbed on the surface, the only trace that Murder had passed that way.

December 1377

A murderously cold wind swept the snow across London with dagger-like gusts of ice and hail. At first it fell in a few white flakes, then thick and heavy, like God's grace pouring from heaven to cover the wounds of that sombre city. The chroniclers in the monasteries on the outskirts of London tried to warm their cold fingers as they squatted in freezing carrels, writing that the terrible weather was God's judgment on the city.

The snow continued to fall, God's judgment or not, to carpet the stinking streets, and the mounds of shit in the lay stalls near the Thames where river pirates, hanging from the low scaffolds, turned hard and black as the river water froze. In savagely cold December, the heavy frost slipped into the city like an assassin to slay the beggars huddled in their rags. The lepers crouching in their filth outside Smithfield cried and moaned as the frost bit their open wounds. Aged, raddled whores were found frosty-faced, cold and dead on the corner of Cock Lane. The streets were empty, and even the rats could not forage; the huge piles of refuse and the open sewers which ran down the middle of every street, usually full and wet with human slime, froze to rock-hard ice.

The blizzards hid the sky and made the nights as black as hell. No God-fearing soul went abroad, especially in Petty Wales and East Smithfield, the area around the Great Tower whose snow-capped turrets thrust defiantly up into the dark night sky. Guards on the ice-covered parapets of the fortress gave up their watch and crouched behind the walls. No sentry stood near the portcullis because the locks and chains had frozen iron hard, and who could open them?

Yet even on a balmy summer's day, the Tower would be avoided. Old hags whispered that the place was the devil's work, and the black ravens, which swooped around its grim turrets, flocks of devils seeking human souls. The crones claimed human blood had been mixed in the mortar of its walls and that beneath its rocky foundations lay the skeletons of human sacrifices murdered by the great Caesar when he first built the fortress. Others, the few who could read, dismissed such stories as nonsense: the Tower and its great White Keep had been built by William the Conqueror to overawe London, and they scoffed at stories told to frighten the children.

Nevertheless, the old hags were correct: the Tower had its macabre secrets. Beneath one of its walls ran cold, green-slimed passageways. Torches, old and blackening, hung listlessly from sconces rusting on the walls. No one had been down there for years, a mysterious warren of tunnels even the soldiers never frequented. Three dungeons were there but only two doors and in the central cell, a square black box of a room, sprawled a decaying skeleton. There was no witness to what it had been when the flesh hung plump on the bones and the blood ran like hot wine through heart and brain. The skeleton was yellowing now; a rat scurried through the rib cage and poked fruitlessly at the empty eye-sockets before scampering along the bony arm which rested against one wall, just beneath the crudely drawn figure of a three-master ship.

The assassin hiding in the shadows on the frozen parapet of the great Bell Tower knew nothing of such secret places, though he realized the Tower held great mysteries. He drew deeper into his cloak.

'"The time has come",' he muttered to himself, quoting the Gospels, '"when all those things hidden in the dark shall be revealed in the light of day".' He squinted up at the sky. 'Blood can only be avenged,' he whispered, 'by blood being spilt!'

Yes, he liked that thought: justice and death walking hand-in-hand. He gazed across at the dark mass of the Chapel of St Peter ad Vincula. Surely God would understand? Did he not brand Cain for slaying Abel, and why should murderers walk free? The assassin did not mind the biting wind, the steadily falling flakes of snow or the lonely, haunting call of the night birds down near the icy river.

'There are things colder than the wind,' he whispered as he turned inwards and meditated on his own bleak soul and the great open sore festering there. Soon it would be Yuletide and Childermass. A time of innocence and warmth, of food roasting slowly on turning spits. Green boughs would decorate rooms; there would be mummers, revelries, games, hot cakes and mulled wine. The assassin smiled. And, like every Christmas, the murderers would gather here in the Tower. He rocked himself gently to and fro. The trial would begin. The warnings were already prepared. He stretched his hands up against the night sky.

'Let the blood flow,' he murmured. 'Let Murder be my weapon!'

The cross of St Peter ad Vincula caught his eye. 'Let God be my judge,' he whispered, thrusting his hands beneath his cloak, his eyes staring into the black night. He remembered the past and rocked himself gently, crooning a song only he understood. Now he felt warm. He would bathe his soul's wounds in the blood of his victims.

Chapter 1

Brother Athelstan stood on the tower of St Erconwald's Church in Southwark and stared up at the sky. He chewed on his lip and quietly cursed. He'd thought the clouds would have broken up by now; they had for a while, and the stars had glittered down like jewels against a velvet cushion. Athelstan had wanted to study the constellations as the longest night of the year approached and see if the writer of the *Equatorie of the Planets* was correct. However, the wind had drawn the snow clouds like a thick veil across the sky.

The friar stamped his sandalled feet and blew on his freezing fingers. He picked up his ink horn, quill, astrolabe and roll of parchment, lifted the trap door and cautiously went down the steps. The church was freezing and dark. He took a tinder and lit the tapers in front of Our Lady's statue, the sconce torches down the nave and the fat, white beeswax candles on the altar. Athelstan went back down the sanctuary steps and under the newly carved chancel screen, freshly painted by Huddle with a tableau depicting Christ leading souls from Limbo. Athelstan admired the painter's vigorous brush strokes in green, red, blue and gold colours.

'The young man has a genius,' he muttered to himself, standing back to scrutinise the figures delineated there. He just wished Huddle had been a little more delicate in his depiction of a young lady with rounded juicy breasts whom Cecily the courtesan claimed was a fair represent-ation of her.

'Well, let's see!' Tab the tinker had shouted out before Ursula the pig woman jabbed a sharp elbow in his ribs.

Athelstan shook his head and went across to warm his hands over the small charcoal brazier, which glowingly offered some heat against the freezing night air. He looked down the nave of the church, noticing the boughs of evergreens, the holly and ivy which Watkin the dung-collector's wife had wound round the great broad pillars. Athelstan was pleased. The roof was mended, the win-dows glazed with horn. 'More like a church now,' he muttered, 'than a long, dark tunnel with holes in the walls.' Soon Advent would be over. The greenery had been placed there to welcome the newborn Christ. 'Evergreen,' the friar murmured. 'For the evergreen Lord.' A small shadow, deeper than the rest, slunk from the darkened aisle.

'You always know when to appear, Bonaventura.'

The great tom cat padded across, stopped and stretched in front of Athelstan, then brushed imploringly against the friar's black robe. Athelstan glanced down.

'No mice here,' he whispered. 'Thank God!'

He'd never forget how Ranulf the rat-catcher had secreted traps in the rushes and Cecily had caught her toe in one of them as she cleaned the church one morning. Athelstan had lived for thirty years and served with sol-diers, but never had he heard such a litany of ripe oaths as those which had poured from Cecily's pretty mouth.

The friar crouched and picked up the cat, studying the great black and white face, the tattered ears. 'Bonaventura the Great Mouser,' he murmured. 'So you have come for your reward.' Athelstan went into one of the darkened transepts and took a bowl of freezing milk and sliced pilchard from the windowsill. 'Whose life is more rewarding, Bonaventura,' he murmured as he crouched to feed the animal, 'a torn cat's in Southwark or that of a Dominican monk who likes the stars but has to work in the mud?'

The cat blinked back, squatted down and gobbled the food from a pewter platter, one eye alert on a small flurry where the rushes lay thick against a pillar. Athelstan returned to the bottom of the sanctuary steps, knelt, crossed himself and began the first prayer of Divine Office.

'*Veni, veni, Emmanuel!*' Come, O come, Emmanuel!

When would Christ come again? Athelstan idly wondered. To heal the wounds and enforce justice... No. He closed his eyes. He'd sworn an oath he wouldn't think of Cranston; he wouldn't dwell on that fat red face and balding head, those mischievous blue eyes, and the great girth which would drain a vineyard dry. He remembered the old story about the devil collecting all the half-hearted prayers of priests, gathering every missing word in a bag for Judgment Day. Athelstan closed his eyes and breathed deeply to calm himself.

He finished his psalms then went into the small, freezing cold sacristy. Washing his hands at the lavarium, he looked round. 'Not purple vestments today,' he murmured, and opened the great missal. 'Today is the Feast of St Lucy.' He unlocked the battered cupboard door and plucked out the gold-covered chasuble with a scarlet cross embroidered in the centre. Unlike the musty cupboard, the chasuble was new and fragrant-smelling. He marvelled at the handiwork and thought of its maker, the widow Benedicta. 'As beautiful as she is,' he murmured. 'Sorry,

sorry!' He whispered an apology for his own distraction and said the prayers which every priest must recite as he dresses for Mass.

Athelstan had trained himself. He knew the dark shadows in his soul threatened to rise and interrupt his morning routine. He must not think of them. The small window in the sacristy clattered as its shutter banged against it. Athelstan started. It was still black as night outside in the cemetery, God's Acre, with its broken wooden crosses guarding the mounds of soil where the ancestors of the good people of the parish slept their eternal dream, waiting for Christ to come again. Yet Athelstan knew there was something else out there. Some dark evil thing which committed terrible blasphemies by dragging corpses from the soil.

The friar shook himself free from his morbid reverie. He opened the strong box and took out the chalice and paten. He placed the white communion wafers on a plate and half filled the goblet with altar wine. Afterwards he picked up the jar and gazed suspiciously at the contents.

'It looks,' he announced to the empty darkness, 'as if our sexton, Watkin the dung-collector, is sampling the wine!' He filled the water bowl for the Lavabo, that part of the Mass when the priest cleanses himself of his sins, and gazed down at the water where thin slivers of ice bobbed. 'What sins?' he whispered. The alabaster-skinned face of Benedicta, veiled by her blue-black hair, sprang to mind. Athelstan felt Bonaventure brush against his leg. 'No sin,' he whispered to the cat. 'Surely it is no sin? She's a friend and I am lonely.' He took a deep breath. 'You're a fool, Athelstan,' he muttered to himself. 'You are a priest, what do you expect?' He continued this line of thought as he finished robing. He had confessed as much to the Father Prior, yet why was he lonely? Despite his moans, Athelstan sought to be loved by the parish and the people he served. But it was his other office, as clerk to Sir John Cranston the coroner, which depressed him. And why? Athelstan absent-mindedly picked up Bonaventura and began to stroke him. He could cope with the violent deaths, the gore and the bloody wounds. It was the others which chilled him – the planned murders, coolly calculated by souls steeped in the black night of mortal sin. Athelstan felt he was on the verge of another such mystery. Something warned him, a sixth sense, as if the evil lurking in the lonely cemetery was waiting to confront him. He stirred himself and kissed Bonaventure on the top of his head.

'There's Mass to be said.'

Athelstan went back into the church, glanced up and saw the first light of dawn through the horn-glazed window. He shivered. Despite the braziers, the church was deathly cold. He reached the altar and stared towards the Pyx holding the Blessed Sacrament, Christ under the appearance of bread, swinging under its golden canopy with only a lonely taper on the altar beneath as a sign that God was present. Behind him the door crashed open and Mugwort the bell cleric waddled in, his bald head and quivering red cheeks concealed beneath woollen rags.

'Good morrow, Father!' he bellowed in a voice Athelstan believed could be heard the length and breadth of the parish.

The friar closed his eyes and prayed for patience as Mugwort began to pull on the bell – more like a tocsin than a summons to prayer. At last the clatter stopped. Benedicta, shrouded in a brown cloak, slipped into the church. She smiled sheepishly at the friar who stood waiting patiently at the foot of the steps. Cecily the courtesan followed. Athelstan knew it was she by the gale of cheap perfume which always preceded her. He closed his eyes and prayed that the only tasks Cecily performed now were to work as a seamstress for Benedicta and to clean the church. He remembered the parish joke: how Cecily had lain down in the cemetery more often than the parish coffin. Pernel, the old Flemish lady, came next; her hair dyed red, her face painted white, a woman of indeterminate background and even more uncertain morals. Athelstan quietly vowed to watch her. He'd heard a story that Pernel did not swallow the host but took it home and placed it in her beehive to keep the bees healthy. If he caught her, he would not offer the Eucharist or accept her silly answer that the honeycombs from her hives were always in the shape of a church! At last Watkin the dung-collector, sexton, warden of St Erconwald's and leader of the parish council, arrived. His ever-growing brood of children clattered down the aisle in their wooden clogs; one of them, Crim, with at least his hands washed, slipped next to Athelstan to serve as altar boy. The friar felt slightly ridiculous, a duty-faced Crim on one side and Bonaventura the cat on the other. Manyer the hangman came last and slammed the door shut.

Athelstan took a deep breath and made the sign of the cross, vowing he would concentrate on the mysteries of the Mass and not on the evils in the cemetery outside.

–

Sir John Cranston, Coroner of the City of London, was standing in Blind Basket Alley off Poor Jewry. The runnel cut like a sliver of ice between the backs of the overhanging houses. The good coroner stamped his feet and blew on his mittened fingers in a futile attempt to warm them.

'Hold that torch higher!' he snapped at the alderman's clerk. Cranston stared at the men around him, dark shapes in the poor light, and then up at the shuttered window of the sombre, desolate house. He saved his most venomous glance for Luke Venables, Alderman of the Ward, who had roused him from a warm bed. Sir John liked his sleep at the best of times, particularly after a strenuous week's work. Two days ago, he had gone to the church of St Stephen in Walbrook to examine the corpse of William Clarke, who had climbed the belfry to look for a pigeon's nest. As the idiot crawled from beam to beam, he'd slipped and fallen, being killed instantly. Cranston had adjudged that the beam was to blame and imposed a fine of fourpence on the angry vicar. Yesterday Cranston had been to West Chepe to examine the corpse of William Pannar, a skinner, found lying near the Conduit. Pannar had been stupid enough to go to a physician with some ailment or other. Of course he had been leeched of blood, so much so that the poor bastard had collapsed on the way home and died on the spot.

Cranston chewed his lip as he banged on the door again. Yet it was not just his work which bothered him. There was something else: his beloved wife Maude was not being honest with him and Cranston suspected she was hiding a dreadful secret. Sir John was infatuated with his wife and could not resist the pleasures of the bed chamber, yet recently, last night included, he had snuggled up next to her only to have his advances rejected. She had whimpered her protests softly in the darkness, would not tell him the reason and refused to be comforted. Now, in the early hours, this idiot Venables had brought him out into the cold in order to force entry into this mysterious house. Cranston hammered on the door again but there was no reply, only the muttered oaths and shuffling feet of his companions.

'So!' Cranston turned to the alderman. 'Tell me again what the problem is.'

Venables knew Sir John and stared anxiously at the be-whiskered red face, the icy-blue eyes and furrowed brow under the great, woollen beaver hat. Sir John was a good man, Venables reflected, but when he lost his temper, he could be the devil incarnate. Venables pointed to the broken ale-stake jutting out just above the door.

'The facts are these, Sir John. The householder here is Simon de Wyxford. This is his ale-house. He had no family, only a servant, Roger Droxford. Eight days ago, master and servant had a violent quarrel which continued all day. On December the sixth the servant, Roger, opened the ale-house as usual, set out the benches and sold wine, but nothing was seen of Simon. The next day neighbours asked Roger where his master was. He replied that Simon had gone to Westminster to recover some debts.' Venables blew out his cheeks and turned to one of the shadowed figures beside him. 'Tell Sir John the rest.'

'Four days ago—' began the neighbour, a small man swathed in robes.

Cranston could see only a pair of timid eyes and a dripping nose above the muffler.

'Speak up!' Cranston roared. 'Remove the muffler from your mouth.'

'Four days ago,' the fellow continued, obeying Sir John with alacrity, 'Roger was seen leaving here, a bundle of possessions slung across his back. We thought he was fleeing but he went to one of our neighbours, Hammo the cook, telling him he was going to seek out Simon, his master, and gave Hammo the key should de Wyxford suddenly return. Last night,' he continued, clearing his throat, 'Francis Boggett, a taverner, came here to recover a debt Master Simon owed him.'

'Come on! Come on!' Cranston interrupted.

'Boggett entered the house,' the alderman intervened smoothly, 'to find no trace of Simon or his servant, so he seized three tuns of wine as recompense for his debt.'

'How did he get in?' Cranston snapped.

'Hammo the cook gave him the key.'

Sir John pursed his lips. 'Boggett is to be fined fivepence for trespass and the cook twopence as his accomplice.' He glared at the alderman. 'You have the key on you?'

Venables nodded. Cranston snapped his fingers and the alderman handed it over. The coroner drew himself up to his full height.

'As coroner of this city,' he grandly announced, 'in view of the mysterious events reported to me, I now authorise our entry to this house to search out the truth. Master Alderman, you will accompany me.'

There was further confusion as Venables asked for a tinder from one of his companions. Sir John unlocked the door and entered the cold darkness of the tavern. The place smelt dirty and musty. They crashed against barrels, stools and tables until Venables struck a tinder and lit two cresset torches, one of which he handed to Cranston. They went from room to room and then upstairs where they found the two chambers ransacked, and coffers and chests with their lids broken or thrown aside, but no trace of any body.

'You know what we are looking for?' Cranston murmured.

Venables nodded. 'But so far nothing, Sir John.'

'There is a cellar?'

The alderman led Cranston downstairs. They searched the darkened taproom until they found a trap door, which Venables pulled back. Both men descended gingerly by wooden ladders. The cellar was a long, oblong box with a trap door at the far end for the carts to unload their barrels through. Cranston told Venables to stand still and walked carefully through the cellar, his great bulk made grotesque by the dim light of the flickering torches. At the far end he stopped, lowered the torch and looked behind three great wine tuns. The light made the spiders' webs which clung to the barrels shimmer like cloth of gold. Cranston leaned over and felt the sticky mess he had spotted. He brought his hand up into the light and looked at the blood which coated his fingers like paste. He forced his arm back further behind the barrels, and scrabbled around.

'Sir John!' the alderman called out. 'All is well?'

'As well as can be expected, Master Venables. I have found the taverner, or at least part of him!' Cranston picked up the decapitated head from behind the barrels and held it aloft as if he was the Tower headsman. The alderman took one look at the blue-white face, the half-closed eyes, sagging blood-stained mouth and the jagged remains of the neck, and sat down heavily on a stone plinth, retching violently. Cranston put down the head and walked back, wiping his fingers on the mildewed wall. As he passed, he patted Venables gently on the shoulder.

'Have some claret, my good alderman, it steadies the stomach and fortifies the heart.' He stopped and took a step back. 'After that, swear out warrants for the arrest of

Roger Droxford. Declare him a wolfshead, and place…'
Cranston screwed up his eyes. 'Yes, place ten pounds'
reward on his head, dead or alive. Have this house sealed,
and in the event of no will or self-proclaimed heir appearing, the city council might find itself a little richer.'

He climbed the ladder and the taproom steps and
emerged on to the bitterly cold street.

'We've found the taverner,' he announced. 'Murdered.
I think the good alderman will need your help to assemble
the corpse.'

Then, hand on his long Welsh dagger, Sir John trudged
back along the ice-packed runnels and alleyways. He
turned into the Mercery and gasped as the icy wind tore
away his breath. 'Oh, for summer!' he wailed to himself.
'For weeds in clumps, for grass lovely and lush.'

He slithered on the icy cobbles and leaned against the
wooden frame of a house, grinning.

'Athelstan should be here helping,' he murmured. 'If
not with headless corpses, then at least by keeping me
steady on the ice.'

He walked on up Cheapside. A dark shape slid from
the shadows to meet him. Cranston half drew his dagger.

'Sir John, for the love of Christ!'

Cranston peered closer at the raw-boned face of the
one-legged beggar who always sold trinkets from his rickety stall on the corner of Milk Street.

'Not in bed, Leif? Looking for a lady, are we?'

'Sir John, I've been robbed!'

'See the sheriff!'

'Sir John, I have no money and no food.'

'Then stay in bed!'

Leif steadied himself against the wall. 'I paid no rent,
so I lost my garret,' he wailed.

'Well, go and beg at St Bartholomew's!' Cranston barked back, and trudged on. He heard Leif hopping behind him.

'Sir John, help me.'

'Bugger off, Leif.'

'Thank you, Sir John,' the beggar answered as coins tinkled to the ground. Leif knew enough about the fat coroner to understand Sir John hated to be seen giving charity.

Cranston stopped before his own house and looked up at the candlelit windows. Leif nearly crashed into him and Cranston shrugged him off. What is the matter with Maude? he wondered. He had always considered marriage similar to dipping one's hand into a bag of eels – it depended on luck what you drew out. Yet he had been so fortunate. He adored Maude, from the mousey hair of her head to the soles of her tiny feet.

As he mused, a figure suddenly emerged from the alleyway which ran alongside Cranston's house.

'By the sod!' he exclaimed. 'Doesn't anyone in this benighted city sleep?'

The fellow approached and Cranston recognised the livery of the Lord Mayor.

'By the sod,' he repeated, 'more trouble!'

The young pursuivant, teeth chattering, hoarsely delivered his message.

'Sir John, the Lord Mayor and his sheriffs wish to see you now at the Guildhall.'

'Go to hell!'

'Thank you, Sir John. The Lord Mayor said your reply would be something like that. Shall I wait for you?' The young man clapped his hands together. 'Sir John, I am cold.'

Still bellowing 'By the sod!' Cranston banged on the door of his house. A thin-faced maid opened it. Behind her stood Maude, now fully dressed, her sweet face tear-stained. Sir John grinned at her to hide his own disquiet.

'Lady wife, I am off to the Guildhall – but not before I break fast.' He dragged the young pursuivant in with him. 'He'll eat too. He looks as if he needs it.'

Cranston spun on his heel, went back outside and re-entered, dragging in Leif by the scruff of his neck. 'This idle bugger will also be joining us. After which, find him a job. He will be spending Yuletide here.' He tapped his broad girth. 'For all of us, hot oatmeal and spiced cakes!' The coroner sniffed the air. 'And some of that white manchet, freshly baked.' He looked slyly at his wife. 'And claret, hot and spiced. Then tell the groom I need a horse!' He grinned broadly, but despite his bluster Cranston noticed how pale and ill his wife looked. He glanced away. Oh God! he thought. Am I to lose Maude? He tossed off his cloak and strode past his wife, touching her gently on the shoulder as he passed.

–

Athelstan was distributing communion, placing the thin white wafers on the tongues of his parishioners. Crim held the silver plate under their chins to catch any crumbs which might fall. Most of the parish council had turned up, some wandering in when Mass was half over.

The friar was about to return to the altar when he heard a tapping on the outside wall of the far aisle. Of course! He had forgotten the lepers, two unfortunates whom he'd allowed to shelter in the musty charnel house in the cemetery. Athelstan provided them with food and drink and a bowl of water infused with mulberry to wash in, but never once had he glimpsed their scabrous white faces, though from his clothes one was definitely a male. He wished he could do more for them but Canon Law was most insistent – a leper was not allowed to take communion with the rest of the congregation but could only receive it through the leper squint, a small hole in the wall of the church.

Crim remembered his duties and, picking up a thin twig of ash, handed it to the friar who placed a host on the end and pushed it through the leper squint. He repeated the action, whispered a prayer, and went back to finish the Mass.

Afterwards Athelstan disrobed in the sacristy, closing his ears to the crashing sounds from the nave as Watkin the dung-collector rearranged the benches for the meeting of the parish council. Athelstan knelt on his *prie dieu*, asked for guidance, and hoped to God his parishioners would overlook the dreadful events happening outside.

As soon as he stepped into the nave, he knew his prayers had been fruitless. Watkin was sitting in pride of place, with the other members on benches on either side of him. Crim had placed Athelstan's chair out of the sanctuary ready for him and, as he took it, Athelstan caught Watkin's self-important look, the ominous flickering of the eyes and the mouth pursed as if on the brink of announcing something very important.

Ursula the pig woman had joined them, bringing her large fat sow into church with her in spite of the protests of the rest. The creature waddled around grunting with pleasure. Athelstan was sure the annoying beast was grinning at him. He did not object to its presence. Better here than outside. Ursula was a garrulous but kindly old

24

woman. Nevertheless, the friar hid a blind hatred for her large, fat-bellied sow which periodically plundered his garden of any vegetables he tried to plant there.

Athelstan said a prayer to the Holy Ghost and leaned back in his chair.

'Brothers and sisters,' he began, 'welcome to this meeting on our holiday feast of St Lucy.' He ignored Watkin's eye. 'We have certain matters to discuss.' He smiled at Benedicta then noticed with alarm how Watkin's wife was glaring at Cecily the courtesan. A mutual antipathy existed between these two women, Watkin's wife in the past loudly wondering why it was necessary for her husband to confer so often with Cecily on the cleaning of the church. Huddle the painter stared vacantly at a blank wall, probably dreaming of the mural he would like to put there if Athelstan gave him the monies.

Most of the parish business was a long litany of mundane items. Pike the ditcher's daughter wished to marry Amisias the fuller's eldest boy. The great Blood Book was consulted to ensure there were no lines of consanguinity. Athelstan was pleased to announce there were not and matters turned to the approaching Yuletide: the Ceremony of the Star, which would take place in the church, the timing of the three Masses for Christmas Day, the non-payment of burial dues, and the children using the holy water stoup as a drinking fountain. Tab the tinker offered to fashion new candlesticks, two large ones, fronted with lions. Gamelyn the clerk volunteered to sing a pleasant carol at the end of each Mass at Yuletide. Athelstan agreed to a mummers' play in the nave on St Stephen's Day, and some discussion was held about who would play the role of the boy bishop at Childermass, the feast of the Holy Innocents, on the twenty-eighth of December.

Athelstan, however, noticed despairingly how Watkin just slumped on his bench, glaring impatiently as he clawed his codpiece and shuffled his muddy boots. Benedicta caught Athelstan's concern and gazed anxiously at this man she loved but could not attain because he was an ordained priest. At last Athelstan ran out of things to say.

'Well, Watkin,' he commented drily. 'You have a matter of great urgency?'

Watkin drew himself up to his full height. His greasy brow was furrowed under a shock of bright red hair, receding fast to leave a bushy fringe. His pale blue eyes, which seemed to fight each other for space next to a bulbous nose, glared around at his colleagues.

'The cemetery has been looted!' he blurted out.

Athelstan groaned and lowered his head.

'What do you mean?' shouted Ranulf the rat-catcher, his face sharp and pointed under a black, tarry hood.

'In the last few days,' Watkin announced, 'corpses have been exhumed!'

Consternation broke out. Athelstan rose and clapped his hands for silence, and kept doing so until the clamour ceased. 'You know,' he began, 'how our cemetery of St Erconwald's is often used for the burial of corpses of strangers – beggars on whom no claim is made. No grave of any parishioner's relative has been disturbed.' He breathed deeply. 'Nevertheless, Watkin is correct. Three graves have been robbed of their bodies. Each had been freshly interred. A young beggar woman, a Brabantine mercenary found dead after a tavern brawl, and an old man seen begging outside the hospital of St Thomas, who was found in the courtyard of the Tabard Inn, frozen dead.' Athelstan licked his lips. 'The ground is hard,' he continued. 'Watkin knows how difficult it is to dig with mattock and hoe to furnish a grave deep enough, so the very shallowness of the graves has assisted these blasphemous robbers.'

'A guard should be placed,' Pike the ditcher called out.

'Will you do it?' Benedicta asked softly. 'Will you spend all night in the cemetery, Pike, and wait for the grave robbers?' Her dark eyes took in the rest of the council. 'Who will stand guard? And who knows,' she continued, 'if the robberies are committed at night? Perhaps they take place in the afternoon or eventide.'

Athelstan glanced at her gratefully. 'I could watch,' he interrupted. 'Indeed, I have done so when I – er...' he faltered.

'When you study the stars, Brother,' Ursula the pig woman broke in, provoking a soft chorus of laughter, for all the parishioners knew of their priest's strange occupation.

Huddle the painter stirred himself. 'You could ask Sir John Cranston to help us. Perhaps he could send soldiers to guard the graves?'

Athelstan shook his head. 'My Lord Coroner,' he replied, 'has no authority to order the King's soldiers hither and thither.'

'What about the beadles?' Watkin's wife bellowed. 'What about the ward watch?'

Yes, what about them? Athelstan bleakly thought. The alderman and officials of the ward scarcely bothered about St Erconwald's, still less about its cemetery, and wouldn't give a fig for the graves of the three unknowns being pillaged.

'Who are they?' Benedicta asked softly. 'Why do they do it? What do they want?'

Her words created a pool of silence. All faces turned to their priest for an answer. This was the moment Athelstan feared. The cemetery was God's Acre. When he had first come to the parish nine months ago, he had been very strict about those who tried to set up market there or with the young boys who played games with the bones dug up by marauding dogs or pigs. 'The cemetery,' he had announced, 'is God's own land where the faithful wait for Christ to come again.' Even then Athelstan had not given the full reason for his strictures; secretly he shared the Church's fears of those who worshipped Satan, the Lord of the Crossroads and Master of the Gibbet, and often practised their black arts in cemeteries. Indeed, he had heard of a case in the parish of St Peter Cornhill where a black magician had used the blood drained from such corpses to raise demons and scorpions.

Athelstan coughed. How could he answer? Then the door was flung open and Cranston, his saviour, swept grandly into the church.

Chapter 2

Sir John pulled back his cloak and tipped his beaver hat to the back of his head.

'Come on, Brother!' he bawled, winking at Benedicta. 'We are needed at the Tower. Apparently Murder does not wait upon the weather.'

For once Athelstan was pleased by Cranston's dramatic style of entry. The friar peered closely at him.

'You have been at the claret, Sir John?'

Cranston tapped the side of his fleshy nose. 'A little,' he slurred.

'What about the cemetery?' Watkin wailed. 'Sir John, our priest has to see to that!'

'Sod off, you smelly little man!'

Watkin's wife rose and looked balefully at Cranston.

'My Lord Coroner, I shall be with you presently,' Athelstan smoothly intervened. 'Watkin, I shall attend to this business on my return. In the meantime, make sure that Bonaventura is fed and the torches doused. Cecily, you will put out food for the lepers?'

The girl stared vacuously and nodded.

'Mind you,' Athelstan muttered, 'they tend to wander and look after themselves during the day.'

He smiled beatifically around his favourite group of parishioners and made a quick departure down the icy steps of the church and across to the priest's house. He cut himself a slice of bread but spat it out as it tasted sour and stale. 'I'll eat on my journey,' he murmured, and packed his saddlebags with vellum, pen cases and ink horns. Philomel, his old war horse, snickered and nudged him, a real nuisance as Athelstan tried to fasten the girths beneath the aged destrier's ponderous belly.

'You're getting more like Cranston every day!' Athelstan muttered.

He led Philomel back to the front of the church and ran up the porch steps. Cranston was leaning against the pillar, leering at Cecily whilst trying to keep Bonaventura from brushing against his leg. The coroner couldn't stand cats ever since his campaigns in France when the French had catapulted their corpses into a small castle he was holding, in an attempt to spread contagious diseases. Bonaventura, however, adored the coroner. The cat seemed to know when he was in the vicinity and always put in an appearance.

Athelstan murmured a few words to Benedicta, and smiled apologetically at Watkin and the rest; he collected his deep-hooded cloak from the sanctuary and returned just in the nick of time to prevent Cranston from toppling head over heels over Ursula's fat-bellied sow. The coroner stormed out, glaring at Athelstan and daring him to laugh. Cranston mounted his horse, roaring oaths about pigs in church and how he would like nothing better than a succulent piece of roast pork. Athelstan swung his saddlebags across Philomel, mounted and, before Cranston could do further damage, led him away from the church into Fennel Alleyway.

'Why the Tower, Sir John?' he asked quickly, trying to divert the coroner's rage.

'In a while, monk!' Cranston rasped back.

'I'm a friar, not a monk,' Athelstan muttered.

Cranston belched and took another swig from his wineskin. 'What was going on back there?' he asked.

'A parish council meeting.'

'No, I mean about the cemetery.'

Athelstan informed him and the coroner's face grew serious.

'Do you think it's Satanists? The Black Lords of the graveyard?' he whispered, reining his horse closer to Athelstan's.

The friar grimaced. 'It may well be.'

'It must be!' Cranston snapped back. 'Who else would be interested in decaying corpses?'

The coroner steadied his horse as Philomel, conscious of the narrowing alleyway, tossed his head angrily at Cranston's mount.

'I'd like to root the lot out!' the coroner slurred. 'In my treatise on the governance of London…' Two blue eyes glared at Athelstan, scrutinising the friar's face for any trace of boredom as the coroner expounded on his favourite theme. 'In my treatise,' he continued, 'anyone practising the black arts would suffer heavy fines for the first offence and death for the second.' He shrugged. 'But perhaps it's just some petty nastiness.'

Athelstan shook his head. 'Such matters are never petty,' he replied. 'I attended an exorcism once at a little church near Blackfriars. A young boy possessed by demons was speaking in strange tongues and levitating himself from the ground. He claimed the demons entered him after a ceremony in which the corpse of a hanged man was the altar.'

Cranston shuddered. 'If you need any help…' the coroner tentatively offered.

Athelstan smiled. 'That's most kind of you, My Lord Coroner. As usual your generosity of spirit takes my breath away.'

'Any friend of the Good Lord is a friend of mine,' Cranston quipped. 'Even if he is a monk.'

'I'm a friar,' Athelstan replied. '*Not* a monk.' He glared at Cranston, but the coroner threw back his head and roared with laughter at his perennial joke against Athelstan.

At last they left the congested alleyways, taking care to avoid the snow which slid from the high, sloped roofs, and turned on to the main thoroughfare down to London Bridge. The cobbled area was sheeted with ice, coated with a thin layer of snow, which a biting wind stirred into sudden, sharp flurries. A few stalls were out, but their keepers hid behind tattered canvas awnings against the biting wind now packing the sky with deep, dark snow clouds.

'A time to keep secret house,' Cranston murmured.

A relic-seller stood outside the Abbot of Hyde's inn trying to sell a staff which, he claimed, had once belonged to Moses. Two prisoners, manacled together and released from the Marshalsea where debtors were held, begged for alms for themselves and other poor unfortunates. Athelstan threw them some pennies, moved to compassion by their ice-blue feet. Both Cranston's and Athelstan's horses were well shod but the few people who were about slipped and slithered on the treacherous black ice. These hardy walkers made their way gingerly along, grasping the frames of the houses they passed. Nevertheless, as Cranston remarked, justice was active; outside the hospital of St Thomas a baker had been fastened on a hurdle as punishment for selling mouldy bread. Athelstan remembered the stale food he had spat out earlier and watched as the unfortunate was pulled along by a donkey. A drunken bagpipe player slipped and slid along behind, playing a raucous tune to hide the baker's groans. In the stocks a taverner, wry-mouthed, was being made to drink sour wine, whilst a whore, fastened to the thews, was whipped by a sweating bailiff who lashed the poor woman's back with long thick twigs of holly.

'Sir John,' Athelstan whispered, 'the poor woman has had enough.'

'Sod her!' Cranston snarled back. 'She probably deserved it!'

Athelstan looked closer at the coroner's round red face.

'Sir John, for pity's sake, what is the matter?'

Beneath the false bonhomie and wine-guzzling, Athelstan sensed the coroner was either very angry or very anxious. Cranston blinked and smiled falsely. He drew his sword and, turning his horse aside, moved over to the whipping post and slashed at the ropes which held the whore. The woman collapsed in a bloody heap on the ice. The bailiff, a snarl making his ugly face more grotesque, walked threateningly towards Cranston. Sir John waved his sword and pulled the muffler from his face.

'I am Cranston the City Coroner!' he yelled.

The man backed off hastily. Sir John delved under his cloak, brought out a few pennies and tossed them to the whore.

'Earn an honest crust!' he snapped.

He glared at his companion, daring him to comment before continuing down past the stews and on to the wide expanse of London Bridge. The entire trackway of the bridge was coated with ice and shrouded in mist. Athelstan stopped, his hand on Cranston's arm.

'Sir John, something is wrong! It's so quiet!'

Cranston grinned. 'Haven't you realised, Brother? Look down, the river is frozen.'

Athelstan stared in disbelief over the railings of the bridge. Usually the water beneath surged and boiled. Now it seemed the river had been replaced by a field of white ice which stretched as far as the eye could see. Athelstan craned his neck and heard the shouts of boys skating there, using the shin bones of an ox for skates. Someone had even opened a stall and Athelstan's stomach clenched with hunger as he caught the fragrant smell of hot beef pies. They continued past the Chapel of St Thomas on to Bridge Street, into Billingsgate and up Botolph's Lane to Eastcheap. The city seemed to be caught under the spell of an ice witch. Few stalls were out and the usual roar of apprentices and merchants had been silenced by winter's vice-like grip. They stopped at a pie shop. Athelstan bought and bit deeply into a hot mince pie, savouring the juices which swirled there and the delightful fragrance of freshly baked pastry and highly spiced meat. Cranston watched him eat.

'You are enjoying that, Brother?'

'Yes, My Lord. Why don't you join me?'

Cranston smiled wickedly. 'I would love to,' he replied. 'But have you not forgotten, friar? It's Advent. You are supposed to abstain from meat!'

Athelstan looked longingly at the half-eaten pie, then smiled, finished his meal and licked his fingers. Cranston shook his head.

'What are we to do?' he wailed mockingly. 'When friars ignore Canon Law.'

Athelstan licked his lips and leaned closer. 'You're wrong, Sir John. Today is the thirteenth of December, a holy day, the feast of St Lucy, virgin and martyr. So I am allowed to eat meat.' He sketched a sign of the cross in the air. 'And you can drink twice as much claret as you usually do!' The friar gathered the reins of the horse in his hands. 'So, Sir John, what takes us to the Tower?'

Cranston pulled aside as a broad-wheeled cart stacked high with sour green apples trundled by.

'Sir Ralph Whitton, Constable of the Tower. You have heard of him?'

Athelstan nodded. 'Who hasn't? He's a redoubtable soldier, a brave crusader, and a personal friend of the Regent, John of Gaunt.'

'Was,' Cranston intervened. 'Early this morning Whitton was found in his chamber in the North Bastion of the Tower, his throat slit from ear to ear and more blood on his chest than you would get from a gutted pig.'

'Any sign of the murderer or the weapon?'

Cranston shook his head, blowing on his ice-edged fingers. 'Nothing,' he grated. 'Whitton had a daughter, Philippa. She was betrothed to Geoffrey Parchmeiner. Apparently Sir Ralph liked the young man and trusted him. Early this morning Geoffrey went to wake his prospective father-in-law and found him murdered.' He took a deep breath. 'More curious still, before his death Sir Ralph, suspected someone had evil designs on his life. Four days prior to his death he received a written warning.'

'What was this?'

'I don't know but apparently the constable became a frightened man. He left his usual chambers in the turret of the White Tower and for security reasons moved to the North Bastion. The stairway to his chamber was guarded by two trusted retainers. The door between the steps and the passageway was locked. Sir Ralph kept a key and so did the guards. The same is true of Sir Ralph's chamber. He locked it from the inside, whilst the two guards had another key.'

Cranston suddenly leaned over and grabbed the bridle of Athelstan's horse, pulling him clear as a huge lump of snow slipped from the sloping roofs above and crashed on to the ice.

'We should move on,' the friar remarked drily. 'Otherwise, Sir John, you may have another corpse on your hands and this time *you* will be the suspect.'

Cranston belched and took a deep swig from his wineskin.

'Is young Geoffrey one of the suspects?' Athelstan enquired.

Cranston shook his head. 'I don't think so. Both doors were still locked; the guards unlocked one, let him through and then locked it again. Apparently, Geoffrey went down the passageway, knocked and tried to rouse Sir Ralph. He failed to do this so came back for the guards who opened Sir Ralph's room. Inside they found the constable sprawled on his bed, his throat cut and the wooden shutters of his window flung wide open.' Cranston turned and spat, clearing his throat. 'One other thing – the guards would never allow anyone through without a rigorous body search, and that included young Geoffrey. No dagger was found on him nor any knife in the room.'

'What was Sir Ralph so fearful of?'

Cranston shook his head. 'God knows! But there's a fine array of suspects. His lieutenant, Gilbert Colebrooke, was on bad terms and wanted Sir Ralph's post for himself. There's the chaplain, William Hammond, whom Sir Ralph caught selling food stocks from the Tower stores. Two friends of Sir Ralph's, hospitaller knights, came as they usually did to spend Christmas with him. Finally, there's a pagan, a mute body servant, a Saracen whom Sir Ralph picked up whilst crusading in Outremer.'

Athelstan pulled his hood closer as the cold wind nipped the corners of his ears. '*Cui bono?*' he asked.

'What does that mean?'

'Cicero's famous question: "Who profits?"'

Cranston pursed his lips. 'A good question, my dear friar. Which brings us to Sir Ralph's brother, Sir Fulke Whitton. He stands to inherit some of his brother's estate.'

Cranston fell silent, half closing his eyes and gently burping after the good breakfast he had eaten. Athelstan, however, prided himself on knowing the fat coroner as well as the palm of his own hand.

'Well, Sir John,' he needled, 'there is more, is there not?'

Cranston opened his eyes. 'Of course there is. Whitton was not liked by the court, nor by the Londoners, nor by the peasants.'

Athelstan felt his heart sink. They had been down this road on numerous occasions.

'You think it may be the Great Community?' he asked.

Cranston nodded. 'It could be. And, remember, Brother, some of your parishioners may be part of it. If the Great Community acts and revolt spreads, the rebels will try to seize the Tower. Whoever controls it controls the river, the city, Westminster and the crown.'

Athelstan pulled the reins closer to him and reflected on what Cranston had said. Matters were not going well in London. The king was a child; John of Gaunt, his uncle, a highly unpopular Regent. The court was dissolute, whilst the peasants were taxed to the hilt and tied to the soil by cruel laws. For some time there had been whispers, rumours carried like leaves on a strong breeze, of how peasants in Kent, Middlesex and Essex had formed a secret society called the Great Community. How its leaders were plotting rebellion and a march on London. Athelstan even vaguely knew one of these leaders – John Ball, a wandering priest; the man was so eloquent he could turn the most placid of peasants into an outright rebel by mouthing phrases such as: 'When Adam delved and Eve span, who was then the gentleman?' Was Whitton's death a preamble to all this? Athelstan wondered. Were any of his parishioners involved? He knew they met in the ale-houses and taverns and, God knew, had legitimate grievances. Harsh taxes and savage laws were cruel enough to provoke a saint to rebellion. And if the revolt came, what should he do? Side with the authorities or, like many priests, join the rebels? He looked sidelong at Cranston. The coroner seemed lost in his own thoughts and once again the friar detected an air of sadness about him.

'Sir John, is there anything wrong?'

'No, no,' the coroner mumbled.

Athelstan left him alone. Perhaps, he concluded, Sir John had drunk too deeply the night before.

They moved down a snow-covered Tower Street past the church where a poor beadsman knelt, making atonement for some sin; the hands clutching his rosary beads were frost-hardened and Athelstan winced at some of the penances his fellow priests imposed on their parishioners. Sir John blew his breath out so it hung like incense in the cold air.

'By the sod!' he muttered. 'When will the sun come again?'

They had turned into Petty Wales when suddenly a woman's voice, clear and lilting, broke into one of Athelstan's favourite carols. They stopped for a moment to listen then crossed the ice-glazed square. Above them soared the Tower's sheer snow-capped walls, turrets, bastions, bulwarks and crenellations. A mass of carved stone, the huge fortress seemed shaped not to defend London but to overawe it.

'A very narrow place,' Cranston muttered. 'The House of the Red Slayer.' He looked quizzically at Athelstan. 'Our old friends Death and Murder lurk here.'

Athelstan shivered and not just from the cold. They crossed the drawbridge. Beneath them the moat, its water and the dirty green slime which always covered it, were frozen hard. They went through the black arch of Middle Tower. The huge gateway stood like an open mouth, its teeth the half-lowered iron portcullis. Above them the severed heads of two pirates taken in the Channel grinned down. Athelstan breathed a prayer.

'God defend us,' he muttered, 'from all devils, demons, scorpions, and those malignant spirits who dwell here!'

'God defend me against the living!' Cranston quipped back. 'I suspect Satan himself weeps at the evil we get up to!'

The gateway was guarded by sentries who stood under the narrow vaulted archway, wrapped in brown serge cloaks.

'Sir John Cranston, Coroner!' he bellowed. 'I hold the King's writ. And this is my clerk, Brother Athelstan, who for his manifest sins is also parish priest of St Erconwald's in Southwark. A place,' the coroner grinned at the outrage in Athelstan's face, 'where virtue and vice rub shoulders and shake hands.'

The sentries nodded, reluctant to move because of the intense cold. Athelstan and Cranston continued past

By-ward Tower and up a cobbled causeway where their horses slithered and slipped on the icy stones. They turned left at Wakefield Tower, going through another of the concentric circles of defences, on to Tower Green. This was now carpeted by a thick white layer of snow which also covered the great machines of war lying there – catapults, battering rams, mangonels and huge iron-ringed carts. On their right stood a massive half-timbered great hall with other rooms built on to it. A sentry half dozed on the steps and didn't even bother to look up as Cranston roared for assistance. A snivelling, red-nosed groom hurried down to take their horses whilst another led them up the steps and into the great hall. Two rough-haired hunting dogs snuffled amongst the mucky rushes. One of them almost cocked a leg against Sir John but growled as the coroner lashed out with his boot.

The hall itself was a large sombre room with a dirty stone floor and brooding, heavy beams. Against the far wall was a fireplace wide enough to roast an ox. The grate was piled high with logs but the chimney must have needed cleaning for some of the smoke had escaped back into the hall to swirl beneath the rafters like a mist. The early morning meal had just been finished; scullions were clearing the table of pewter and wooden platters. In one corner, two men were idly baiting a badger with a dog and other groups were huddled round the fire. Athelstan gazed around. The heavy pall of death hung over the room. He recognised its stench, the suspicion and unspoken terrors which always followed a violent, mysterious slaying. One of the figures near the fire rose and hurried across as Cranston bellowed his title once again. The fellow was tall and lanky, red-haired, with eyes pink-lidded and devoid of lashes. An aquiline nose dominated his half-shaven, lantern-shaped face.

'I am Gilbert Colebrooke, the lieutenant. Sir John, you are most welcome.' His bleary eyes swung to Athelstan.

'My clerk,' Cranston blandly announced. The coroner nodded to the group round the fire. 'The constable's household, I suspect?'

'Yes,' Colebrooke snapped.

'Well, man, introduce us!'

As they moved across, the people crouching on stools near the fire rose to greet them. Introductions were made, and inevitably Cranston immediately dominated the proceedings. As usual Athelstan hung back, studying the people he would soon interrogate. He would dig out their secrets, perhaps even reveal scandals best left hidden. First the chaplain, Master William Hammond, thin and sombre in his dark black robes. He moved with a birdlike stoop, his face sallow with an unhealthy colour, balding head covered with greasy grey wisps of hair. A bitter man, Athelstan concluded, with a nose as sharp as a dagger point, small black eyes and lips thin as a miser's purse.

On the chaplain's right stood Sir Fulke Whitton, the dead man's brother, sleek and fat, with a pleasant face and corn-coloured hair. His handshake was firm and the man curved his considerable girth with the grace and speed of an athlete.

Beside him was the dead constable's daughter, Philippa. No great beauty, she was broad-featured with pleasant brown eyes and neat auburn hair. She was rather plump and reminded Athelstan of an over-fed capon. Next to her stood, or rather swayed, her betrothed, Geoffrey Parchmeiner, hair black as night though oiled and dressed like that of a woman. He seemed a pleasant enough fellow, strong-featured though his smooth-shaven face was slightly flushed with the blood-red claret he slopped around in a deep-bowled goblet. A merry fellow, Athelstan thought, and gazed with amusement at Geoffrey's tight hose and protuberant codpiece: the shin beneath the tawny cloak dripped with frills under the sarcenet doublet, and the toes of the shoes were so long and pointed they were tied up by a scarlet cord wound around the knees. God knows how he walks on ice, Athelstan thought. He recognized the type – a young man who aped the dandies of the court. A parchment-seller with a shop in some London street, Geoffrey would have the money to act like a courtier.

The two hospitaller knights whom Cranston had mentioned, Sir Gerard Mowbray and Sir Brian Fitzormonde, could have been brothers, each dressed in the grey garb of their Order, cloaks emblazoned with broad white pointed crosses. Athelstan knew the fearsome reputation of these knight monks and had on occasion even acted as confessor at their stronghold in Clerkenwell. Both Gerard and Brian were middle-aged, and every inch soldiers with their neat clipped beards, sharp eyes and close-cropped hair. They moved like cats, men conscious of their own prowess. Warriors, Athelstan mused, men who would kill if they thought the cause just.

Between them stood a lithe-figured dark man, his hair and beard liberally oiled. He was dressed in blue loose-fitting trousers and a heavy military cloak over his doublet. His eyes moved constantly and he watched Cranston and Athelstan as if they were enemies. The coroner barked a question at him, but the fellow just looked dumbly back, opened his mouth and pointed with his finger. Athelstan looked away in pity from the black space where the man's tongue should have been.

'Rastani is a mute.' The girl, Philippa, spoke up, her voice surprisingly deep and husky. 'He was a Muslim, though now converted to our faith. He is…' She bit her lip. 'He was my father's servant.' Her eyes filled with tears and she clutched the arm of her betrothed, though the young man was more unsteady on his feet than she.

Once the introductions were made, Colebrook shouted for more stools and, catching the greedy gaze of Sir John directed towards the young man's wine cup, goblets of hot posset. Cranston and Athelstan sat in the middle of the group. Sir John had no inhibitions but threw back his cloak, stretched out his log-like legs and revelled in the warmth from the fire. The posset he drained in one gulp, held out his cup to be refilled and slurped noisily from it, smacking his lips and staring around as if all his companions were close bosom friends. Athelstan muttered a silent prayer, as he rearranged the writing tray on his lap, that the Good Lord would keep Cranston both sober and awake. Geoffrey sniggered whilst the two knights stared in utter disbelief.

'You are the King's Coroner?' Sir Fulke loudly asked.

'Yes, he is,' Athelstan intervened. 'And Sir John is not always as he appears.'

Cranston smacked his lips again.

'No, no, I am not,' he murmured. 'And I suspect the same is true of everyone here. Always remember a useful dictum: every man born of woman is three persons: what he appears to be, what he claims to be and,' he beamed round, 'what he really is.' He grinned lecherously at Philippa. 'The same is true of the fairer sex.' He suddenly remembered Maude and the thought sobered him quicker than a douche of cold water. 'The same,' he continued crossly, 'is true of the murderer of Sir Ralph Whitton, Constable of this Tower.'

'You suspect someone here?' Sir Fulke said, his face now drained of good humour.

'Yes, I do!' Cranston snapped.

'That's an insult!' the chaplain blurted out. 'My Lord Coroner, you are in your cups! You swagger in here, you know us not...'

Athelstan placed his hand on the coroner's arm. He sensed Sir John was in a dangerous mood and noticed how the hospitallers had both opened their cloaks to display the daggers hooked in their belts. Cranston heeded the warning.

'I make no accusations,' he replied softly. 'But it usually transpires that murder, like charity, begins at home.'

'We face three problems,' Athelstan diplomatically intervened. 'Who killed Sir Ralph, why, and how?'

The lieutenant made a rude sound with his tongue. Cranston leaned forward.

'You wish to say something, sir?'

'Yes, I do. Sir Ralph could have been killed by any rebel from London, by a peasant from the hundreds of villages around us, or by some secret assassin sent in to perform the ghastly deed.'

Cranston nodded and smiled at him.

'Perhaps,' he replied sweetly, 'but I shall return to your theory later. In the meantime, none of you will leave the Tower.' He looked around the sombre hall. 'After I have viewed the corpse, I wish to see all of you, though in more suitable surroundings.'

The lieutenant agreed. 'St John's Chapel in the White Tower,' he announced. 'It is warm, secure, and affords some privacy.'

'Good! Good!' Cranston replied. He smiled falsely at the group. 'In a while, I shall see you all there. Now I wish to inspect Sir Ralph's body.'

'In the North Bastion,' Colebrooke retorted and, rising abruptly, led them out of the hall.

Sir John swayed like a galleon behind him whilst Athelstan hastily packed pen, inkhorn and parchment. The friar was pleased; he had names, first impressions, and Cranston had played his usual favourite trick of alienating everyone. The coroner was as crafty as a fox.

'If you handle suspects roughly,' he had once proclaimed, 'they are less likely to waste time on lies. And, as you know, Brother, most murderers are liars.'

Colebrook waited at the bottom of the steps of the great hall and silently led them past the soaring White Tower which shimmered in the thick snow packed around its base, traces of frost and slush on every shelf, cornice and windowsill. Athelstan stopped and looked up.

'Magnificent!' he murmured. 'How great are the works of man!'

'And how terrible,' Cranston added.

They both stood for a few seconds admiring the sheer white stone of the great tower. They were about to move on when a door at the foot of the keep, built under a flight of outside steps, was flung open. A fantastical hunchbacked creature with a shock of white hair appeared before them. For a moment, he stood as if frozen. His face was pallid, his body covered in a gaudy mass of dirty rags with oversized boots on his feet. Finally he scampered towards them on all fours like a dog, sending flurries of snow flying up on either side. The lieutenant cursed and turned away.

'Welcome to the Tower!' the creature shrieked. 'Welcome to my kingdom! Welcome to the Valley of the Shadow of Death!'

Athelstan looked down at the twisted white face and milky eyes of the albino crouching before him.

'Good morrow, sir,' he replied. 'And you are?'

'Red Hand. Red Hand,' the fellow muttered. He parted his blue-tinged lips, dirty yellow teeth chattering with the cold. 'My name is Red Hand.'

'Well, you're a funny bugger, Red Hand!' Cranston barked.

The mad eyes slyly studied the coroner.

'Madness is as madness does!' Red Hand muttered. 'Twice as mad as some and half as mad as others.' He brought his hand from behind his back and shook a stick with a dirty, inflated pig's bladder tied on the end. 'So, my darlings, you want to play with Red Hand?'

'Piss off, Red Hand!' the lieutenant growled, taking a threatening step towards him.

The albino just glared at Colebrooke.

'Old Red Hand knows things,' he said. 'Old Red Hand is not as stupid as he appears.' Grimy, claw-like fingers stretched out towards Athelstan. 'Red Hand can be your friend, for a price.'

Athelstan unloosed his purse and put two coins in the madman's hands. 'There,' he said softly. 'Now you can be both Sir John's friend and mine.'

'What do you know?' Cranston asked.

The albino jumped up and down. 'Sir Ralph is dead. Executed by God's finger. The Dark Shadows are here. A man's past is always with him. Sir Ralph should have heeded that.' The madman glared at the lieutenant. 'So should others! So should others!' he exclaimed. 'But Red Hand is busy, Red Hand must go.'

'My Lord Coroner, Brother Athelstan,' the lieutenant interrupted, 'Sir Ralph's corpse awaits us.'

'Off to see the gore and blood, are we?' Red Hand cried, jumping up and down. 'An evil man, Sir Ralph. He deserved what he got!'

The lieutenant lashed out with his boot, but Red Hand scampered away, shrieking with laughter.

'Who is he?' Athelstan whispered.

'A former mason here. His wife and child were killed in an accident many years ago.'

'And Sir Ralph let him stay here?'

'Sir Ralph hated the sight of him but could do very little about it. Red Hand is a royal beneficiary. He was a master mason to the old king and has a pension and the right to live here in the Tower.'

'Why Red Hand?' Athelstan asked.

'He lives in the dungeons, and scrubs the torture instruments and the killing block after executions.'

Athelstan shivered and wrapped his cloak more firmly about him. Truly, he thought, this was the Valley of Shadows, a place of violence and sudden death. The lieutenant was about to walk on, but Cranston caught him by the arm.

'What did Red Hand mean about Sir Ralph being an evil man who got his just deserts?'

Colebrooke's bleary eyes looked away. 'Sir Ralph was a strange man,' he muttered. 'Sometimes I think he had demons lurking in his soul.'

Chapter 3

Athelstan and Cranston followed Colebrooke around the half-timbered sheds and outbuildings, under the archway of the inner curtain wall and across the frozen yard to a huge tower which bulged out over the moat. He stopped and pointed.

'There are dungeons beneath ground level, and above them steps leading to the upper tier which has one chamber.' He shrugged. 'That's where Sir Ralph died.'

'Was murdered!' Cranston interrupted.

'Are there other chambers?' Athelstan asked.

'There used to be a second tier, but the doorway was sealed off.'

Athelstan looked up at the snow-capped crenellations and drew in his breath quickly.

'A tower of silence,' he murmured. 'A bleak place to die.'

They walked up the steps. Inside two guards squatted on stools round a brazier. Colebrooke nodded at them. They climbed another steep staircase, pulled back the half-open door, and a dark, musty passageway stretched before them. Quietly cursing to himself, Colebrooke took a tinder from a stone shelf and the sconce torches flared into life. They walked along the cold corridor. Athelstan noticed the pile of fallen masonry, loose bricks and shale which sealed off the former entrance to the upper storey.

Colebrooke searched amongst some keys he had brought out from beneath his cloak, opened the door and, with a half-mocking gesture, waved Athelstan and Cranston inside.

The chamber was a stone-vaulted room. The first impression was one of brooding greyness. No hangings or tapestries on the walls, nothing except the gaunt figure of a dying Christ on a black, wooden crucifix. Pride of place was given to a huge four-poster bed, its begrimed, tawny curtains tightly closed. There was a table, stools and three or four wooden pegs driven into the wall next to the bed. A cloak, heavy jerkin and broad leather sword belt still hung there. On the other side of the bed stood a wooden lavarium with a cracked pewter bowl and jug over which a soiled napkin had been placed. A small hooded fireplace would have afforded some warmth, but only cold powdery ash lay there. A brazier full of half-burnt charcoal stood forlornly in the centre of the room. Athelstan was sure it was colder in here than outside. Cranston snapped his fingers at the open shutters.

'By the Devil's tits, man!' he exclaimed. 'It's freezing!'

'We left things as we found them, My Lord Coroner,' Colebrooke snapped back.

Athelstan nodded towards the window. 'Is that where the assassin is supposed to have climbed in?'

He stared at the huge diamond-shaped opening.

'It could have been the only way,' Colebrooke muttered, going across and slamming the shutters firmly together. Athelstan stared round the room. He recognized the fetid stench of death and noticed with distaste the soiled rushes on the floor and the cracked chamber pot full of night stools and urine.

'By the sod!' Cranston barked, tapping it with his boot. 'Get that removed or the place will stink like a plague pit!'

The coroner crossed to the bed and pulled the curtains back. Athelstan took one look and stepped away in horror. The corpse sprawled there, white and bloodless against the grimy bolsters and sheets; rigid hands still clutched the blood-soaked bedcovers and the man's head was thrust back, face contorted in the rictus of death. The heavy-lidded eyes of the corpse were half-open and seemed to be staring down at the terrible slash which ran from one ear to the other. The blood had poured out like wine from a cracked barrel and lay in a thick congealed mess across the dead man's chest and bedclothes. Athelstan pulled the sheets back and gazed at the half-naked, white body.

'The cause of death,' he muttered, 'is obvious. No other wounds or bruise marks.' He silently made the sign of the cross over the corpse and stepped back.

Colebrooke wisely stood well away. 'Sir Ralph feared such a death,' he murmured.

'When did this fear begin?' Athelstan asked.

'Oh, three to four days ago.'

'Why?' Cranston queried. 'What did Sir Ralph fear?'

Colebrooke shrugged. 'God knows! Perhaps his daughter or kinsman will tell you that. All I know is that before he died, Sir Ralph believed the Angel of Death stood at his elbow.'

Cranston walked across to the window, pulled back the shutters and leaned out into the chill air.

'A sheer drop,' he commented, drawing himself back, much to Athelstan's relief. He alone realized how much the good coroner had drunk. Cranston slammed the shutters closed.

'Who would make such a climb at the dead of night and in the depths of winter?'

'Oh, there are steps cut in the wall,' Colebrooke answered smugly. 'Although few people know they are there.'

'Why?' Athelstan asked.

'They're really just footholds,' Colebrooke answered. 'A precaution of the mason who built the tower. If anyone fell in the moat, they could climb out.'

'So,' Cranston mumbled, slumping down on to the stool and wiping his forehead, 'you are saying someone, probably a soldier or paid assassin, used these footholds and climbed to the window.' He turned and looked at the shutters. 'According to you,' the coroner continued, 'the killer prized a dagger through the crack to lift the catch, got in, and slashed Sir Ralph's throat.'

Colebrooke nodded slowly. 'I suppose so, Sir John.'

'And I suppose,' Cranston added sarcastically, 'Sir Ralph just allowed his assassin entry, didn't even get out of his bed but lay back like a lamb and allowed his throat to be cut?'

Colebrooke went across to the shutters, and, pushing the wooden clasp back into place, locked them shut. He then took out his dagger, slid it into the crack between the shutters and gently levered the clasp open. He drew the shutters wide, turned and smiled at Cranston.

'It can be done, My Lord Coroner,' he observed gaily. 'The assassin, quiet-footed, crossed the chamber. It only takes seconds to cut a man's throat, especially someone who has drunk deeply.'

Athelstan reflected on what the lieutenant had said. It did make sense. Both he and Cranston knew about the Nightshades, robbers who could enter a house under cover of darkness and plunder it beneath the sleeping noses of burgesses, wives, children, and even dogs. Why should this be any different? Athelstan studied the chamber carefully: the heavy granite walls, the stone-vaulted ceiling and cold rag stone floor beneath the rushes.

'No, Brother!' Colebrooke called out as if reading the friar's thoughts. 'No secret passageways exist. There are two ways to enter this chamber – by the window or by the door. However, there were guards in the lower chamber, we passed them as we came up, and the upper storey is blocked off by a fall of masonry.'

'Were any traces of blood found?' Athelstan asked. He saw the lieutenant smirk and glance sideways at the gory corpse sprawled on the bed. 'No,' Athelstan continued crossly, 'I mean elsewhere. Near the window or the door. When the assassin walked away, his knife or sword must have been coated with blood.'

Colebrooke shook his head. 'Look for yourself, Brother. I found no trace.'

Athelstan glanced despairingly at Cranston who now sat like a sagging sack on the stool, eyes half-closed after his morning's heavy drinking and vigorous exertions in the cold. The friar conducted his search thoroughly: the bedclothes and corpse were soaked in dried blood but he found no traces near the window, in the rushes or around the door.

'Did you find anything else disturbed?'

Colebrooke shook his head. Cranston suddenly stirred himself.

'Why did Sir Ralph come here?' he asked abruptly. 'These were not his usual chambers.'

'He thought he would be safe. The North Bastion is one of the most inaccessible in the fortress. The constable's usual lodgings are in the royal apartments in the White Tower.'

'And he was safe,' Athelstan concluded, 'until the moat froze over.'

'Yes,' Colebrooke replied. 'Neither I nor anyone else thought of that.'

'Wouldn't an assassin be seen?' Cranston interrupted.

'I doubt it, Sir John. At the dead of night, the Tower is shrouded in darkness. There were no guards on the North Bastion, whilst those on the curtain wall would spend most of their time trying to keep warm.'

'So,' Cranston narrowed his eyes, 'before we meet the others, let's establish the sequence of events.'

'Sir Ralph dined in the great hall and drank deeply. Geoffrey Parchmeiner and the two guards escorted him over here. The latter searched this chamber, the passageway and the room below. All was in good order.'

'Then what?'

'Sir Ralph secured the door behind him. The guards outside heard that. They escorted Geoffrey out of the passageway, locked the door at the far end and began their vigil. They were at their posts all night and noticed nothing untoward. Neither did I on my usual nightly rounds.'

Athelstan held up his hand. 'This business of the keys?'

'Sir Ralph had a key to his own chamber, as did the guards, on a key ring below.'

'And the door at the end of that passage?'

'Again, both Sir Ralph and the guard had a key. You will see them when you go below, hanging from pegs driven into the wall.'

'Go on, Lieutenant, what happened then?'

'Just after Prime this morning, Geoffrey Parchmeiner…' The lieutenant looked slyly at Athelstan. 'You have met him? The beloved prospective son-in-law? Well, he came across to waken Sir Ralph.'

'Why Geoffrey?'

'Sir Ralph trusted him.'

'Did he bring food or drink?'

'No. He wanted to, but because of the cold weather Sir Ralph said he wished to be aroused with Geoffrey in attendance. They would plan the day, and breakfast with the rest of the company in the hall.'

'Continue,' Cranston blurted crossly, stamping his feet against the cold.

'Well, the guards led Geoffrey up the stairs, let him through the passageway door and locked it behind him. They heard him go down the corridor, knock on the door and shout, but Sir Ralph could not be roused. After a while Geoffrey came back. "Sir Ralph cannot be woken," he proclaimed.' Colebrooke stopped, scratched his head and closed his eyes in an attempt to recall events. 'Geoffrey took the key to Sir Ralph's chamber from the peg but changed his mind and came for me. I was in the great hall. I hurried here, collected the keys and unlocked the door.' The lieutenant gestured towards the bed. 'We found Sir Ralph as you did.'

'And the shutters were open?' Cranston asked.

'Yes.'

'How long has the moat been frozen solid?' Athelstan queried.

'About three days.' Colebrooke rubbed his hands together vigorously. 'Surely, Sir John, we need not stay here?' he pleaded. 'There are warmer places to ask such questions.'

Cranston stood and stretched.

'In a little while,' he murmured. 'How long had Sir Ralph been constable?'

'Oh, about four years.'

'Did you like him?'

'No, I did not. He was a martinet, a stickler for discipline – except where his daughter or her lover were concerned.'

Cranston nodded and went back to look at the corpse. 'I suppose,' he muttered, 'there's no sign of any murder weapon? Perhaps, Athelstan, you could check again?'

The friar groaned, but with Colebrooke's help carried out a quick survey of the room, raking back the rushes with their feet, and sifting amongst the cold ash in the fireplace.

'Nothing,' Colebrooke declared. 'It would be hard to hide a pin here.'

Athelstan went across and pulled the sword from Sir Ralph's sword belt. 'There are no blood stains here,' he commented. 'Not a jot, not a speck. Sir John, we should go.'

Outside, they stopped to examine a stain on the passage floor but it was only oil. They were halfway down the stairs when Athelstan suddenly pulled the lieutenant back. 'The two guards?' he whispered. 'They are the same sentries as last night?'

'Yes. Professional mercenaries who served Sir Ralph when he was in the household of His Grace the Regent.'

'They would be loyal?'

Colebrooke made a face. 'I should think so. They took a personal oath. More importantly, Sir Ralph had doubled their wages. They had nothing to gain from his death and a great deal to lose.'

'Do *you* have anything to gain?' Cranston asked thickly.

Colebrooke's hand fell to his dagger hilt. 'Sir John, I resent that, though I confess I did not like Whitton, notwithstanding His Grace the Regent did.'

'Did you want Whitton's post?'

'Of course. I believe I am the better man.'

'But the Regent disagreed?'

'John of Gaunt kept his own private counsel,' Colebrooke sourly observed. 'Though I hope he will now appoint me as Whitton's successor.'

'Why?' Athelstan asked softly.

Colebrooke looked surprised. 'I am loyal, and if trouble comes, I shall hold the Tower to my dying breath!'

Cranston grinned and tapped him gently on the chest. 'Now, my good lieutenant, you have it. We think the same on this. Sir Ralph's death may be linked to the conspiracies which flourish like weeds in the villages and hamlets around London.'

Colebrooke nodded. 'Whitton was a hard taskmaster,' he replied, 'and the Great Community's paid assassin would have found such a task fairly easy to accomplish.'

Athelstan too smiled and patted Colebrooke on the shoulder. 'You may be right, Master Colebrooke, but there is only one thing wrong with such a theory.'

The lieutenant gazed dumbly back.

'Can't you see?' Athelstan murmured. 'Someone in the Tower must have told such an assassin where, when and how Sir Ralph could be found!'

A now crestfallen lieutenant led them down the stairs. The two burly, thick-set guards still squatted with hands outstretched towards the fiery red brazier. They hardly moved as Colebrooke approached and Athelstan sensed their disdain for a junior officer suddenly thrust into authority.

'You were on guard last night?'

The soldiers nodded.

'You saw nothing untoward?'

Again the nods, accompanied by supercilious smiles as if they found Athelstan slightly amusing and rather boring.

'Stand up!' Cranston roared. 'Stand up. You whore-begotten sons of bitches! By the sod, I've had better men tied to trees and whipped till their backs were red!'

The two soldiers jumped up at the steely menace in Cranston's voice.

'That's better,' the coroner purred. 'Now, my buckos, answer my clerk's questions properly and all will be well.' He grasped one by the shoulder. 'Otherwise, I may put it about that in the dead of night you killed your master.'

'That's not true!' the fellow grated. 'We were loyal to Sir Ralph. We saw nothing, knew nothing, until the popinjay—' the guard shrugged '—the constable's prospective son-in-law, comes rushing down, exclaiming he can't rouse Sir Ralph. He grabs the key and is about to return, but the coward thinks better of it and sends for the lieutenant here.'

'You heard him knock on the door and call Sir Ralph?' Athelstan asked.

'Of course we did.'

'But he did not enter?'

'The key was down here,' the guard replied, pointing to a peg driven into the wall. 'It was hanging before our eyes. There were only two. One here, and Sir Ralph had the other.'

'You are certain of that?' Cranston asked.

'Yes, yes,' the fellow confirmed. 'I found the other key on the table next to the constable's bed as soon as I opened the door. I have it now.'

Cranston nodded. 'Ah, well,' he breathed, 'enough is enough. Let us see the tower from the outside.'

As they left the North Bastion, they suddenly heard an awesome din from the inner bailey. They followed the lieutenant as he hurried under the arch, staring across the snow-capped green. The noise came from a building in between the great hall and the White Tower. At first Athelstan couldn't distinguish what was happening. He saw figures running about, dogs leaping and yelping in the snow. Colebrooke breathed deeply and relaxed.

'It's only him,' he murmured. 'Look!'

Athelstan and Cranston watched in stupefaction as a great brown shaggy-haired bear lurched into full view. The beast stood on its hind legs, its paws pummelling the air.

'I have seen bears before,' Cranston murmured, 'rough-haired little beasts attacked by dogs, but nothing as majestic as that.'

The bear roared and Athelstan saw the great chains which swung from the iron collar round its neck, each held by a keeper as the lunatic Red Hand led the animal across the bailey to be fastened to a huge stake at the far side of the great hall.

'It's magnificent!' Athelstan murmured.

'A present,' the lieutenant replied, 'from a Norwegian prince to the present king's grandfather, God bless him! It is called Ursus Magnus.'

'Ah!' Athelstan smiled. 'After the constellation.'

Colebrooke looked dumb.

'The stars,' Athelstan persisted. 'A constellation in the heavens.'

Colebrooke smiled thinly and led them back to a postern gate in the outer curtain wall. He pulled back bolts and the hinges shrieked in protest as he threw open the solid, creaking gate.

No one, Athelstan thought, has gone through this gate for months.

They stepped gingerly on to the frozen moat, the very quietness and heavy mist creating an eerie, unreal feeling.

'The only time you'll ever walk on water, Priest!' Cranston muttered.

Athelstan grinned. 'A strange feeling,' he replied, then looked at the drawn face of Colebrooke. 'Why is the gate here?'

The lieutenant shrugged. 'It's used very rarely. Sometimes a spy or a secret messenger slips across the moat, or someone who wishes to leave the Tower unnoticed. Now,' he tapped his boot on the thick, heavy ice, 'it makes no difference.'

Athelstan stared around. Behind him the great soaring curtain wall stretched up to the snow-laden clouds, whilst the far side of the moat was hidden in a thick mist. Nothing stirred. There was no sound except their own breathing and the scraping noise of their boots on the ice. They walked gingerly, carefully, as if expecting the ice to crack and the water to reappear. They followed the sheer curtain wall round to the North Bastion.

'Where are these footholds?' Cranston asked.

Colebrooke beckoned them forward and pointed to the brickwork. At first the holds in the wall could hardly be detected, but at last they saw them, like the claw marks of a huge bird embedded deeply in the stonework. Cranston pushed his hand into one of them.

'Yes,' he muttered, 'someone has been here. Look, the ice is broken.'

Athelstan inspected the icy apertures and agreed. He followed the trail of the footholds up until they, like the top of the tower, were lost in the clinging mist.

'A hard climb,' he observed. 'Most dangerous in the dead of night.' He looked at the frost-covered snow and, stooping down, picked up something, hiding it in the palm of his hand until Colebrooke turned to go back.

'What is it?' Cranston slurred. 'What did you find there?'

The friar opened his hand and Cranston smiled at the silver-gilt buckle glinting in his palm.

'So,' Cranston mumbled, 'someone was here. All we have to do is match the buckle with its wearer, then it's heigh-ho to King's Bench, a swift trial, and a more prolonged execution.'

Athelstan shook his head. 'Oh, Sir John,' he whispered, 'if things were only so simple.' They went back through the postern gate and into the inner bailey. The Tower had now come to life even though the frost still held and there was still no sign of any break in the weather. Farriers had fired the forges and the bailey rang with the clang of the hammer and the whoosh of bellows as ragged apprentices worked hard to fan the forge fires to life. A butcher was slicing up a gutted pig and scullions ran, shaking the blood from the meat, to stick it into fat-bellied tubs of salt and brine so it would last through to the spring. A groom trotted a lame horse, roaring at his companions to look for any defect, whilst scullions and maids soaked piles of grease-stained pewter plates in vats of scalding water. The lieutenant watched the scene and grinned.

'Soon be Christmas!' he announced. 'All must be clean and ready.'

Athelstan nodded, watching three boys drag holly and other evergreen shrubs across the snow to the steps of the great keep.

'You will celebrate Christmas?' Athelstan asked, nodding to a high-wheeled cart from which soldiers were now unloading huge tuns of wine.

'Of course,' Colebrooke replied. 'Death is no stranger to the Tower, and Sir Ralph will be buried before Christmas Eve.' He walked on as if tired of their questions.

Athelstan winked at Cranston, stood his ground and called out: 'Master Colebrooke?'

The lieutenant turned, trying hard to hide his irritation. 'Yes, Brother?'

'Why are so many people here? I mean the hospitallers, Master Geoffrey, Sir Fulke?'

Colebrooke shrugged. 'The constable's kinsman always stay here.'

'And young Geoffrey?'

Colebrooke smirked. 'I think he's as hot for Mistress Philippa as she is for him. Sir Ralph invited him to the Tower for Christmas, and why not? This great frost has stopped all business in the city and Sir Ralph insisted, especially when he grew strangely fearful, that his daughter's betrothed stay with him.'

'The two hospitallers?' Cranston asked.

'Old friends,' Colebrooke replied. 'They come here each Christmas and go through the same ritual. They arrive two weeks before Yuletide, and every Christmas Eve go to sup at the Golden Mitre tavern outside the

Tower. They always stay till Twelfth Night and leave after the Feast of the Epiphany. Three times they've done so, though God knows why!' He turned and spat a globule of yellow phlegm on to the white snow. 'As I have said, Sir Ralph had his secrets and I never pried.'

Cranston fidgeted, a sign he was growing bored as well as tired of the cold, so Athelstan allowed Colebrooke to take them back into the White Tower, up a stone spiral staircase, through an antechamber and into the Chapel of St John.

Athelstan immediately relaxed as he caught the fragrant scent of incense. He walked into the nave with its soaring hammer-beamed roof and wide aisles, each flanked by twelve circular pillars around which thick green and scarlet velvet ribbons had been tied. The floor was polished, the strange red flagstones seeming to give off their own warmth, whilst the delicate paintings on the walls and the huge glazed windows caught the blinding white light of the snow and bathed both sanctuary and nave in a warm, glowing hue. Braziers, sprinkled with herbs, stood next to each pillar, making the air thick with the cloying sweetness of summer. Athelstan felt warm, comfortable and at peace, even though he studied the church enviously. If only, he thought, he had such decorations at St Erconwald! He saw the great silver star pinned above the chancel screen and, muttering with delight, walked into the silent sanctuary, marvelling at the marble steps and magnificent altar carved out of pure white alabaster.

'So serene,' he murmured, coming back to join his companions.

Colebrooke smiled self-consciously. 'Before we left the hall, I ordered servants to prepare the place,' he announced, and looked around. 'By some trick or artifice of the architects, whether it be the thickness of the stone or its location in the Tower, this chapel is always warm.'

'I need refreshment,' Cranston solemnly announced. 'I have walked up many stairs, studied a ghastly corpse, balanced on freezing ice, and now I've had enough! Master Lieutenant, you seem a goodly man. You will gather the rest here and, seeing it's the Yuletide season, bring a jug of claret for myself and my clerk.'

Colebrooke agreed and hurried off, but not before he and Athelstan had rearranged the chapel stools into a wide semicircle. Once he'd gone, Athelstan brought a polished table from the sanctuary and laid out pen, inkhorn and parchment. He took care to warm the ink over the brazier so it would run smooth and clear from his quill. Cranston just squatted on his chair, throwing back his cloak and revelling in the fragrant warmth. Athelstan studied him carefully.

'Sir John,' he murmured, 'take care with the wine. You have drunk enough and are tired.'

'Sod off, Athelstan!' Cranston slurred angrily. 'I'll drink what I damned well like!'

Athelstan closed his eyes and breathed a prayer for help. So far Sir John had behaved himself, but the wine in his belly might rouse the devil in his heart and only the Good Lord knew what mischief might then occur. Colebrooke hurried back. Behind him, much to Athelstan's despair, a servant carried a huge jug of claret and two deep-bowled goblets. Cranston seized the jug like a thirsty man and downed two cupfuls as the rest of the constable's household entered the chapel and sat on the stools before him. At last Cranston closed his eyes, gave a deep rich belch and pronounced himself satisfied. His reluctant guests stared in disbelief at the red face of the King's Coroner as he sprawled slack-limbed on the chair before them. Athelstan was torn between anger and admiration. Something had upset Cranston, though God only knew what. Nevertheless, the coroner's ability to drink a vineyard dry and still keep his wits about him always fascinated Athelstan.

The Dominican quickly scanned the assembled people. The two hospitallers looked aloof and disdainful. Philippa clung more closely to her now tipsy betrothed who grinned benevolently back at Cranston. Rastani, the servant, looked ill at ease, fearful of the huge cross which hung from one of the beams above him, and Athelstan wondered if the Muslim's conversion to the true faith was genuine. Sir Fulke looked bored, as if he wished to be free of such tiresome proceedings, whilst the chaplain's exasperation at being so abruptly summoned was barely suppressed.

'I do thank you,' Athelstan began smoothly, 'for coming here. Mistress Philippa, please accept our condolences on the sudden and ghastly loss of your father.' Athelstan toyed with the stem of his goose-quilled pen. 'We now know the details surrounding your father's death.'

'Murder!' Philippa strained forward, her ample bosom heaving under her thick taffeta dress. 'Murder, Brother! My father was murdered!'

'Yes, yes, so he was,' Cranston slurred. 'But by whom, eh? Why and how?' He sat up straight and drunkenly tapped the side of his fiery red nose. 'Do not worry, Mistress! The murderer will be found and do his last final dance on Tyburn scaffold.'

'Your father,' Athelstan interrupted, 'seemed most fearful, Mistress Philippa. He moved from his usual quarters and shut himself up in the North Bastion. Why? What frightened him?'

The group fell strangely silent, tensing at this intrusion into the very heart of their secrets.

'I asked a question,' Athelstan repeated softly. 'What was Sir Ralph so frightened of that he locked himself up in a chamber, doubled the wages of his guards, and insisted that visitors be searched? Who was it,' he continued, 'that wanted Sir Ralph's death so much he crossed an icy moat in the dead of night, climbed the sheer wall of a tower, and entered a guarded chamber to commit foul, midnight murder?'

'The rebels!' Colebrooke broke in. 'Traitors who wanted to remove a man who would protect the young King to the last drop of his blood!'

'Nonsense!' snapped Athelstan. 'His Grace the Regent, John of Gaunt, will as you said yourself, Master Colebrooke, appoint a successor no less fervent in his loyalty.'

'My father was special,' Philippa blurted out.

'Mistress,' Athelstan caught and held her tearful glance, 'God knows your father was special, both in his life and in his secrets. You know about those, so why not tell us?'

The girl's eyes fell away. She brought her hand from beneath her cloak and tossed a yellowing piece of parchment on to the table. 'That changed my father's life,' she stammered. 'Though God knows why!'

Athelstan picked up the parchment and quickly gazed at the people sitting around him. He noticed the hospitallers were suddenly tense. The friar smiled secretly to himself. Good, he thought. Now the mystery unfolds.

Chapter 4

The parchment was greasy and finger-stained, a six-inch square with a three-masted ship crudely drawn in the centre and a large black cross in each corner.

'Is that all?' Athelstan asked, passing the parchment back.

The girl tensed. Her lower lip trembled, tears pricked her eyes.

'There was something else,' Athelstan continued. 'Wasn't there?'

Philippa nodded. Geoffrey took her hand and held it, stroking it gently as if she was a child.

'There was a sesame seed cake.'

'What?' Cranston barked.

'A seed cake like a biscuit, a dirty yellow colour.'

'What happened to it?' Cranston asked.

'I saw my father walk along the parapet. He seemed very agitated. He brought his arm back and threw the cake into the moat. After that he was a changed man, keeping everyone away from him and insisting on moving to the North Bastion tower.'

'Is that correct?' Cranston asked the rest of the group.

'Of course it is!' the chaplain snapped. 'Mistress Philippa is not a liar.'

'Then, Father,' Cranston asked silkily, 'did Sir Ralph share his secrets with you?' He held up a podgy hand. 'I know about the seal of confession. All I'm asking is, did he confide in you?'

'I think not,' Colebrooke sniggered. 'Sir Ralph had certain questions to ask the chaplain about stores and provisions which appear to have gone missing.'

The priest turned on him, his lip curling like that of an angry dog.

'Watch your tongue, Lieutenant!' he rasped. 'True, things have gone missing, but that does not mean that I am the thief. There are others,' he added meaningfully, 'with access to the Wardrobe Tower.'

'Meaning?' Colebrooke shouted.

'Oh, shut up!' Cranston ordered. 'We are not here about stores but about a man's life. I ask all of you, on your allegiance to the King – for this could be a matter of treason – did Sir Ralph confide in one of you? Does this parchment mean anything to any of you?'

A chorus of 'No's' greeted the coroner's demands though Athelstan noticed that the hospitallers looked away as they mumbled their responses.

'I hope you are telling the truth,' Cranston tartly observed. 'Sir Ralph may have been slain by peasant leaders plotting rebellion. Your father, Mistress Philippa, was a close friend and trusted ally of the court.'

Athelstan intervened, trying to calm the situation. 'Mistress Philippa, tell me about your father.'

The girl laced her fingers together nervously and looked at the floor.

'He was always a soldier,' she began. 'He served in Prussia against the Latvians, on the Caspian, and then travelled to Outremer, Egypt, Palestine and Cyprus.' She blinked and nodded at the hospitallers. 'They can tell you more about that than I.' She took a deep breath. 'Fifteen years ago,' she continued, 'he was in Egypt in the army of the Caliph and then he came home covered in glory, a rich man. I was three years old. My mother died a year later and we entered the household of John of Gaunt. My father became one of his principal retainers; four years ago, he was appointed Constable of the Tower.'

Athelstan smiled understandingly. He knew Sir Ralph's type: a professional soldier, a mercenary who would crusade for the faith but was not averse to serving in the armies of the infidel. Athelstan stared round the group. How quiet and calm they appeared, though he sensed something was wrong. They were hiding mutual dislikes and rivalries in their over-eagerness to answer his questions.

'I suppose,' he remarked drily, 'you have already been through Sir Ralph's papers?'

Athelstan looked at Sir Fulke, who nodded.

'Of course I have been through my brother's documents, household accounts, memoranda and letters. I found nothing untoward. I am, after all,' he added, glaring round the room as if expecting a challenge, 'the executor of Sir Ralph's will.'

'Of course, of course,' Cranston assured him.

Athelstan groaned to himself. Yes, he thought, and if there was anything damaging, it will have been removed. He stared at the young man next to Philippa.

'How long, sir, have you known your betrothed?'

Geoffrey's wine-flushed face was wreathed in smiles as he gripped her hand more firmly. 'Two years.'

Athelstan noticed the conspiratorial smiles the two lovers exchanged.

Cranston leered at the girl whilst he considered the incongruous couple. Geoffrey was outstandingly handsome and probably quite wealthy, yet Philippa was almost plain. Moreover, Sir Ralph had been a soldier and Geoffrey was not, at first glance, the sort of man likely to be welcomed into such a family. Cranston then remembered Maude and his own passionate courting of her. Love was strange, as Athelstan kept reminding him, and opposites were often attracted to each other.

'Tell me, Geoffrey, why did you stay in the Tower?'

The young man belched and blinked his eyes as if he was on the point of falling asleep. 'Well,' he mumbled, 'the great frost has killed all trade in the city. Sir Ralph wished me to stay during the Yuletide season – even more so after he became distraught and upset.'

'Did you know the reason for his anxiety?'

'No,' Geoffrey slurred. 'Why should I?'

'Did you like Sir Ralph?'

'I loved him as a son does a father.'

Cranston switched his attention to Sir Fulke, who was beginning openly to fidget.

'Sir Fulke, you say you are the executor of Sir Ralph's will?'

'Yes, I am. And, before you ask, I am also a beneficiary, after the will is approved in the Court of Probate.'

'What does the will provide?'

'Well, Sir Ralph had property next to the Charterhouse in St Giles. This and all of the monies banked with the Lombards in Cornhill will go to Philippa.'

'And to you?'

'Meadows and pastures in the Manor of Holywell outside Oxford.'

'A rich holding?'

'Yes, Sir John, a rich holding, but not rich enough to murder for.'

'I didn't say that.'

'You implied it.'

'Sir Ralph,' Athelstan hurriedly interrupted, 'was a wealthy man?'

'He amassed wealth in his travels,' Sir Fulke snapped back. 'And he was careful with his monies.' Athelstan noticed the sour smile on the chaplain's face. Sir Ralph, he thought, was probably a miser. The friar looked sideways at Cranston and quietly groaned. The good coroner was taking one of his short naps, his great belly sagging, mouth half-open. Oh, Lord, Athelstan quietly prayed, please make sure he doesn't snore!

'Why do you live in the Tower, a bleak dwelling place for any man?' Athelstan abruptly asked.

Sir Fulke shrugged. 'My brother paid me to help him in an unofficial capacity.'

Both he and Athelstan chose to ignore the snorting laughter of Colebrooke. Cranston was now quietly nodding, belching softly and smacking his lips. Mistress Philippa tightened her mouth and Athelstan cursed; he did not wish his interrogation to end in mocking laughter.

'Sir Gerard, Sir Brian,' he almost shouted in an attempt to rouse Cranston, 'how long have you been in the Tower?'

'Two weeks,' Fitzormonde replied. 'We come every year.'

'It's a ritual,' Mowbray added, 'ever since we served with Sir Ralph in Egypt. We met to discuss old times.'

'So you were close friends of Sir Ralph?'

'In a sense. Colleagues, veterans from old wars.' Mowbray stroked his evenly clipped beard. 'But, I'll be honest with you, Sir Ralph was a man more feared and respected than loved.'

Athelstan picked up the yellowing piece of parchment and thrust it at them.

'Do you know what this drawing means or the significance of the seed cake?'

Both knights shook their heads, but Athelstan was sure they were lying. He leaned forward. 'Why?' he whispered. 'Why should Sir Ralph be so terrified of this?' He stared slowly round the rest of the group.

'A cup of sack!' Cranston muttered thickly.

'Who found this?' Athelstan quickly asked.

Sir Fulke pointed to Rastani, who sat with his dark face fearful and anxious. Athelstan leaned forward. 'What does this mean, Rastani?'

The eyes stared blankly back.

'Where did you find it?'

The fellow suddenly made strange gestures with his fingers.

'He can hear but not speak,' Philippa reminded the friar.

Fascinated, Athelstan watched the strange hand signs which Philippa translated for him.

'He found it on a table in my father's chamber,' she announced. 'Four days ago. Early on the morning of the ninth of December – that and the hard-baked seed cake.'

Athelstan caught and held Rastani's glance.

'You were a faithful servant to Sir Ralph?'

The man nodded in response.

'Why didn't you move with your master to the North Bastion?' Athelstan continued.

The fellow's mouth opened and shut like a landed carp's.

'I can answer that,' Philippa said. 'When the message was received, my father distanced himself from Rastani, though God knows why.' She gently stroked the man's hand. 'As I have said, Father became strange. Even I did not recognise him from his actions.'

Cranston smacked his lips and suddenly stirred.

'Yes, yes, very good!' he bawled. 'But did any of you approach the North Bastion tower the night Sir Ralph was killed?'

A series of firm denials greeted his question.

'So you can all account for your movements?'

'I can,' the kinsman spoke up. 'Rastani and I were out of the Tower. We were sent to buy stores from a merchant in Cripplegate. Or, at least, that's where the warehouse is. You can ask Master Christopher Manley in Heyward Lane near All Hallows.'

'That's near the Tower?'

'Yes, it is, Sir John.'

'And when did you leave?'

'Before dinner, and did not return until after Prime this morning when we heard of Sir Ralph's death. Rastani and I can vouch for each other. If you doubt that, speak to Master Manley. He saw us take lodgings at a tavern in Muswell Street.'

Sir John rose and stretched.

'Well, well! Now my clerk and I,' he trumpeted, 'would like to question each of you alone. Though,' he smiled at the girl, 'Mistress Philippa and Geoffrey had best stay together. Master Colebrooke, there's a chamber below. Perhaps our guests could wait there?'

There were mumbled protests and groans but Cranston, refreshed after his nap, glared round beneath thick furrowed brows. Led by Colebrooke, all left except for Philippa and Geoffrey.

'Your chamber, Master Geoffrey?' Athelstan asked. 'Where is it?'

'Above the gatehouse.'

'And you stayed there all night?'

The young man smiled weakly. 'You're a perceptive man, Sir John. That's why you asked me to stay, I suppose? I spent the night with Philippa.'

The girl looked away, blushing. Cranston smiled and tapped the man gently on the shoulder. 'Why did you not rouse Sir Ralph yourself?'

The young man rubbed his eyes. 'As I have said before, I didn't have a key and, God be my witness, I knew there was something wrong. The corridor was cold, with no sound from Sir Ralph's chamber.' He smiled bleakly at Athelstan. 'I am not the bravest of men, I'll be honest. I did not like Sir Ralph using me as a page boy but he distrusted the others.'

'You mean Colebrooke and the rest?'

'Yes, I think so.'

Cranston stared at Philippa. 'Had your father been in such dark spirits before?'

'Yes, about three years ago, just before Christmas. But it passed when he met his companions, as was their custom, and supped at the Golden Mitre.'

'Who were your father's companions?' Athelstan asked.

'Well, the two hospitallers, Sir Gerard Mowbray and Sir Brian Fitzormonde, and Sir Adam Horne – he's a merchant in the city.'

'Did these include all your father's comrades-in-arms?'

'Oh, there was someone called Bartholomew. Bartholomew...' the girl repeated, biting her lip '...Burghgesh, I believe. But he never came.'

'Why?'

'I don't know.' She half laughed. 'I think he's dead.'

'Why did your father insist on meeting his friends every year just before Christmas?'

'I don't know. Some pact they made a long time ago.'

Athelstan scrutinised the girl carefully. He was sure she was hiding something. 'Tell me,' he said, changing tack, 'is there more than one postern gate on to the moat?'

'Oh, yes,' Philippa replied. 'Quite a number.'

Athelstan glanced at Cranston. 'My Lord Coroner, do you have any questions?'

'No,' Sir John replied. 'Enough is enough! Ask Master William Hammond to come in.'

The priest entered in a surly, disgruntled way, biting his thumb nail to the quick as he gave curt answers to Athelstan's questions. Yes, he had been in the fortress that evening, but in his chamber in the Beauchamp Tower near the Church of St Peter ad Vincula.

The two hospitaller knights were more courteous but equally adamant. They had chambers in Martin Tower and spent most of the evening drinking or trying their hand at chess.

'I assure you, Sir John,' Mowbray rasped, 'we can hardly find our way around the Tower in the full light of day, never mind on a freezing winter's night.'

'But you know what this means, don't you?' Athelstan accused, picking up the piece of yellow parchment.

'By heaven, we do not!' Fitzormonde replied.

'Sir,' Athelstan retorted, 'I think you do, as you also know about the seed cake.'

The two hospitallers shook their heads.

'Oh, come,' Athelstan continued. 'Let's not be coy. You are monks and knights. Your Order fights for the cross in Outremer. My Order, too, has brothers who serve there.

75

They bring back tales which they relate over the dinner table at Blackfriars.'

'What tales?' Mowbray challenged.

'How in the mountains of Palestine live a secret sect of infidels called the Assassins, ruled by a chieftain called the Old Man of the Mountain. This coven deals in secret assassination. They are fed on drugs and despatched by their master with golden daggers to kill whomever he has marked down for destruction.'

Cranston watched the two knights tense and, for the first time, show a flicker of nervousness, Fitzormonde particularly.

'Now these assassins,' Athelstan continued, 'always give their victim fair warning. They do not leave a picture but a flat seed cake as a sign that violent death will soon be upon them.' Athelstan stood up and stretched to ease the cramp in his thighs and legs. 'I ask myself, why is this secret sect which flourishes in the Middle Sea, carrying out murder in the cold and sombre chambers of the Tower of London?'

'Are you accusing us?' Mowbray shouted. 'If so, do it!'

'I am not accusing anyone, just remarking on a strange coincidence.'

'Rastani is from Palestine!' Mowbray cried. 'Sir Ralph did distance himself from his so-called faithful servant.'

'Why do you say "so-called"?' Cranston quickly asked.

'Because I do not believe Rastani's conversion to our faith was genuine. Such men bear grudges. They wait years to settle accounts.'

'But Rastani was absent from the Tower?'

'He could have slipped back.'

'No, no, no!' Athelstan sat down and shook his head. 'Sir Ralph's death is more complex than that. You served with him?'

'Yes, we did. The Caliph of Cairo hired us to crush revolts in the city of Alexandria.'

'And after that?'

'Sir Ralph came home. We stayed a while longer before returning to our house in Clerkenwell.'

'Have you ever returned across the seas?' Cranston asked.

Mowbray shook his head. 'No, Fitzormonde is slightly wrong. When we served with Sir Ralph, we were not hospitallers. We joined after we left him. The Order sent us back to England. I am at Clerkenwell, Fitzormonde in our house at Rievaulx near York.'

Athelstan stared at the closed, set faces of both knights. 'Forgive me,' Athelstan said quietly, 'I do not wish to call you liars, but there is a great mystery here and you are party to it.' He leaned over and suddenly pulled back Mowbray's cloak. 'You wear chained mail? And you, too, Sir Brian. Why? Do you also fear the assassin's dagger? How well do you sleep at night? What secrets did you share with Sir Ralph?'

'By the Rood!' Sir Brian suddenly stood up. 'I have heard enough. We have told you what we can. Leave it at that!'

Both hospitallers swept out of the room. Cranston slumped on the stool and stretched out his legs.

'A pretty mess, eh, Friar? What have we here? Treason by persons unknown or foul midnight murder?'

'I don't know.' Athelstan replaced the stopper in the ink horn as he rearranged his writing materials. 'But we do have the buckle we found on the icy moat, and I know who it belongs to.'

'By the sod!' Cranston cried. 'For a monk you are sharp-eyed, Athelstan.'

'For a friar I am very quick, My Lord Coroner, and so would you be if you drank less claret!'

'I drink to drown my sorrows.' Cranston looked away. What would Maude be doing now? he fretted. What was she hiding? Why wouldn't she just tell him instead of giving those long, mournful glances? Cranston glared at the small statue in a niche, the Virgin and Child; secretly, the coroner hated Christmas. Yuletide always brought back the memories of little Matthew, taken by the plague, but not before the mite had shown Sir John the wonder with which every child greeted Christmas. Did Maude also have her memories?

'Sir John!'

Cranston blinked to hide his tears and grinned over at Athelstan.

'I have a need of refreshment, monk!'

Athelstan saw the pain in his friend's face and looked away.

'In a while, Sir John. First, let us see Sir Fulke. I wish to search Sir Ralph's bed chamber here in the White Tower.'

Cranston nodded and lumbered off whilst Athelstan packed his writing tray away. The friar sat for a while admiring the beauty of St John's Chapel, comparing it to the grimness of St Erconwald's. He thought of Benedicta. How lovely she had looked at the early morning Mass. He wondered if Huddle would use her in the painting of the Visitation he was planning for one of the aisles. What, Athelstan wondered, would she do at Christmas? She had mentioned a brother in Colchester. Perhaps she might stay in Southwark and agree to go for a walk, or at least sit and share a goblet of wine with him and gossip about the past. Christmas could be so lonely… Athelstan's eye caught a crucifix and he suddenly remembered the horrors being perpetrated in the cemetery at St Erconwald's. He must get to the bottom of that matter. Who could it be, and why?

'Brother Athelstan! Brother Athelstan!' Cranston stood, leering down at him. 'You drink too much claret, priest,' the coroner mockingly announced. 'Come, we must visit the late constable's chamber. Colebrooke and Sir Fulke are on their way.'

Sir Ralph's quarters were up a polished wooden staircase in one of the turrets of the White Tower, a pleasant, sweet-smelling chamber in sharp contrast to the grim cell over in the North Bastion. Two small bay windows with cushioned seats below and an oriel window, glazed with stained glass depicting the Agnus Dei, provided light. The walls were of plaster, painted soft green and decorated with silver and gold lozenges. A thick tapestry hung just above the small canopied fireplace, the floor had been polished smooth, and the great bed was covered by a gold-tasselled counterpane. At the foot of the four-poster, with its lid thrown back, stood Sir Ralph's huge personal coffer.

'It's luxurious,' Cranston whispered. 'What terrified Sir Ralph so much he had to move from here to that bleak prison cell?'

Cranston and Athelstan squatted down before the coffer and began to go through Sir Ralph's personal papers, but they found nothing about his years in Outremer. Every document concerned his office as constable or his service in the retinue of John of Gaunt. They must have spent an hour sifting through letters, indentures and memoranda. Only a Book of Hours caught Athelstan's attention. Each page was decorated with delicate filigree-like scrollwork in a range of dazzling colours: on one page lightly drawn angel figures, on another a priest sprinkling a shrouded corpse with holy water as he committed it to the grave. The Nativity, with Mary and Joseph bowing over a sleeping child; Christ's walk through Limbo, driving away black-faced demons with the power of his golden eye. Athelstan became engrossed, fascinated by its beauty. He looked inside the cover and noticed how Sir Ralph had scrawled prayer after prayer to St Julian. 'St Julian, pray for me! St Julian, avert God's anger! St Julian, intercede for me with Christ's mother!' Each of the blank pages at the back of the book was filled with similar phrases. Athelstan read them all, ignoring Cranston's mutterings and the angry boot-tapping of Sir Fulke. Finally Athelstan closed the coffer and stood up.

'You are finished, friar?' the kinsman snapped.

Athelstan looked sharply at him: Sir Fulke was apparently a man who hid behind a veil of bonhomie and good humour but now he looked angry, suspicious, and resentful of their intrusion.

'Am I finished?' Athelstan echoed. 'Yes and no, Sir Fulke.'

The knight blew out his cheeks. 'The day is passing, friar,' he observed tartly, glaring out of the window. 'I am a busy man with matters to attend to. What more do you want?'

'You wear boots, Sir Fulke?'

'Yes, I wear boots!' came the mimicking reply.

'And there are buckles on your boots?'

The colour drained from Sir Fulke's face.

'Yes,' he mumbled.

'Well,' Athelstan pulled from his wallet the buckle he had found on the frozen moat, 'I believe this is yours. We found it on the ice outside the North Bastion tower, yet you said you were in the city all night.'

Sir Ralph's kinsman paled, the arrogance draining from his face. 'I lost the buckle yesterday.'

'Were you on the ice?'

Sir Fulke suddenly smiled. 'Yes, I was. I went there early this morning. You are not the only one, Brother, to think the assassins scaled the tower at dead of night to murder Sir Ralph.'

Athelstan tossed the buckle at him and Sir Fulke caught it clumsily.

'Then, Sir John, we are finished here. Perhaps some refreshment?'

They met Colebrooke in the passageway outside, thanked him for his attentions and went down the outside steps into the Tower bailey. Athelstan gauged it to be about two o'clock in the afternoon and this was confirmed by a servant who bumped into them as they passed the great hall. They were on the point of going under the Archway of Wakefield when Athelstan caught sight of the great brown bear chained to the wall in the corner near Bell Tower.

'I have never seen a bear so huge, Sir John!' he exclaimed.

Cranston clapped him on the shoulder. 'Then, my lad, it's time you did!'

The friar was fascinated by Ursus. The bear scarcely repaid the compliment but sat on his hindquarters, hungrily stuffing his great muzzle from a pile of scraps thrown around him. Cranston clapped his hands and the beast raised his huge, dark head. One paw came up and

Athelstan stood, riveted by the great, slavering jaws, the teeth – long, white and pointed like a row of daggers – and the insane ferocity blazing in those red-brown eyes. The bear lurched slightly towards them, growling softly in his throat. Cranston grabbed Athelstan's arm and pulled him back. The animal, alarmed by such rapid movement, now sprang to his full height, his great unsheathed paws beating the air as he strained at the massive steel collar around his neck. Both the coroner and his companion saw the chain fastened to the wall strain at its clasps.

'That chain,' Athelstan murmured, 'is not as secure as it should be.'

'Goodbye, Ursus,' Cranston whispered. 'Let's go, Athelstan. Very softly!'

They collected their horses and made their way out of the Tower into Petty Wales. A few stalls stood uncovered and some brave souls made their way through the ankle-deep, mucky slush. Two beggar children, arms and legs as thin as sticks, stood beside a brazier singing a carol. Cranston tossed them a penny, and turned to watch as a woman condemned as a scold was led by a beadle up to the stocks in Tower Street, a steel brank fastened tightly around her head. Down the dirt-filled alleyways business was thriving for the red-wigged whores and their constant stream of clients from the Tower garrison.

Cranston asked directions from a one-eyed beggar man and came back beaming from ear to ear.

'I have found it!' he announced. 'The Golden Mitre tavern! You know, the one Sir Ralph and the hospitallers went to every year for their banquet.'

The tavern was just near the Custom House on the corner of Thames Street, a grand, spacious affair with a green-leaved ale-stake pushed under the eaves from which hung a huge, gaudily painted sign. A red-nosed ostler took their horses. Inside, the tap room was airy and warmed by a fire. The rushes on the floor were clean and sprinkled with rosemary and thyme. The walls were lime-washed to keep off insects, and the hams which hung from the blackened beams gave off a sweet crisp smell which made Cranston smack his lips. They hired a table between the fire and the great polished wine butts. The landlord, a small, red-faced, balding fellow with a surprisingly clean apron draped across his expansive front, took one look at Sir John and brought across a deep bowl brimming with blood-red claret.

'Sir John!' he exclaimed. 'You remember me?'

Cranston seized the bowl by its two silver handles and half drained it at a gulp. 'Yes, I do,' he replied, smacking his lips and glaring over the rim. 'You are Miles Talbot who once worked as an ale-conner in the taverns round St Paul's.' Cranston put down the bowl and shook the landlord's hand. 'Let me introduce an honest man, Brother Athelstan. Talbot always knew when a blackjack of ale had been watered down. Well, well, well!' Cranston unclasped his cloak and basked in the sweet odours and warmth of the tavern. 'What can you serve us, Master Talbot? And don't give me fish. We know the river is frozen and the roads blocked, so anything from the water must be weeks old!'

The landlord grinned, listed the contents of his larder, and within the half-hour served a couple of pullets stuffed with herbs and covered with a piquant sauce of sweet butter and wild berries, a skillet pasty, an apple tansy, and a prodigious marrow pudding. Athelstan sat in complete stupefaction, drinking his beer, as Cranston cleared every platter, washing it all down with another bowl of claret.

At last Cranston belched, stretched, and beamed round the tavern, snapping his fingers to call Talbot over.

'Master Miles, a favour!'

'Anything you wish, Sir John.'

'Your house is frequented, or rather was frequented, by the late Constable of the Tower, Sir Ralph Whitton?'

Talbot's face became guarded. 'Now and again,' he mumbled. 'He used to meet here every Yuletide – he, two hospitallers, and others.'

'Oh, come, Miles. I'm not your enemy, you can trust me. What did they talk about?'

Talbot tapped the table with his stubby fingers. 'They sat here like you do, Sir John, well away from the rest. When I or any of the servants came near, they always fell silent.'

'And their demeanour? Were they sad or happy?'

'Sometimes they would laugh but they were generally very secretive. Often the two hospitallers would be locked in argument with Sir Ralph, and he would become quite hostile and snap back at them.'

'Anything else?'

Talbot shook his head and turned away. Cranston made a face at Athelstan and shrugged. Suddenly the taverner came back to the table.

'One thing,' he announced. 'Only one strange thing: about three years ago, around Christmas, a stranger came here.'

'What did he look like?'

'Oh, I can't remember his appearance but there was something about him. He was cowled and hooded, but he spoke like a soldier. He wanted to know if Sir Ralph drank here. I told him I knew nothing. He went on his way and

I never saw him again.' Talbot smiled apologetically. 'Sir John, on my oath, that's all I know.'

The coroner sat with lips pursed, staring down at the empty platters and dishes as if wishing the food he had devoured would magically reappear. Athelstan studied him carefully, rather concerned, for by now Sir John would usually have been shouting for more claret or sack.

'My Lord Coroner?'

'Yes, Brother Athelstan.'

'We must formulate some conclusions about Sir Ralph's death.'

Cranston blew noisily through his lips. 'What can we say?'

'First, you will agree that Sir Ralph was not murdered because he was Constable of the Tower. I mean, by peasant knaves plotting treason and rebellion?'

'I agree, Brother, but the assassin might have come from outside. He could have been a professional. There are plenty of ex-soldiers for hire in the city who would cut their mothers' throats if the price was right.'

Athelstan skimmed the rim of the wine goblet with his finger.

'I would like to believe that, Sir John, but it strikes me as false.' He shrugged. 'Yet, for the sake of argument, we will accept that the assassin crossed the frozen moat, climbed the North Bastion, undid the wooden shutters and quietly slashed Sir Ralph's throat.'

'It can and has been done, my good priest.'

'Of course,' Athelstan continued, 'the assassin may have been someone in the Tower who knew where Sir Ralph lay, and seized the opportunity of the moat freezing over to gain access to the footholds on the North Bastion.

Accordingly, either the murderer did this himself or paid someone else to do it.'

Cranston took a deep gulp from the wine bowl. 'Let us put the two together,' he said, cracking his knuckles softly. 'Let us say, for the sake of argument, that the plotter and the assassin are one and the same person. Virtually everyone we questioned, including Mistress Philippa, who may be plump but is very light on her feet, young and agile, could have climbed that tower.'

'Yet, in the main, they all have stories to explain their whereabouts.'

Cranston nodded. 'So they have. And it would be the devil's own job to prove any of them a liar. Moreover, have you noticed how each, apart from the chaplain, has someone to confirm their tale? Which means,' Cranston concluded, 'we could be hunting two murderers, not one: the two hospitallers, Sir Fulke and Rastani, Philippa and her young swain, Colebrooke and one of the guards.'

Athelstan stared idly up at one of the hams turning on its skewer from one of the rafters. 'In reality, we know nothing,' the friar concluded. 'We have no idea who the murderer is or how he or she gained access to Sir Ralph, though we did find Sir Fulke's buckle.'

'And yet he claims he walked on the frozen moat this morning before our arrival.'

'I believe him,' Athelstan answered. 'But remember how he said he lost the buckle the previous day.'

'What are you saying, friar?'

'Either he lost it as he crept across the moat to kill Sir Ralph or else someone put it there. I believe the latter. Sir Fulke's honesty in admitting he walked on the frozen moat saved him from suspicion. If he had denied it, and we later proved he had been on the moat, then it would have been a different matter.'

'How do we know he's honest?' Cranston barked. 'Did you notice the postern gate we used to gain access to the moat? Its hinges were rusty. Before we did, no one had used that door for years. Sir Fulke could be lying.'

'Or he could have used another postern gate.'

'An interesting thought, Brother, but let's look at motives.'

Athelstan spread his hands. 'There are as many motives as there are people in the Tower, Sir John. Was Sir Fulke greedy? Was the chaplain angry at being called a thief? Did Colebrooke want Sir Ralph's post? Did Philippa and her lover see Sir Ralph as an obstacle to their marriage or to Mistress Philippa's inheritance?'

'Which brings us,' Cranston concluded, 'to the two hospitallers. Now we know they are not telling the truth. Somehow or other that piece of parchment and the seed cake lie at the very heart of the murder and they must know something about both. Sir Ralph's death note bore the impression of a three-masted ship, the type often used in the Middle Sea, whilst the seed cake is the mark of the Assassins. Ergo, Sir Ralph's death must be linked to some mystery in his past, something connected with his days as a warrior in Outremer.'

Athelstan put his blackjack down on the table. He opened and shut his mouth.

'What's the matter, friar?'

'There's only one conclusion we can reach, Master Coroner – Sir Ralph might not be the first person to die in the Tower before Yuletide comes.'

Chapter 5

They stayed in the tavern a little longer. Athelstan expected Cranston to mount his horse and ride back to Cheapside but the coroner shook his head.

'I want to go back to your damned graveyard,' he snorted. 'You need a keen brain to plumb the mysteries there.'

'But Lady Maude will be waiting.'

'Let her!'

'Sir John, tell me, is there anything wrong?'

Cranston scowled and looked away.

'Is it Matthew?' Athelstan asked gently. 'Is it the anniversary of his death?'

Cranston stood up and linked his arm through Athelstan's as they went out to stand at the door whilst the ostler saddled their horses. 'Tell me. Brother, when you ran away from your order as a novice and took your younger brother to the wars in France, were you happy?'

Athelstan felt his own heart lurch. 'Of course.' He smiled thinly. 'I was young then. The blood boiled in my veins for some great adventure.'

'And when you found your brother dead, cold as ice in that battlefield, and trailed back to England to confess your deeds to your parents, what then?'

Athelstan looked across the darkening yard. 'In the Gospels, Sir John, Christ says that at the end of the world the very heavens will rock and the planets fall to earth in a fiery blaze.' Athelstan closed his eyes. He sensed Francis's ghost very close to him now. 'When I found my brother dead,' he continued, 'my heaven fell to earth.' He shrugged. 'I suppose it was the end of my world.'

'And what did you think of life then?'

Athelstan rubbed his mouth with his thumb and gazed directly at Cranston's sorrowful face. 'I felt betrayed by it,' he whispered.

Cranston tapped him gently on the shoulder. 'Aye, Brother, always remember the carmined kiss of the traitor is ever the sweetest. You remember that, as I shall.'

Athelstan gazed speechlessly back. He had never seen Cranston like this before. By now the coroner should have been singing some lewd song at the top of his voice, bellowing abuse at the landlord, or urging Athelstan to come back to his house in Cheapside.

They mounted their horses and made their way quietly up snow-packed Billingsgate, turning left into the approaches to London Bridge. A large crowd milled there despite the cold wind which lashed face and hand. Under a sky shrouded by deep snow clouds, some boys threw snowballs at each other, shrieking with laughter as they hit their target. A legless beggar pulled himself along through the slush on wooden slats. A group of tattered watermen muttered abuse at the frozen river and cursed the great frost which had taken their livelihood from them. Others, hooded and cowled, pushed forward into the city or joined Athelstan and Cranston in crossing the narrow frozen bridge to Southwark.

The coroner suddenly reined in his horse, staring back at a group of dark figures who had just slipped by. Were they a group, he wondered, or just individuals travelling together for comfort and security? He was sure he had glimpsed Lady Maude amongst them, her pale face peering out from beneath her hood. But what would she have been doing in Southwark? Apart from Athelstan she knew no one there, and Southwark was a dangerous place to visit on a dark winter's day.

'Sir John, is all well?'

Cranston stared once more at the group receding into the darkness. Should he go back? But then a great metal-rimmed cart came crashing by, and the people behind Cranston began to mutter and moan, so the coroner nodded at his companion that they should continue on their way. They crossed the bridge, passing the Priory of St Mary Overy at the far end, and took the main highway into Southwark. The two men rode down the narrow alleyways where the great four-storey houses were interspaced with the ramshackle cottages and lean-tos of the workmen and artisans. The coroner caught the acrid tang of dog urine.

'The snow doesn't hide the stench!' he muttered, twitching his nose.

Athelstan agreed, pulling the cowl of his hood closer against the sight of rotting refuse, and discarded food and human excrement tossed out in night pots, mixed with the sweepings from the houses as the citizens prepared for a festive season. Southwark, of course, never rested. The artisans and cottagers continually plied their trades: chandlers making tallow from pig fat; skinners, cheesemongers, capmakers, blacksmiths, and at night, when the stalls came down, the raw-boned villains of the underworld who scrounged for easy pickings amongst the brothels and stew sides of the Thames. No one, however, approached

Cranston or Athelstan. The friar was well respected whilst Cranston was more feared than the Chief Justice himself.

They found St Erconwald's in darkness. Athelstan was pleased that Watkin had doused the lights. He was about to lead Sir John through the wicket gate to the priest's house when a dark shape jumped from the shadows and grabbed Philomel by the bridle. Athelstan stared down at the long, white face under its tarry black hood.

'Ranulf, for God's sake, what's the matter?'

'Father, I have been waiting for you all afternoon.'

'Tell him to bugger off, Athelstan! I'm cold!'

'Never mind Sir John,' Athelstan replied soothingly. 'What do you want, Ranulf?'

The rat-catcher licked bloodless lips. 'I have an idea, Father. You know how the great Guilds across the river have their own churches? St Mary Le Bow for the mercers, St Paul's for the parchment-makers?'

'Yes. So?'

The rat-catcher looked up pleadingly.

'Go on, Ranulf, what do you want?'

'Well, Father, I and the other rat-catchers wondered whether St Erconwald's could be the church for our guild fraternity?'

Athelstan hid a smile, glanced at Cranston's glowering face and bunched the reins in his hands. 'A guild of rat-catchers, Ranulf? With St Erconwald's as your chancery church and I your chaplain?'

'Yes, Father.'

Athelstan dismounted. 'Of course.'

'We would pay our tithes.'

'In what?' Cranston bellowed. 'A tenth of the rats you catch?'

Ranulf flashed the coroner a dagger glance but Cranston was already rocking to and fro in the saddle, laughing uproariously at his own joke.

'I think it an excellent idea,' Athelstan murmured. 'And we shall talk about it again. You have my agreement in principle, Ranulf, but for the moment Sir John and I are both busily engaged on other matters. If you could stable our horses, give them some hay?'

The rat-catcher nodded vigorously and, gathering the reins of Sir John's horse, trotted into the darkness. Philomel followed, moving a little faster as he sensed feeding time was very close. Athelstan led Cranston round the church, stopped, and told the coroner to wait until he fetched a sconce torch. He hurried back to the priest's house, plucked one from the wall, lit it with a tinder and ran back before Cranston's litany of curses became too audible.

They crossed into the cemetery. Even in summertime it was a sombre place. Now, under a carpet of white snow, the branches of the yew trees spread like huge white claws over the forlorn mounds of earth, crude crosses and decaying headstones. Athelstan felt a deep sense of isolation. An eerie stillness hung like a cloud and even the breeze seemed softer. The trees were motionless. No night bird sounded. In places, the shadows seemed oppressively dark, sinister hiding-places where some demon or evil sprite might lurk. Athelstan held up his torch and Cranston looked around this most benighted of God's acres.

'By the sod, Athelstan!' he whispered. 'Who would come here in the dead of night, never mind pluck corpses from their final resting place? Where are the graves?'

Athelstan showed him the forlorn, shallow holes in the ground, the mud piled high on either side as if some demented creature had clawed the corpses out. Cranston knelt down next to them and whistled softly through his teeth. He looked up, his fat face distorted by the torchlight.

'Brother, you said that only the corpses of beggars and strangers have been stolen?'

'Yes, Sir John.'

'And how were they buried?'

'The corpse, wrapped in canvas, is placed on a piece of wickerwork in the parish coffin. During the funeral ceremony this is covered by a purple canopy and removed when the body is lowered into the soil.'

'And you found no trace of the grave robbers?'

'None whatsoever.'

Cranston stood up, wiping the slushy mud from his hands. 'We have three possibilities, Brother. First, it could be a macabre joke. Some of our idle rich young fops think it funny to place such a corpse in the bed of a friend, but there's no rumour of such an evil prank recently. Secondly, it could be animals, either four-footed or human. Oh, yes,' he murmured at Athelstan's shocked expression. 'When I served in France, I witnessed such abominations outside Poitou. However,' he stamped his feet and looked up at the darkened mass of the church, 'no one, not even in Southwark, can be *that* degenerate. Finally, there are Satanists, the Astrasoi, those born under an evil star.' He shrugged. 'You know more about such people than I do, Brother. The corpse may be used as an altar or the blood drained to raise a demon or they may need one of the limbs. You have heard of the hand of glory?'

Athelstan shook his head.

'The hand of the corpse is hacked off; the name of the person whom the witch or warlock wishes to hurt is placed between its fingers and then it's buried at the foot of a gibbet on the first stroke of midnight.'

Athelstan rubbed his face. 'But how can I stop such desecration, Sir John? The ward bailiffs and beadles are not interested. No citizen will guard our cemetery.'

'I will see what I can do,' Cranston murmured. He turned quickly. 'There's someone here.' He pointed to two dark shapes over near the charnel house at the far side of the cemetery. 'Look there!' He strode across the snow-covered grass like a charging bullock, Athelstan hurrying behind him.

'Stop!' Sir John bellowed. 'In the King's name, stop!'

Two cloaked figures turned and slowly walked towards them. At the sound of the clatter of wooden sticks and the soft tinkle of a bell, Cranston hurriedly stepped back.

'Lepers!' he whispered, and grabbing Athelstan's torch, held it up before him. 'By the sod!' Cranston breathed, and stared pityingly at the white-hooded faces. He looked round at Athelstan. 'You let them stay here?'

He nodded. 'During the day. At night it is easier for them to wander unmolested.'

'Have they seen anything?'

Athelstan shook his head. 'They are mutes, but I doubt if they would become involved. It would be a brave man, Sir John, never mind a healthy one, who would confront grave robbers.'

'You are sure they are lepers?' Cranston whispered.

Athelstan grinned in the darkness. 'They have letters from the bishops. Look at their wrists and hands. However, if you wish to examine them…?'

Cranston cursed and tossed a coin at one of the creatures then strode back to the house, bellowing that he had seen enough. Ranulf the rat-catcher had apparently disappeared, as indeed did any of Athelstan's parishioners when the coroner appeared.

'You will stay for a bowl of soup, Sir John? I have some fine claret.'

Cranston, huffing and puffing, checked the saddle girths of his horse. 'I would like to, Brother,' he replied over his shoulder, 'but I must return.'

Cranston did not wish Athelstan to probe his anxieties about the Lady Maude. 'I need to reflect upon what we saw at the Tower.' He pointed to the graveyard. 'I'll see what I can do to help you there.' He swung himself on to his horse, and with an airy wave clattered into the darkness.

Athelstan sighed and went round to unlock the church. It was cold inside, but the friar was pleased that it had lost its musty smell. He revelled in the fragrance of the green boughs so lovingly placed along the nave and sanctuary steps. He remembered the Chapel of St John and wondered what lies he had been told there. Athelstan was sure the murderer was in the Tower and equally certain that some evil deed from the past had finally caught up with Sir Ralph.

He took a tinder from his pouch, lit two sconce torches in the nave and collected his battered prayer book from the sacristy. He knelt on the sanctuary steps and began the Divine Office. He reached the line in the psalm 'My God, my God, why have you forsaken me?' and stopped. He stared into the flickering light of the candle, leaning back on his heels. Had God forsaken him? Why did things such as the desecration of the cemetery, Sir Ralph's murder or

Cranston's sadness happen? Oh, Athelstan knew about the problem of evil but sometimes he wondered, especially when he stared into the darkness, was there really anyone listening to him? What if there was not? What if Christ had not risen from the dead, and religion was mere hocus-pocus?

Painfully, Athelstan drew back from the precipice of doubt and depression. He finished his prayers, made the sign of the cross, and crouched with his back against the chancel screen. He took deep breaths, trying to calm his mind and soul so he could concentrate on the recent events in the Tower.

'What happens,' he asked the darkness, 'if Sir Ralph has been killed by secret peasant leaders? And if the revolt comes...?'

–

He dozed for an hour until a warm, furry body slid under his hand. 'Good evening, Bonaventura!' he whispered. 'A cold day for a gentleman of leisure.'

He sat up and stroked the cat gently, scratching between the backs of its ears, making Bonaventura purr with pleasure. 'So, you have been visiting all your ladies in the neighbourhood?' Athelstan knew about Bonaventure's sexual prowess. Sometimes the cat even brought his 'ladies' back to the church steps to sing their own eerie vespers to a cold silver moon. 'What will happen, Bonaventura, when the rebellion comes? Will we side with Pike the ditcher and the other dispossessed?'

Bonaventura grinned in a fine display of pink gums and sharp ivory teeth. Pike the ditcher! Strange, Athelstan thought, but there it was. He had no proof but he was certain the ditcher was a member of the Great Community and carried secret messages to its leaders. Athelstan tensed as the church door opened.

'Brother Athelstan? Brother Athelstan?'

The friar smiled. Benedicta. Perhaps she would share his supper? They could exchange gossip about the parish; anything to distract his mind. He put Bonaventura down, stood, and broadened his smile, to hide his disappointment. Beside Benedicta stood a tall man, his features quite clear in the torchlight. His face was burnt dark by the sun, his raven-black hair tied in a knot at the back of his head. He was dressed in a long blue robe which reached down to snow-flecked boots. Athelstan went along the nave to meet him. The man was strikingly good-looking, he thought, with the sharp features of a hunting peregrine, vivid cherry-brown eyes, a hooked nose and neatly clipped moustache and beard. Athelstan saw the pearl pendant which hung on a gold chain from one ear lobe.

'This is Doctor Vincentius,' Benedicta exclaimed.

Athelstan clasped a strong, brown hand. 'Good evening, sir. I have heard of you.'

And who hadn't? Athelstan wondered. The physician lived in Duckets Lane off Windmill Street, on the other side of the Tabard Inn. He had recently bought a huge house there with a garden which bordered on the river, directly opposite Botolph's Wharf. Vincentius had won himself a name as a reputable physician. His fees were petty and he didn't bleed his patients with leeches or use strange zodiac charts and stupid incantations. Instead he preferred to emphasise cleanliness, the importance of a sensible diet, the efficacy of boiled water, and the need to keep wounds clean. Cecily the courtesan had even intimated that he used an ointment which was most effective in curing certain sores on the most delicate parts of the body.

Athelstan studied the extraordinarily handsome face and the beaming smile on Benedicta's. The friar felt a twinge of jealousy.

'I have heard of you, Father,' the doctor smiled.

Athelstan shrugged. 'I am a priest, a friar, one amongst thousands.'

The doctor spread his hands and the rings on his fingers sparkled. 'But there again, it is written on many tombstones… "I was a healthy man until I met a physician".'

Athelstan laughed, immediately liking the man. 'I don't see you in church,' he teased.

'Perhaps one day, Father.'

'Doctor Vincentius so wanted to meet you.' Benedicta spoke as coyly as a young girl. 'I wonder, Father, if you could join us for supper?'

Athelstan felt like refusing, but that would have been churlish. He clapped his hands briskly. 'I would love to.' He doused the lights in the church and locked the door, leaving Bonaventure to hunt in the darkness. He went across to the house whilst Benedicta and her strange visitor waited on the church steps. Philomel was still munching noisily on his oats. Athelstan patted him gently, took his cloak from the house and rejoined Benedicta and Vincentius.

They walked through the silent, icy streets into Flete Lane, near Holyrood Walk, where the widow lived. This was the first time Athelstan had been to Benedicta's house, a two-storeyed building which stood alone, an alleyway on either side and a garden beyond. On the ground floor was a huge kitchen, parlour and storeroom. The kitchen had no rushes on the floor but the flagstones were scrubbed and wiped clean. Two box-chairs were pushed near the roaring log fire. Above the hearth ran a broad oaken shelf containing silver and pewter cups which shimmered by the light of two multi-branched candelabra; woollen rugs of dark murrey hung against the white-washed walls. A warm, homely place, Athelstan thought. Indeed, very much as he had imagined it. They both helped Benedicta prepare and serve the meal. First jussell, composed of eggs and spiced bread. Then succulent hare cooked in wine, a jelly moulded in the form of a castle, and a jug of chilled white wine and claret which Cranston would have downed in a trice.

Vincentius quietly dominated the conversation. Athelstan found his courtly manners and soft, well-modulated voice fascinating. Perhaps Vincentius realised he talked too much and, changing the conversation, asked about the friar's day. Athelstan described his journey to the Tower and Sir Ralph Whitton's death.

'He will not be missed,' Vincentius observed. 'A dour, war-like man.'

'You met him?'

The physician smiled. 'I know of him, though it's the Tower I find more interesting. I went there yesterday. A wonderful testimony to the subtlety of the human mind, especially when it comes to engines and places of war.' Vincentius sipped from his goblet. 'You say Sir Ralph's throat was slashed?'

'Yes,' Athelstan replied. 'Why?'

'How was the body when it was found?'

'What do you mean?'

'Was it cold? Was the blood congealed?'

'Yes, it was,' Athelstan replied, though he remembered he had not asked that question himself at the time. 'Where are you from, Doctor?' he deftly turned the conversation. The physician carefully put his wine cup back on the table.

'I was born in Greece, of Frankish parents. They later returned to England. I studied at Cambridge, then Santiago and Salerno.' He grinned. 'At Salerno,' he continued, 'I spent most of my time trying to forget what I had learnt at Cambridge. The Arabs have a more thorough grasp of medicine than we. They know more about the human body and have proper Greek translations of Galen's *Art of Medicine* and Hippocrates' *Book of Symptoms*.'

'What brought you back to Southwark?' Benedicta asked.

The physician smiled as if relishing some private jest.

'Why not?' he joked. 'Wealth? I have enough. And as you know, Brother, the poor need any help they can get.' He leaned across the table and studied Athelstan's face carefully.

'What are you going to recommend, Physician?' Athelstan teased. 'The eagle's remedy for bad eyesight?'

'What's that?' Benedicta asked.

'Brother Athelstan jokes,' Vincentius replied. 'The charlatans say the eagle gets its keen eyesight by eating raw lettuce. So they claim rubbing the eyes with the juice of the lettuce will clear up any eye infection.'

'And will it?'

'A bag of nonsense!' Vincentius snapped. 'Warm water and a clean cloth will do more! No, Brother,' he tapped Athelstan lightly on the fingers, 'what you need is more sleep. And if you have any lettuce, eat it. It will do you good.'

Athelstan laughed. 'If I can find it! The frost has killed everything in my garden, and Ursula's pig scoffs the rest.'

Whilst Benedicta described Ursula and her malevolent sow, Athelstan felt tempted to talk to Vincentius about the desecration of the cemetery but concluded it was not a topic suitable for the table. He looked across at the hour candle and saw it was growing late. He rose and made his farewells, politely refusing Benedicta's invitation to stay longer. He had enjoyed the meal but was glad to be gone, reminding himself that he was a priest and Benedicta was the mistress of her own life. He left her house and trudged wearily through the snow. The night was cold and black but when he stopped and looked up between the black overhanging gables of the houses, he was pleased to see the clouds beginning to break up. He would have gone straight home but made a short diversion when he found Pike the ditcher drunk as a bishop on the corner of the trackway leading down to the church. Athelstan helped his errant parishioner to his feet.

'Good evening, Father.'

Athelstan flinched at the ale fumes which billowed towards him.

'Pike! Pike!' he hissed. 'You great fool. You should be home in your bed with your wife.'

Pike staggered away from him, tapping his nose drunkenly. 'I have been seeing people, Father.'

'I know you have, Pike.' Athelstan grasped him by the arm. 'For God's sake, man, be careful! Do you want to end your life swinging on the end of some gibbet as the crows come to peck your eyes out?'

'We'll rule like kings,' Pike slurred. He struggled free of the friar's grip and danced a quick jig. 'When Adam delved and Eve span,' he chanted, 'who was then the gentleman?' Pike smiled drunkenly at Athelstan. 'But you'll be safe, Father. You, your cat, and your bloody stars!' He laughed. 'You're a jewel. You charge no tithes. I just wish you'd bloody well laugh sometimes!'

'I'll bloody well laugh,' Athelstan hissed, seizing the drunken man by the arm, 'when you're sober!'

And he hustled the ditcher back to his angry wife waiting in their tenement in Crooked Lane.

Athelstan thankfully reached St Erconwald's, made sure everything was locked up and walked over to his house. It was only when he was lying on his pallet bed trying to pray and not be distracted by Benedicta's fair face, that Athelstan suddenly remembered what Vincentius had said. What had the good physician been doing at the Tower? Moreover, Vincentius admitted he had been educated in the area around the Middle Sea where Sir Ralph and the others had also served. Was there any connection? Athelstan wondered. He was still pondering on the problem when he drifted into a deep and dreamless sleep.

Cranston, too, was thinking about events in the Tower but was too anxious to concentrate on the problems they posed. The coroner sat forlornly at the desk in his chamber, his little chancery or writing office as he called it, a place he loved, at the back of the house away from noisy Cheapside. He stared around. The floor had been specially tiled with small red and white lozenge-shaped stones and covered with woollen rugs. The windows were glazed and tightly shuttered against piercing draughts. Pine logs crackled and snapped in the small fireplace and warming dishes stood on stands at either end of the great writing desk. Sir John loved to spend time here, concentrating on his great treatise on the governance of the city. Yet tonight he could not relax; he was too distracted, ill at ease with the atmosphere in his own household. Oh, he had found Maude a little happier, they had exchanged the usual pleasantries, but Cranston still sensed that she was hiding something. He stirred as below stairs the maid tinkled a bell, the sign for dinner. Sir John groaned as he eased his bulk up and sorrowfully waddled down to the aroma-filled kitchen. Leif, the beggar, was crouched in the inglenook, stuffing his mouth full of richly sauced venison. He grinned at Sir John, then stared in surprise as Cranston mournfully passed by. Leif was astonished. Usually Sir John would greet him with a stream of good-natured abuse.

The beggar shrugged and went back to his meal. He was enjoying himself. Lady Maude had given him a few pennies and tomorrow he planned to see his friend in Crabbe Street. They'd dine in an eating-house and go to Moorfields where foaming bears, huge-tusked hogs and fat bulls were baited by bloody-mouthed mastiffs.

In the linen-panelled dining chamber, the table had been specially laid, covered by a white cloth of lawn with gold embossed candlesticks placed at either end. Cranston looked suspiciously at his wife. She seemed too happy. He noticed the colour high in her cheeks whilst her eyes danced with pleasure. Sir John grew more mournful. Had Lady Maude found someone else? he wondered. A young swain more virile and lusty than he? Oh, he knew such practices were common. The bored wives of old men and burgesses often found happiness in the arms of some court dandy or noble fop.

Sir John eased himself into his great chair at the top of the table and gloomily reflected on the past. Yes, his marriage had been an arranged one. Maude Philpott, daughter of a cutler, solemnly betrothed to the young Cranston. Young? He had been fifteen years her senior when they met at the church door but he had been slimmer then, fleet as a greyhound, a veritable Hector on the battlefield and a Paris in the bedchamber. Sir John looked soulfully at his wife, who smiled back. Should he raise the matter? Sir John gulped. He dare not. Cranston was frightened of no one; he had the body of a bullock and the heart of a lion. Yet, secretly, he was wary of his miniature, doll-like wife. Oh, she never shouted or threw things at him. Just the opposite. She would sit and answer back, stripping away his pomposity as she would the layers of an onion, before going into a sulk which could last for days.

'Sir John, all is well?'

'Yes, My Lady,' Cranston mumbled.

The maid served dinner: beef stew pie, the pastry crisp and golden. The meat within was garnished with herbs and cooked in a rich onion sauce. Cranston's mood receded, aided and abetted by two generous cups of claret.

'You were at the Tower today, Sir John?'

'Yes, and all the fault of Sir Ralph Whitton, the constable. Last night he had a throat, tonight both throat and life have gone.'

Lady Maude nodded, remarking how she had heard that Sir Ralph was a hard, cruel man.

'And you, My Lady?'

'Oh, this morning I did the accounts, and later went to take the air.'

'Where?'

'In Cheapside. Why?'

'You didn't go to Southwark?'

'By the Mass, Sir John, no! Why do you ask?' Cranston shook his head and looked away. He had caught the tremor in her voice. His heart lurched and he splashed his goblet full to the brim with dark red claret.

—

In the darkness of the Tower, the hospitaller, Gerard Mowbray, walked along the high parapet which stretched between Broad Arrow Tower and Salt Tower on the inner curtain wall. The night wind whipped his grey cropped hair, bit at his ears and cheeks and clawed at the grey robe wrapped round his body. Sir Gerard ignored the cold. He always came here. This was his favourite walk. He would stand and stare into the darkness trying to see the old ruins of Caesar's time, but not tonight, as the mist was too thick. To the north he could glimpse the beacon light in the Tower of St Mary Grace's, and to the south the fires and torch flames from the Hospital of St Katherine. Sir Gerard looked up at the sky. The clouds were beginning to break, revealing a storm of stars across the heavens. Strange, he thought. In Outremer the stars seemed closer, the velvet darkness of the heavens so near you felt you could stand on tiptoe and pluck the lights from the sky.

Mowbray leaned against the crenellated wall. Oh, they had been happier times! He remembered the hot burning sands outside Alexandria where he, Sir Brian, Sir Ralph, and the others had been a band of carefree knights only too happy to take the gold of the enemy. Mowbray recalled the climax of their campaign. There had been a revolt in Alexandria and the Caliph's army, Mowbray's group amongst them, had massed outside the city: the air thick with the beat of their kettledrums, the wind snapping at the huge green banners, and the silver crescents on the standards dazzling in the scorching sunlight. The city had been besieged for months but at last a breach had been forced in one of the walls. He and Sir Brian had gone in first to stand shoulder to shoulder, their comrades around them, a fighting circle of steel slowly edging into the city. Behind them the massed troops of the Caliph, their battle cries rising and falling like a demoniac chorus. The knights had forced their way through the gap and along the wall to the steps leading to the parapet above the main gate.

Sir Gerard's mind slipped eagerly back into the past. He remembered the intense heat, the sunlight dancing off sword and dagger points, the roar of battle, and the blood which pumped like a thousand fountains as men fell screaming from horrible wounds in head, body or thigh. Slowly he and his companions had edged up the steps, hacking their way through flesh until they reached a point above the main gate. Now who had it been? Of course! As always, Bartholomew. He'd jumped down, engaging in combat with a huge Mameluke. Bartholomew had moved with the grace of a dancer, his sword a silver hissing snake. One false feint to the groin, then up and round in a semi-arc to slice the enemy between helmet and hauberk. Ralph had followed. He had been an honourable knight then.

The great bar to the gate was lifted and the Caliph's men had poured into the city. What a bloodletting! No quarter was asked and none was given. The narrow, hot streets dinned with the silver bray of trumpets and the shrieks of dying men and women. At least the knights had not been party to the massacre; they had achieved their task and now looked for suitable reward. They eventually found themselves in a huge square where a white marble fountain played in the centre. Nearby stood the banker's empty house. Oh, the treasure they had found there! Adam had run knee-deep in silver ducats and jewelled goblets full of pearls!

Mowbray suddenly shook himself free from his memories. He thought he'd heard a sound, there towards the end of the parapet at the top of the steps. No, he concluded, it was only the wind. He went back to his memories. Strange, Mowbray pondered, that Adam had not come to see them this Christmas. Perhaps he was too frightened. Had the dead Sir Ralph and the now wealthy burgess Adam known something he did not? What had happened three years ago to frighten the Constable so much?

'We are all frightened,' Mowbray whispered to himself. This fear had changed them all. That's what evil did to you, he thought. It corroded the will, rotted the soul, and fouled the chambers and passageways of the mind. What had been done in Outremer so many years ago had been evil! Bartholomew had been their leader. Half the treasure was rightfully his, and he had trusted them – a terrible mistake. Betrayal! Treachery! The words shrieked like tormented ghosts in the dark recesses of Mowbray's soul. Ralph had planned it but they had all been party to his evil. Mowbray stirred against the cold. Oh, he had confessed his sins, walked barefoot to the shrine of St James at Compostela and both he and Fitzormonde had become hospitallers to make reparation. He stared out into the darkness.

'Oh, sweet Christ!' he murmured. 'Wasn't that enough?' The hospitaller felt the black demons of Hell closing in around him. What terrors did the pit hold for traitors? To be basted with pitch in a dark pen full of brimstone where adders would suck at his eyes and snakes curl round his lying tongue! What could he do to break free of such phantasms? Tell Cranston? No! Perhaps Brother Athelstan? Mowbray remembered the dark eyes and closed face of the Dominican monk. Mowbray had met such men before; some of his commanders in the knights hospitaller had the same gift as Athelstan of sensing every thought. The friar knew there was something wrong, something evil and rotten, behind Sir Ralph's death.

Mowbray jumped as a night bird shrieked beyond the Tower walls. A dog howled in protest. Was it a dog? he wondered. Or one of Satan's scouts calling up the legions of the damned from the abyss of Hell? A bell clanged. Mowbray moaned in fear, caught now in his own fancies. The bell boomed as though it came from the bowels of the earth. He cursed and calmed himself.

The bell was the tocsin in the Tower! Mowbray's hand fell to his sword hilt as he realised that great brass tongue only tolled when the Tower was under attack. He gripped the hilt of his sword tightly. Perhaps he had been wrong? Perhaps Sir Ralph's death had been the work of rebels and now they were back? He ran along the gravel-strewn parapet. He wanted to fight. He wanted to kill, give vent to the fury boiling within him. Suddenly he stumbled. His arms flailed out like the wings of a bird, black against the sky, then he tipped and fell, his mind still gripped by delirium. He was a boy again, leaping from a rock into one of the sweet rivers of Yorkshire. He was the brave young knight storming the parapet of Alexandria, crying out for the rest to join him. Then, darkness.

Mowbray's body crashed against the earth, his brains spattering as the sharp, icy cobbles crushed his skull. His body twitched then lay still, even as the dying hand edged towards the wallet containing a yellow piece of parchment depicting a crudely etched ship with dark crosses drawn in each corner.

Chapter 6

Athelstan stood outside his church and stared in pleasant disbelief at the blue-washed sky and the early morning sun as its rays danced and shimmered over the snow-covered roofs of his parish. The friar took a deep breath and sighed. He had slept well, woken early, said Office, celebrated Mass, broken fast and then swept both his house and Philomel's stable. He had been to the cemetery. The lepers had gone and none of the graves had been disturbed. Athelstan felt pleased, even more so as the great frost had been broken by this sudden bright snap as if Christ himself wanted the weather to improve for his great feast day. He looked over his shoulder and smiled at Cecily the courtesan as she swept the porch of the church. She simpered back before looking, sloe-eyed, towards a dreamy-faced Huddle, now sketching in charcoal the outlines of one of his vigorous paintings on the wall of the nave.

'Keep your mind on the task in hand, Cecily,' Athelstan murmured. He stretched, turning his face up to the sun. 'Praise to thee, Lord,' he muttered, 'for Brother Day. Praise to thee, Lord,' he continued St Francis of Assisi's Canticle of the Sun, 'for our sister, Mother Earth.' Athelstan sniffed and wrinkled his nose. 'Even though,' he whispered, 'in Southwark she smells of sour vegetables and putrid refuse!' He suddenly remembered other beautiful mornings at his father's farm in Sussex and the sun seemed to lose some of its brightness.

'You are happy, Father?'

Athelstan grinned at Benedicta. 'Yes, I am. You left Mass early?' he queried.

'I had to, Father, have you forgotten?'

Athelstan remembered the date and winced. No, he hadn't forgotten Simon the carpenter, one of his more errant parishioners, a florid-faced, thick-set man with an evil temper and a long Welsh dagger. Two weeks ago, Simon had raped a girl whilst carousing in Old Fish Street then compounded his crime by brutally beating her. He had been tried for his life at the Guildhall and tomorrow would hang. Simon had neither family nor friends and three days ago the parish council had begged Athelstan and Benedicta to visit the unfortunate. The friar had even made a vain plea to Cranston to have the sentence commuted but the coroner had sorrowfully shaken his head.

'Brother,' he had replied, 'I can do very little, even if I wanted to. The girl was only twelve and she'll never walk again. The fellow has to die.'

Athelstan stared up at the sky. 'God have mercy on Simon,' he whispered. 'And God help his poor victim!'

'What was that, Father?'

'Nothing, Benedicta, nothing.' Athelstan turned to go back into his church just as a young pursuivant turned the corner of the alley, slipping and sliding on the ice as he bellowed the friar's name. Athelstan groaned. 'What is it, man?' As if he didn't know already.

'Sir John Cranston awaits you, Father, at the Golden Lamb tavern near the Guildhall. Father, he says it is urgent. You must go there now!'

Athelstan fished in his purse and flicked a penny at the young man. 'Go tell Sir John to stay where he is and not to drink too much. I'll be there shortly!'

Athelstan took the keys of the church, tied by a piece of string to the cord round his waist, and pressed them into Benedicta's soft, warm hand.

'Look after the church,' he pleaded.

Her eyes rounded with mock wonderment. 'A woman in charge of the church, Father? Next you'll be saying that God favours women more than men because he created Eve in Paradise, rather than before, as He did Adam.'

'They also say the serpent had a woman's face.'

'Aye, and a man's lying heart!'

'You'll lock the church?'

'Such trust, Father.'

Athelstan smiled. 'I believe you would do a better job than any of the men. Seriously, Benedicta, make sure Ranulf the rat-catcher doesn't take Bonaventure. The children are not to play snowballs in the porch. Try to keep Ursula's pig away from what is left of my garden, and above all watch Cecily! I think she is about to fall in love again.' He ran down the steps and turned. 'Oh, Benedicta?'

'Yes, Father.'

'Last night – the delicious meal, thank you. A strange man, Doctor Vincentius.'

Benedicta grinned. 'Not as strange as some priests I have met!'

Athelstan glowered back in mock anger whilst she turned and skipped like a young girl into the church.

He roused and saddled a snoring Philomel and took the road to London Bridge. He found the stews around the riverside as busy as an overturned ant heap in summer as boatmen, sailors and fishermen flocked down to the riverbank to watch the ice thaw. Athelstan gently nudged Philomel through the press around the bridge. He refused to look to either side; crossing the bridge on the pleasantest of days could be a frightening experience and more so now as the ice below split and cracked. Instead Athelstan looked across the river at the ships plying along the quays of Billingsgate and Queenhithe in a scene of frenetic activity. Galleys from Gascony laden with casks of wine, woad ships for Picardy, the whelk boats of Essex, and the great vessels of Alamein and Norway making ready for sea. Fishing boats, barges and lighters were busy around the ships, full of men smashing the ice with picks, hammers and mallets. From the high-stemmed poop of a Genoese cog, a boy sang a hymn to the Virgin in thanksgiving for the change in the weather whilst sailors in a Greek galley chanted their prayer for mercy: '*Kyrie Eleison, Christe Eleison, Kyrie Eleison.*' Lord, have mercy, Christ have mercy, Lord have mercy. The chant was so beautiful Athelstan stopped, closing his eyes to listen, until a rough-mouthed carter flicked his whip, bellowing how some men had to work and couldn't laze around like stupid priests. Athelstan sketched a blessing in the air at his tormentor, dismounted and led Philomel past the church of St Magnus on the corner of Bridge Street.

They turned into Candlewick, now thronged with carts, pack horses and wagons as virtually every tradesman in the city seized the opportunity afforded by the break in the weather. Athelstan continued into Walbrook. On one side of the street ran a sluggish stream in a deep channel cut through the earth. The water was black, ice-filled, and two youths were fighting with quarter-staffs on one of the shit-strewn footbridges. Athelstan and Philomel pressed forward though, for a while, both were forced into the shadows of the overhanging houses as a group of aldermen rode pompously down the street. A herald went before them, a silver trumpet to his lips, whilst two serjeants-at-arms cleared the way with sharp knocks from their staffs. Above the aldermen the city banner snapped in a glorious splash of bright vermilion, whilst the figure of St Paul, embroidered in gold, seemed to glow with its own special light. At the corner of Walbrook the rakers were out, their great wooden rods moving piles of slush and refuse into high, stinking heaps. A bailiff had found a pig wandering where it shouldn't and, according to city regulations, had promptly cut the animal's throat. The blood gushed out in hot, scarlet streams whilst its owner, a little balding man, threatened the official with a stream of horrible oaths. Athelstan remembered Ursula and her great, fat sow and wondered if the bailiff would cross to Southwark. The city parasites were also massing as thick as flies over a turd: smooth-skinned lads, cloak-twitchers, quacks, night wanderers, mimes and petty sorcerers.

At last Athelstan found the Golden Lamb, a little tavern on the corner of an alleyway. The dark taproom was dominated by a morose Cranston, who sat slumped on a bench with his back against the wall. The empty ale-jacks scattered on the table before him made the coroner look like an angry Bacchus surrounded by votive offerings. Athelstan walked across and Cranston's eyes swivelled to meet him.

'Where have you been?' the coroner snapped.

'I came as fast as I could.'

'It wasn't fast enough!'

Athelstan silently prayed for patience and sat down on the stool opposite Sir John. He didn't like the appearance of the coroner one bit. Cranston was a drinker but was usually a jovial soul, conscious of his own sins, faults and failings, and so tolerant of those of others. Now he looked positively sinister, his eyes continually flashing around as if seeking a challenge. His lips moved wordlessly and even the white whiskers bristled with some inner fury.

'Do you want some wine, Priest?'

'No, Sir John, I don't, and I think you've drunk enough.'

'Sod off!'

Athelstan leaned forward. 'Sir John, please, what is wrong? Perhaps I could help?'

'Mind your own business!'

Athelstan coughed and backed away. 'This,' he murmured, 'is going to be a very trying day. You said the mayor and the sheriffs wished to see us?'

'They have seen me. They got tired of waiting for you!'

'And what did they say, Sir John?' Athelstan asked sweetly.

The coroner shook himself, sat up and smiled shame-facedly at Athelstan. 'Forgive me, Brother,' he mumbled. 'A bad night, and I've got an aching head.'

And a filthy temper to boot, Athelstan thought, but decided to keep his own counsel. Sir John would talk soon enough.

Cranston chewed his lip and glared into a corner where a huge rat gnawed at a bloody globule of fat glistening amongst the dirty rushes. 'Is it the black or brown rat which carries infection?' he suddenly asked.

Athelstan followed Cranston's gaze and shuddered in disgust.

'Both, I think, so I'm not eating here, Sir John, and I suggest that neither should you. Anyway, tell me what's happened.'

'There's been more bloodshed in the Tower. Sir Gerard Mowbray, who also received a death warning, slipped from a parapet and fell.'

'Anything else?'

'About the same time that Mowbray died, the great tocsin of the Tower sounded, convincing the garrison it was under attack.'

'But there was no attack?' Athelstan replied. 'And, I am sure, no sign of a bell ringer?'

'Apparently.'

'And the business of the Mayor?'

Athelstan jumped as a fierce tom cat slunk out of the shadows, grasped the rat by its leg and pulled it squealing into the centre of the room.

'For God's sake!' Cranston bellowed at the taverner.

The fellow wandered over waving a broomstick and the cat, its quarry still swinging from his mouth, fled up the spiral, wooden staircase. Cranston lifted the ale-jack, remembered the rat, and slammed it back on the table.

'The business of the Mayor, my dear Athelstan, is that Sir Adam Horne, burgess, alderman and close friend of the late Sir Ralph, has received a drawing of a three-masted cog, together with a flat sesame seed cake.'

'And where is Horne now?'

'At his warehouse along the Thames. Horne did not tell the mayor about this, his wife did. Both message and cake were delivered anonymously to her. She handed them over to her husband and was terrified by his reaction. He became pale and ill as if taken by a sudden seizure.'

'When was this?'

'Earlier today. The wife immediately went to see one of the sheriffs. The rest you know.'

'Lady Horne acted very quickly?'

'Yes, the mayor himself is suspicious. He still believes Lady Horne knows more than she claims.'

Athelstan stared towards the door as a group of pedlars, battered trays slung round their necks, bustled in, raucously shouting for ale. A one-eyed beggar followed and, for a penny, agreed to do a dance. His skeletal body clothed in dirty rags looked grotesque as he hopped from foot to foot, to the mocking laughter of the tinkers.

'Isn't it strange, Sir John,' Athelstan murmured, 'how we men take such a delight in the humiliation of others?'

Cranston remembered Lady Maude, blinked and looked away.

Athelstan stirred. 'So, Sir John, do we question Horne or go to the Tower?'

Cranston rose. 'My office is to enquire as to the cause of death,' he announced pompously. 'Not to run errands for the powerful ones of this city. So we go to the Tower. After all, as the good book says, "Where the body lies, the vultures will gather".'

'Sir John?' Athelstan scratched his head. 'This warning – the seed cake and the ship, still troubles me.'

'What do you mean?' Cranston slurred, swaying dangerously against the table.

'Well, apparently Horne, for example, recognised the seed cake as a death threat, but why does the crude drawing of a ship hold such terrors for him and others?'

'All men are fearful because they're liars!' Cranston snapped. 'No one tells the truth!' He glared at Athelstan under bristling brows.

'What's wrong, Sir John?' Athelstan insisted. 'I can feel the fury and the hurt seething within you. You must tell me.'

'In a while,' the coroner muttered. 'Let's go!'

They collected their horses from the stables and led them through the cold, bustling streets. Every Londoner seemed to be out of doors: the stall-holders were busy making up for lost trade and the air was thick with savoury smells from taverns and cookshops. They went to Cornhill, past Leadenhall and into Aldgate, pausing where a crowd had gathered round a speaker on the corner of Poor Jewry. He was a striking figure with a long, dour face, the head completely shaven, his thin body clothed from head to toe in a black gown and cloak. The speaker paused as he glimpsed Cranston, and his mouth and jaw tensed with fury. The anger in his face made his eyes glow, reminding Athelstan of the figure of St John the Baptist in a mummer's play. The man's eyes never left Cranston's as he drew a deep breath, one bony finger pointing upwards to the clear blue sky.

'Woe to this city!' the preacher rasped. 'Woe to its corrupt officials! Woe to those they serve who are clad in silk, loll on couches, and fill their bellies with the best of food and the richness of wine. They will not escape the fury which is coming! How can we eat and drink when our poor brothers starve? What will their answer be then?'

Cranston angrily stepped forward, but Athelstan caught him by the sleeve.

'Not now, Sir John!'

'Who is it?' Cranston rasped.

'The hedge priest, John Ball. A great preacher,' Athelstan muttered. 'Sir John,' he advised, 'the man is well liked. This is neither the time nor the place!'

Cranston took a deep breath, spun on his heel and walked on. The preacher's fiery words pursued them as they passed the house of Crutched Friars and turned left down an alleyway towards the Tower.

'One day,' Cranston grated, 'I'll see that bastard hang!'

'Sir John, he speaks the truth.'

The coroner turned. His face and body sagged as the fury drained from him.

'What can I do, Athelstan? How can I feed the poor of Kent? I may eat too much, I know I drink too much, but I pursue justice and do the best I can.' Cranston's great fat hands flapped like the wings of a wounded bird and Athelstan saw the hurt in his eyes. 'By the sod, Brother, I can't even govern my own house.'

'Lady Maude?' Athelstan queried.

Cranston nodded. 'I fear she has met someone else,' he blurted out. 'Perhaps a fop from the court.'

Athelstan stared back in disbelief. 'Lady Maude? Never! Sir John, you are a fool!'

'If any other man said that, I'd kill him!'

'Well, I say it, Sir John. Lady Maude is an honourable woman, she loves you deeply. Though,' Athelstan snarled in genuine anger, 'sometimes I wonder how she can!' He grasped the fat coroner by his cloak. 'What proof do you have?'

'Last night I saw her coming across London Bridge from Southwark, yet when I asked her where she had been, she replied no further than Cheapside.'

Athelstan was about to snarl a further retort when the coroner's words suddenly quickened his own memories. Sir John might be right. A week ago, just before the feast of the Virgin, Athelstan had seen the Lady Maude near the

Tabard in Southwark. At the time he'd thought it strange but then forgot about it. Cranston narrowed his eyes.

'You know something, don't you, you bloody monk?'

Athelstan looked away. 'I'm a friar,' he replied softly. 'Sir John, I know nothing except that I honour you and the Lady Maude. I also know she would never betray you.'

Cranston brushed by him. 'Come on!' he barked. 'We have business to do.'

They reached the bottom of the alleyway, went up the hill and into the Tower through a rear postern gate. One of the sentries took their horses and led them across Tower Green, now ankle-deep in icy slush, to where a depressed-looking Colebrooke was waiting.

'More deaths,' the lieutenant announced mournfully. 'Sir John, I wish I could say you were welcome.' He took them out, stopped and stared up at the ravens cawing raucously against the blue sky. He pointed up at them. 'You have heard the legends, Sir John? While the ravens are here the Tower will never fall. And that when they caw so stridently, it's always a sign of impending death.' Colebrooke blew on the tips of his fingers. 'Unfortunately, the ravens' song is turning into a constant hymn.'

'Did anyone know that Mowbray had received the same warning as Sir Ralph?' Cranston abruptly asked.

Colebrooke shook his head. 'No. Mowbray was uneasy but, following Sir Ralph's death, so were we all. He and Sir Brian kept to themselves. Last night Mowbray went for his usual walk on the parapet between the Salt and Broad Arrow Towers. He was still there when the tocsin sounded. Mowbray apparently heard the alarm, ran, slipped and fell to his death.'

'There was no one else on the parapet with him?'

'No. Indeed, if it wasn't for the warning we found in his pouch, we would have assumed it was a simple accident.'

'Was the parapet slippery?'

'No, of course not, Sir John. You are a soldier. Sir Ralph was most strict on such matters. As soon as the weather worsens, sand and gravel are strewn on every step.'

'Then who rang the bell?' Athelstan asked.

'Ah, that's the mystery. Come, I'll show you.'

They walked into the centre of Tower Green. The snow was relatively unmarked here, packed high around a great wooden post with a beam jutting out like a scaffold. The tocsin bell was balanced on an iron ring and from its great brass tongue hung a long piece of cord.

'You see,' Colebrooke said, pointing up to the bell, 'this is only sounded when the Tower is under direct attack. If you touch the rope even, the bell is angled so as to sound continuously.'

Sir John looked up and nodded wisely. 'Of course,' he said. 'I have seen such a mechanism before. If the guard is wounded, once he starts the bell, it will swing and toll until someone stops it.'

'Exactly!' Colebrooke exclaimed. 'And that's the real mystery. I stopped the bell myself. No one else was about.'

'But someone could have rung it and run off?' Cranston queried.

Colebrooke shook his head. 'Impossible. I came out here with a sconce torch. I stopped the bell but, when I examined the snow, found no other footprints around.'

'What?' Cranston barked. 'None at all?'

'None, Sir John.' Colebrooke pointed to the surrounding carpet of snow. 'Because this bell is so important,' he explained, 'no one is allowed anywhere near it. Even the soldiers, when they are drunk, keep clear of the area in case they stumble and start the bell tolling.'

'And nothing else was found?'

'Nothing except the claw marks of the ravens.'

'But that's impossible,' Athelstan said.

Colebrooke sighed. 'I agree, Father, and what makes it even more mysterious is that we also had guards patrolling the green. They saw no one approach the bell. They found no footprints.' Colebrooke turned away and spat. 'A time of death,' he mourned. 'The ravens' song is the only one we hear.'

'And where was everyone?' Cranston snapped.

'Oh, Mistress Philippa had invited us all for supper in Beauchamp Tower.'

'All of you?' Athelstan asked.

'Well, the two hospitallers demurred. Rastani did not come, and I left occasionally to make my rounds. I'd just returned to Mistress Philippa's when the bell began to sound.'

'And you found no one?' Cranston repeated.

'No one at all,' Colebrooke muttered. 'Now the soldiers are uneasy. They talk darkly of demons and ghosts and the Tower is not a popular garrison. You know soldiers, Sir John, they're worse than sailors. They repeat stories of how the Tower was built on a place used for ancient sacrifice. How blood is mixed with the mortar, and men were nailed to the earth in its foundation.'

'Nonsense!' Cranston barked. 'What do you think, Brother?'

Athelstan shrugged. 'The lieutenant may be right, Sir John. There are more forces under heaven than we know.'

'So you believe the nonsense about ghosts?'

'Of course not! But the Tower is a bloody place. Men and women have died horrible deaths here.'

Athelstan stared round the green and shivered despite the bright sunshine.

'Fear is the real ghost,' he continued. 'It saps harmony of the mind and disturbs the soul. It creates an air of danger, of threatening menace. Our murderer is highly skilled and intelligent. He is achieving exactly what he wants.'

'Who found the corpse?' Cranston queried.

'Fitzormonde did. When the bell was sounded, people were running around all over the place, checking gates and doors. Fitzormonde went looking for Mowbray and found his corpse.'

'We'll check the parapet walk,' Athelstan muttered.

'Master Lieutenant, I would be grateful if you could gather everyone in Mistress Philippa's chamber. Please give my apologies and excuses to the lady, but it's important to meet where you all were last night when the tocsin was sounded.'

Cranston and Athelstan watched Colebrooke stride away.

'Do you think there's any connection?' Cranston asked.

'Between what?'

'Between the bell chiming and Mowbray's fall.'

'Of course, Sir John.' Athelstan tugged him by the sleeve and they made their way across the deserted bailey to the steps leading up to the parapet walk. They stopped at the foot and stared up at the curtain wall rising above them.

'A terrible fall,' Athelstan whispered.

'You said there was a connection?' Cranston replied testily, 'between the bell sounding and Mowbray falling.'

'A mere hypothesis, Sir John. Mowbray went on to the parapet walk. Like many old soldiers he liked to be by himself, to reflect well away from others. He stands there staring into the darkness. He has already received warnings of his own impending doom so is lost in his own thoughts, fears and anxieties. Suddenly the tocsin sounds, proclaiming the greatest fortress in the realm to be under attack.' Athelstan stared into Sir John's soulful eyes. 'If you had been Mowbray, what would you have done? Remember, Sir John,' Athelstan added slyly, 'you too are a warrior, a soldier.'

Cranston pushed back the beaverskin hat on his head, scratched his balding pate and pursed his lips as if he was a veritable Alexander. 'I'd run to find the cause,' he replied ponderously. 'Yes, that's what I'd do.' He stared at Athelstan. 'Of course, Mowbray would have done the same, but then what happened? Did he slip? Or was he pushed?'

'I don't think he slipped. Mowbray would have been too careful, and I doubt he would have let someone push him off the parapet walk without a struggle.'

'So how?'

'I don't know, Sir John. Let's study the evidence first.'

They were about to climb the steps when a voice suddenly sang out: 'Good morrow, friends!' Red Hand, his gaudy rags fluttering around him, jumped through the slush towards them. 'Good morrow, Master Coroner. Good morrow, Sir Priest,' he repeated. 'Do you like old Red Hand?'

Athelstan saw the chicken struggling in Red Hand's grip. The poor bird squawked and scrabbled, its claws beating the madman's stomach, ripping his rags still further, but Red Hand held it firmly by the neck.

'Death has come again!' he chanted, his colourless eyes dancing with mischievous glee. 'The old Red Slayer has returned and more will die. You wait and see. Death will come, snap, like this.'

And before Athelstan or Cranston could do anything, the madman bit into the hen's neck and tore its throat out. The bird squawked, struggled and lay limp. Red Hand stared up, his mouth ringed with blood, gore and feathers.

'Slay! Slay! Slay!' he chanted.

'Go away!' Cranston barked. 'Sod off, you little bugger!'

Red Hand turned and ran, the blood from the freshly killed chicken spraying the greying slush on every side. Cranston watched him disappear behind a wall.

'In my treatise, Brother,' he said softly, 'I will suggest houses for such men. Though I do wonder...'

'What, Sir John?'

'Well, if Red Hand is as mad as he claims to be.'

Athelstan shrugged. 'Who decides who is mad, Sir John? Red Hand may think he is the only sane man around here.'

They climbed the steep steps, Athelstan going first. Behind him followed Sir John, breathing heavily and muttering a litany of dark curses. The wind whipped their faces; halfway up Athelstan stopped and, stooping, picked up the thick sand mixed with gravel which carpeted every step.

'This would stop anyone from slipping, Sir John.'

'Unless he was drunk or careless,' Cranston replied.

'Aye, Sir John. A sober soldier is a rarity indeed.'

'Aye, monk, very rare, but not as rare as a holy priest.'

Athelstan grinned and continued climbing. They reached the parapet walk. It was about four feet wide and as carefully coated with sand and pebbles as the step. They leaned against the curtain wall. Cranston, breathing heavily, looked down, curiously watching the figures below as they scurried around like black ants on the various tasks of the garrison. He then stared up at the blue sky. The clouds were now only faint wisps lit by the strong mid-day sun. The coroner suddenly felt rather giddy and quietly cursed himself for drinking so much.

'Old age,' he murmured.

'Sir John?'

'*In media vitae, sumus in morte,*' Cranston replied. 'In the midst of life, we are in death, Brother. I do not feel too safe here, yet in France when I was younger but not so wise, I held one of these parapet walks against the best the French could send.' Cranston felt self-pity seep through him. Did Maude also think him old? he wondered. Was that it? Sir John breathed deeply, trying to control the spasm of rage and fear which shot through him. 'Go on, Athelstan,' he muttered. 'Make your careful, bloody study.'

'Stay there, Sir John,' Athelstan replied softly. The friar glanced despondently down at the sand and gravel. 'I suppose so many have been up here since Mowbray's fall, I doubt we will find anything.'

Athelstan walked gingerly along the parapet, using the crenellated wall as his guide. He walked slowly, not daring to look at the drop on his right and becoming ever more aware of the cold, biting wind and eerie sense of loneliness, as if he hung halfway between heaven and earth. On either side of the parapet walk were two towers. Near the Salt Tower he found the gravel-strewn slush had been disturbed, indicating someone had stood there for some time. Athelstan studied this spot for a while.

'What have you found, Brother?' Cranston bellowed.

Athelstan walked carefully back. 'Mowbray stood where I stopped. Now, Sir John, if you go first?'

Cranston went back to the top of the steps. Athelstan followed behind.

'Go on, Sir John. Stand on the top step.'

Cranston obliged, closing his eyes for he had begun to feel rather dizzy.

'What is it, Brother?' he rasped.

Athelstan crouched and stared closely where the sand and gravel had been scattered. 'I suspect Mowbray fell from here,' he replied. 'But why, and how?' The friar examined the crenellations from which an archer would shoot if the wall was under attack. 'Strange,' he murmured. 'There's a fresh mark in the wall as if an axe has been swung against it. And look, Sir John.' Athelstan carefully picked up some splinters of wood. 'These are fresh.'

Cranston opened his eyes. 'Yes, Brother, but what do they mean?'

'I don't know, but it would appear that someone took an axe and drove it hard against the wall, with such force the stone was marked and the wooden handle of the axe shattered.'

Cranston shook his head in disbelief.

'What it all means,' Athelstan murmured, 'I don't know. I cannot make the connection between Mowbray's fall and these fragments of evidence.' The Dominican looked suspiciously at the white, haggard face of Cranston, the bleary red eyes, and the way he was swaying rather dangerously on the top step. 'Come on, Sir John,' he said gently. 'We are finished here and others await.'

They made their way gingerly down the steps. At the bottom Cranston immediately felt better, turned and beamed at Athelstan.

'Thank God!' he bellowed. 'You don't do that every day, eh, Brother?'

Thank God, Athelstan thought, you are not in such a mood every day. The friar looked around. The Tower garrison was now busy: soldiers in half-armour lounged on benches. Despite the cold they wished to revel in the sunshine. A few played dice, others shared a wineskin. A scullion ran across with a basket of fresh-cooked meat, taking it to one of the kitchens where it would hang to be cured, diced, salted and stored for the duration of the winter. The clanging from the blacksmith's rang like a bell through the air, as somewhere a child cried, the son or daughter of one of the garrison. In the outer bailey an officer was shouting orders about a gate being oiled. A dog barked and they heard laughter from the kitchens. Athelstan smiled and relaxed.

He must not forget the small things of life, he concluded. They kept you sane. He linked his arm through Sir John's and they ambled across Tower Green, making their way carefully through the soft, dirty slush, alert for the icy patches which hadn't thawed. A guard ushered them into the Beauchamp Tower and up into Mistress Philippa's chamber on the second floor. It was a spacious room with a deep bay window overlooking Tower Green. The seats were cushioned and quilted, the windows glazed with fragments of stained glass. As soon as he entered, Athelstan sensed it was a woman's chamber – hand-woven tapestries hung on the walls, with one depicting a golden dragon locked in combat with a silver wyvern. Another portrayed the Infant Jesus smiling, arms outstretched, in the manger at Bethlehem where Christ's mother stood in a dress of gold and a mantle of deep sky blue. The bricks in the wall had been painted alternately white and red; large cupboards stood with doors half-open displaying gowns, dresses, hoods and mantles, of various colours and different fabrics. A small pine log fire blazed in the canopied hearth. In one corner stood a spinning wheel, the threads still pulled tight. In the other, curtained off from the rest of the room, was the bed chamber. A long, polished table stood in the centre of the room. On it were placed chafing dishes full of glowing charcoal, spices and herbs. Their perfume reminded Athelstan of a fresh spring morning on his father's farm in Sussex. He also noticed the other door in the far side wall, peeping out from behind the thick red arras. Athelstan grinned and winked at Sir John.

'A lady's bower, My Lord Coroner,' he whispered.

Cranston smiled, then remembered Lady Maude and his face grew long.

Mistress Philippa rose as they entered. In temperament, though not in looks, she reminded Athelstan of Benedicta; she had the same quiet composure and he had glimpsed the steely look in her eyes. Was Philippa strong and ruthless enough, he wondered, to commit murder? Athelstan stared round at the rest mumbling quietly like people who wanted to maintain appearances, though he sensed their tension. The conversation died abruptly as Cranston lurched across the room. Perhaps Philippa or the femininity of her chamber had reminded Cranston of Maude, for the coroner suddenly became bellicose with the girl.

'Another bloody murder!' he roared. 'What now, eh?'

Geoffrey Parchmeiner, Philippa's betrothed, stood up and walked out of the darkness near the wall. He looked anxious, more white-faced and sober than the last time Athelstan had seen him.

'Murder, My Lord Coroner?' he stammered. 'What proof do you have? You swagger in here, into my lady's chamber, and shout allegations yet show no evidence. What can we make of that?'

Athelstan looked around. Sir Fulke seemed subdued and remained slouched in his chair. The chaplain, crouched on a stool near the fireplace, stared into the flames wringing his hands whilst Rastani, the silent, dark servant, sat with his back to the wall as if he wished the very stones would open and swallow him. The other hospitaller, Fitzormonde, stood near the window, his hands folded, staring at the floor as if totally unaware of Cranston's presence. Colebrooke looked embarrassed, tapping his foot and whistling softly under his breath.

'My betrothed asked a question,' Philippa demanded. 'How do you know the knight was murdered? And what difference does it make, Sir Coroner? So was my father, and are you any nearer to finding his killer?'

'Your father's murder will be avenged,' Cranston snapped. 'As for Mowbray, he had that bloody parchment on him and the fragments of a seed cake. What further proof do you need?'

Philippa stared coolly back.

'Well!' Cranston shouted. 'I have answered one of your bloody questions!'

'Sir John,' she replied icily, 'moderate your language. My father,' her voice nearly broke, 'now lies sheeted in a coffin in the Chapel of St Peter ad Vincula. I, his daughter, grieve and demand justice, but all I get is the offensive language of the alleys and runnels of Southwark. Sir, I am a lady.'

Cranston's eyes narrowed evilly.

'So bloody what?' he answered before Athelstan could intervene. 'Show me a lady and I'll show you a whore!'

The girl gasped. Her betrothed leapt back to his feet, his hand going to the knife at his belt, but Cranston just dismissed him with a contemptuous flicker of his eyes. Athelstan watched the hospitaller suddenly stir and noticed with alarm how the knight now grasped one of his gloves in his hand.

Good Lord, the friar thought, not here, not now! The last thing Sir John needs is a challenge to the death.

'Sir John!' he snapped. 'Mistress Philippa is correct. You are the King's Coroner. She is a lady of high birth who has lost her father and now sees one of his friends meet a similar terrible death.' He grasped the coroner's arm and swung him round, keeping an eye on the hospitaller now standing behind them.

'Sir John! Control yourself, please,' he murmured. 'For my sake.'

Cranston stared at Athelstan with red-rimmed eyes. He reminded the friar of the great, shaggy bear squatting in the courtyard below. The friar touched Cranston's hand gently.

'Sir John,' he whispered, 'please. You are a gentleman and a knight.'

The coroner closed his eyes, took a deep breath, opened them and grinned.

'When you are around, monk,' he muttered, 'I don't need a bloody conscience.' He turned to Philippa. 'My lady,' he said, 'before Sir Brian or Sir Fulke,' he glanced contemptuously at the girl's uncle who still sat slumped in his chair, 'challenge me to a duel, I apologise profusely.' He gave her a dazzling smile. 'There are old men, Mistress,' he continued, 'and there are fools. But there's nothing worse than an old fool.' He stretched out his hand, took the girl's unresisting fingers and kissed them in a way the most professional courtier would have envied.

'I was most discourteous,' he bellowed. 'You must forgive me, especially at this time when your father's body is not yet buried.'

Chapter 7

The atmosphere in the room relaxed. Athelstan closed his eyes. Good God, he prayed, oh thank you! The hospitaller had been on the verge of striking Sir John and, once that happened, well, Athelstan knew Cranston. It would be a duel *à outrance*, to the death! Mistress Philippa smiled and stepped forward into the light and Athelstan realised just how boorish Cranston had been.

The girl's face was white as snow, her eyes red–rimmed and circled with deep shadows, but she sensed Cranston's insult had not been intended. She leaned over and kissed Sir John gently on the cheek. This only discomfited the coroner further. He stared down at the floor and shuffled his feet like some clumsy schoolboy. Philippa went across to a tray of goblets, filled two and brought them back. She gave one to Athelstan and pressed the other into Sir John's great paw. The coroner smiled at the wine, lifted the cup and downed it in one gulp. He smacked his lips, winked at the girl and held out the goblet to be refilled. Philippa smilingly obliged and Athelstan groaned. He didn't know what was worse, Cranston sulking or Cranston in his cups.

Sir John took the goblet and went over to the window, staring out at the sun dazzling the snow on Tower Green. Athelstan busied himself arranging his writing tray on the table. The rest of the group hardly moved, as if absorbed in everything the coroner said or did. They watched him intently, like a group of schoolboys would a fearsome master. Cranston watched the sunlight shimmer on the great tocsin bell then turned around abruptly.

'Mowbray,' he announced, 'was murdered. Well, at least I believe he was. He received the same message as Sir Ralph. I think he went on to the parapet and the tocsin was sounded to make him run. Now, I have examined the parapet most carefully...'

Athelstan remembered how Cranston had slouched against the wall and hid his smile.

'I have examined the parapet most carefully,' Cranston continued, glaring at Athelstan. 'Mowbray did not slip accidentally. The sand and gravel there are at least an inch thick. Someone planned his fall.'

'Did Mowbray drink?' Athelstan asked.

Cranston turned and glanced at the other hospitaller. Sir Brian shook his head.

'He was a seasoned warrior,' the knight replied. 'He could run along such a parapet in a blinding snowstorm.'

'Tell me,' Cranston said, 'what happened yesterday evening? I mean, before Mowbray fell?'

'We were all here,' Sir Fulke spoke up. He smiled. 'Mistress Philippa had invited us for supper.'

'I wasn't!' snapped Fitzormonde. 'I was in my own chamber, awaiting poor Mowbray's return.'

'And, of course, Rastani,' the chaplain stuttered, squirming on his stool.

'Yes,' Fitzormonde murmured. 'The Morisco wasn't here.' Athelstan left his desk and squatted in front of Rastani. He stared into the silent, fear-filled face.

'My Lady Philippa,' Athelstan murmured over his shoulder, 'I wish to talk to Rastani though I think he knows what I am going to ask.'

'So do I!' Sir Fulke shouted. 'I will answer for him.'

'No, sir, you won't!' Cranston barked.

Athelstan touched Rastani's hand, which was as cold as ice. The friar gazed into his liquid dark eyes. The man was terrified, but of what? Detection? Discovery?

'Where were you, Rastani?' Athelstan asked.

Beside him, Philippa made strange gestures with her fingers and Rastani replied in the same sign language.

'He says he was freezing cold,' Philippa explained. 'And stayed in my father's old chamber in the White Tower.'

'He's silent-footed as a cat,' Cranston observed. 'He could creep round this fortress and no one would notice.'

'What are you implying, Sir John?' Philippa snapped.

'Rastani could have rung the bell.'

'How on earth could he have done that when there were no footprints?' Geoffrey mocked, moving to stand beside Philippa.

Cranston smiled. 'A snowball?'

Colebrooke snorted with laughter. 'I have told you, Sir John, the area around the bell could be seen by sentries. They saw no one approach.'

Cranston sniffed loudly and looked longingly at his now empty wine goblet.

'Before you continue, Sir John,' Fitzormonde spoke up, 'and you start speculating on where I was, all I can say is that I was in my own chamber but no one saw me there.' He glared fiercely at Cranston. 'However, I am a priest, a knight and a gentleman. I am not a liar!'

'Why did you stay there, Sir Brian?' Athelstan tactfully interrupted.

Sir Brian shrugged. 'I was frightened. I, too, have received a letter of death.' He drew out a piece of parchment from beneath his cloak and Cranston almost snatched it from his hand.

The hospitaller was right. The same sketch Sir Ralph Whitton and Mowbray had received: a crudely drawn ship in full sail and, in each corner, a small black cross.

'I also had the seed cake,' Fitzormonde murmured. 'But I threw it away.'

'When Mowbray fell,' Cranston suddenly asked, 'did anyone else inspect the parapet?'

'I, Fitzormonde and Colebrooke did,' Fulke replied. 'When the tocsin sounded, we all left this room. The hospitaller was with us when Mowbray's body was found. Our young gallant here,' he waved his hand contemptuously at Geoffrey, 'was asked to accompany us to the parapet but it's well known he's terrified of heights.'

Geoffrey flushed with embarrassment and looked away.

'Uncle!' Philippa murmured. 'That's not fair.'

'What's not fair,' Cranston interrupted, 'is that we know so little about last night Mistress Philippa. What time did your guests assemble?'

'Oh, just after Vespers, about eight o'clock.'

'And all except Rastani and the hospitaller came?'

'Yes, yes, that's correct.'

Cranston turned to the hospitaller. 'And where did you say you were?'

'In my chamber.'

'And Mowbray?'

'On the parapet walk.'

'So,' Cranston heaved a sigh, 'as Mowbray brooded, the rest of you except Fitzormonde gathered here?'

'Yes.'

'And how long till the tocsin sounded?'

'About two to three hours.'

'And no one left?'

'Only Colebrooke on his round and others to the privy, but that's along the passageway.' The girl smiled wanly.

'We all drank deep.'

Athelstan raised a hand. 'Never mind that.' The friar, snatching the parchment from Cranston's hand, went and stood over the hospitaller. Athelstan pushed the drawing under the knight's face. 'Sir Brian, what does this mean?'

The knight looked away.

'Sir Brian Fitzormonde,' Athelstan repeated, 'soon you will appear before God's tribunal. I ask you, on your oath as a knight, what does this parchment signify?'

The hospitaller glanced up with his red-rimmed eyes in a drawn, pale face. Athelstan felt he was looking at a man already under the shadow of Death's soft, black wing. The friar leaned closer until he could see the small red veins in the knight's eyes and the grey, dusty pallor of his cheeks. Fitzormonde was probably a brave man but Athelstan could almost taste the stench of fear which emanated from him.

'On your oath to Christ,' Athelstan whispered, 'tell me the truth.'

Sir Brian suddenly lifted his face and whispered in Athelstan's ear. The Dominican stood back in surprise but then nodded.

'What did he say?' Cranston barked.

'Later, Sir John.' Athelstan turned to the rest of the group. 'What did happen here last night?' he asked, trying to divert the conversation.

Sir Fulke, his face now suffused with his usual false bonhomie, leaned forward. 'My niece,' he said, 'wished to thank us for our kindness following the death of Sir

Ralph. We sat and dined like a group of friends. We talked of old times and what might happen in the future.'

'And no one left?'

'Not until the tocsin sounded.'

'No, Sir Fulke,' Geoffrey interrupted. 'Remember, you drank deeply.' He smiled falsely. 'Perhaps too deeply to remember. The priest left.' Geoffrey pointed to where the chaplain, William Hammond, dressed like a crow, sat perched on his stool near the fire. 'Don't you remember, Father, you left?'

'I went back to my room,' the chaplain announced. 'I had a gift of some wine.' He glared maliciously at Geoffrey and then at Colebrooke. 'A parishioner gave it to me. It's not from the Tower stores if that's what you're thinking.' He shrugged. 'Yes, I too drank deeply and I was unsteady and slow in returning. I was about to re-enter Beauchamp Tower when the bell began to toll.'

'What happened then?' Athelstan asked. He glanced at Colebrooke and realised the lieutenant had told them little of his own movements. 'Well, Lieutenant?' Athelstan repeated. 'What did happen?'

'Well, the bell tolled. I and the others left Mistress Philippa. The garrison was roused and all gates were checked. We then scattered, trying to find what was wrong. Fitzormonde discovered Mowbray's body. We joined him then Master Parchmeiner came. We examined the corpse and I went up on to the parapet.'

'And?' Cranston barked.

'I found nothing. We were more concerned that the tocsin had been sounded.'

'But you found no trace of the bell ringer?' Athelstan asked.

'No, I have told you that.'

Athelstan gazed round in desperation. How, he wondered, could a bell ring and no one be seen pulling it? Or, indeed, any trace of someone being near the bell? What did happen? And how could the bell ringer run undetected across the Tower to arrange Mowbray's fall? Athelstan drew a deep breath.

'Where is Mowbray's body now?'

'It's already sheeted,' Philippa replied. 'It lies in its coffin before the chancel screen in the Chapel of St Peter ad Vincula.'

'And I will join him there,' Fitzormonde murmured. He looked up and smiled wanly. 'Oh, yes, I have the mark of death upon me.'

His statement hung like an arrow in the air, just before it turns and begins its fatal descent.

Athelstan whirled round as a loud snore from Cranston broke the silence. He heard Geoffrey giggle, even white-faced Philippa smiled, and the chaplain grinned sourly whilst Fulke snorted with laughter.

'Sir John has many problems to exhaust him,' Athelstan announced. 'Mistress Philippa, may we be your guests for a while?' He looked at Colebrooke. 'Master Lieutenant, I need words with Sir Brian. Is there a chamber here?'

Philippa pointed to the door in the far wall. 'There's a small one at the end of the corridor.' She blushed slightly. 'Just past the privy. The chamber will be warm. I had a brazier put there this morning.'

Athelstan bowed, smiled thinly at the rest of the group, glanced despairingly at the snoring Cranston and led Sir Brian down the corridor. On the left was the privy, covered by a curtain which hung from a metal rod. Athelstan pulled the curtain back and wrinkled his nose at the smell. The privy was crude, a small recess in the wall with a latrine seat, just under a tiny, open, oval-shaped window which looked down over the green.

'It drains down to the moat,' Sir Brian mumbled.

Athelstan nodded, let the curtain fall and walked on. The chamber at the end of the passage was more fragrant and clean. The walls were lime-washed, the windows closely shuttered. Athelstan sat down on a stool and gestured to a bench which ran along the wall.

'Sit down, Sir Brian. Now, tell me, what do you want?'

Sir Brian suddenly knelt at Athelstan's feet and sketched the sign of the cross in the air. Athelstan glanced around despairingly. He suspected what was coming.

'Bless me, Father,' Fitzormonde murmured, 'for I have sinned. And this is my confession.'

Athelstan drew back, the legs of the stool scraping the hard stone floor. 'I cannot,' he whispered. 'Sir Brian, you have tricked me! Whatever you tell me now will be covered by the seal of Confession.'

'I know!' Fitzormonde hissed. 'But my soul is steeped in the blackest sin.'

Athelstan shook his head and made to rise. 'I cannot,' the friar repeated. 'Whatever you tell me, I can only reveal on the orders of the Holy Father, the Pope in Avignon. Sir Brian, you are most unfair. Why this trickery?'

Fitzormonde glanced up, his eyes gleaming. 'No mummery,' he said. 'Father, I wish to confess. You must shrive me. I am a sinner *in periculo mortis*!'

Athelstan sighed. Sir Brian was right. Canon Law was most strict on this: a priest was bound to hear the confession of any man who believed he was in danger of death. To refuse would be a terrible sin. 'I agree,' Athelstan whispered.

Sir Brian made the sign of the cross again.

'Bless me, Father, for I have sinned. It is many years since my last confession and I confess in the face of God and in the hope of his divine mercy at the imminent approach of death.'

Athelstan closed his eyes and leaned back. He listened to the litany of sins: impure thoughts and actions, the lusts of the flesh, avarice, bad temper, foul language, as well as the petty bickerings which take place in any community. Sir Brian confessed about his fight against sin, his will to do good and his constant failures to carry this through. Athelstan, a skilled confessor, perceived Sir Brian was a good but deeply troubled man. At last the hospitaller finished and leaned back on his heels though he kept his head bowed.

'I am a sinner, Father,' he whispered.

'God knows,' Athelstan replied, 'we are all sinners, Sir Brian. There are those who know they are sinners, confess and try to pursue the good. You are one of these. There are others like the Pharisees who cannot be forgiven, for they believe they never do wrong!' Athelstan leaned closer. 'Now you wish absolution?' The friar raised his hand. '*Absolvo te*,' he intoned. 'I absolve you.'

'Stop!' Sir Brian lifted his head and Athelstan saw the tears on the white, haggard cheeks.

'Sir Brian, there is more?' he asked gently.

'Of course there is!' Fitzormonde hissed. 'I am a murderer, Father. An assassin. I took my friend's life. No! No!' He shook his head as if talking to himself. 'I was party to a murder. I turned my face the other way.'

Athelstan tensed, trying to hide that inner tingle of excitement, the deep curiosity aroused in a priest who, in confession, has the unique opportunity to see a soul bare itself.

'Whose murder?' he asked softly.

Sir Brian shook his head, sobbing like a child.

'Sir Brian.' Athelstan tapped him gently on the shoulder. 'Sit down, man! Come, sit down!'

Sir Brian slumped on the bench. Athelstan looked round the chamber and saw the wine jug and goblets on the chest. He got up, filled one of these and thrust it into Fitzormonde's hand.

'There's nothing in Canon Law,' Athelstan smiled, 'which says a man cannot have a drink during confession.' He wiped his sweat-stained hands on his robe. 'Or,' he continued, 'as St Paul says, "Take a little wine for the stomach's sake".'

Sir Brian sipped from the goblet and smiled. 'Aye, Father,' he replied. 'And, as the Romans put it, "*In vino veritas*". In wine there is truth.'

Athelstan nodded, pushed the stool nearer and sat down. 'Tell me, Sir Brian, in your own words and at your own time, the truth about this murder.'

'Many years ago,' Fitzormonde began, 'I was a wild, young man, a knight with visions of becoming a crusader. My friends were of a similar disposition. We all served in London or hereabouts: Ralph Whitton, Gerard Mowbray, Adam Horne, and...' The man's voice trailed off.

'And who?'

'Our leader, Bartholomew Burghgesh, of Woodforde in Essex.' Fitzormonde took a deep breath. 'The war in France was finished. Du Guesclin was reorganising the French armies, our old king was doddering and there was no need for English swords in France, so we sailed for Outremer. We offered our swords to the King of Cyprus. We spent two years there, becoming steeped in blood. Eventually, the Cypriot king dispensed with our services and we had nothing to show for it but our clothes, horses, armour, and the wounds of battle. So we became mercenaries in the armies of the Caliph of Egypt.'

'All of you?' Athelstan asked.

'Yes, yes. We were still a band of brothers. David and Jonathan to each other.' Fitzormonde smiled to himself. 'We feared nothing. We had each other and we always shared. Now there was a revolt in Alexandria. Our leader, Bartholomew, was hired by the Caliph to join his satraps in suppressing the uprising.' Fitzormonde stopped and gulped from the cup. 'It was a bloody business but eventually a breach was forced in the defences and Bartholomew led us through.' The hospitaller's eyes caught Athelstan's. 'We hacked our way through a wall of living flesh. Do you know, the cobblestones couldn't be seen for the blood which swilled like water? The Caliph's armies followed us in and the real killing began. Men, women and children were put to the sword.' Fitzormonde paused and wiped his mouth on the back of his hand. 'That, too, Father, I confess, though we were not party to it. Bartholomew led us away. We found a merchant's house full of treasure.' Fitzormonde licked his lips and closed his eyes tightly, trying to remember events in that sun-drenched city so many years ago. 'Now the Caliph's rules were strict,' he continued. 'As mercenaries we were allowed no plunder, so most of the treasure was useless to us, but Bartholomew found a heavy purse of gold.' The knight stopped speaking and pointed to the cord tied round Athelstan's waist. 'Think of that ten times thicker, Father. Two heavy pieces of leather sewn together and stuffed with money. Every coin was of pure gold. A king's ransom in a leather belt. There must have been thousands.'

Fitzormonde paused again. He was back in time, standing battered and blood-stained, gazing open-mouthed at the belt Bartholomew had found hidden beneath the tiled floor.

'What happened?' Athelstan asked.

Fitzormonde smiled. 'Bartholomew did a brave thing. He said he would wait to see if the Caliph would reward us for forcing the breach. He didn't, so Bartholomew kept the purse.'

'Why was that brave?'

'Well, if he had been caught, Bartholomew would have been sliced from neck to crotch, his genitals ripped off and stuffed into his mouth, and his decapitated head placed on a spike above the city gates. Now Bartholomew agreed to conceal the purse on condition that he had half the treasure whilst we shared the rest. We agreed, and by night fled the Caliph's armies and crossed the sea to Cyprus.'

'Is that the connection with the ship?' Athelstan asked.

'Oh, no. We reached Cyprus safely but the Caliph sent assassins after us. These were the Hashishoni, the followers of the Old Man of the Mountain, skilled killers who came by night. They were so confident they even sent us fair warning of their arrival.'

'A flat sesame seed cake?' Athelstan interrupted.

'Yes, but Bartholomew was waiting for them. One night they crept into our house but he had arranged for us to sleep on the roof whilst through a crack he could watch our sleeping chamber. Do you know,' Fitzormonde said in a dream-like voice, 'Bartholomew showed no fear? He trapped all three in that room and killed them.' Sir Brian's voice broke. 'He was the best – Bartholomew, I mean – honourable and fair. I have never met a more redoubtable fighter, yet we murdered him!'

Athelstan rose, took the wine jug and refilled the man's cup.

'Continue, Sir Brian.'

'Bartholomew wanted to go home, return to his manor at Woodforde. His wife was sickly and he also feared for his young son's life. At the same time, he had difficulties with Sir Ralph Whitton.' Fitzormonde glared into his wine cup. 'Ralph was the canker in the rose. I think he was secretly jealous of Bartholomew. He began to object to the way the treasure was being shared out, but Bartholomew failed to take him seriously. He said a bargain was a bargain; he had found the treasure, he had risked the Caliph's wrath, and he had killed the three assassins. However, he said he trusted his blood brothers and left the treasure with us when he took ship from Cyprus.' Fitzormonde stared at Athelstan and the friar began to suspect the true reason behind the drawing on the pieces of parchment.

'What happened to that ship, Sir Brian?'

The knight emptied the wine goblet in one gulp. 'A few days later we learnt Whitton had sent a secret message to the Caliph.' He shrugged. 'The rest is obvious. The ship Bartholomew was travelling on was intercepted and sunk.'

Athelstan whirled round as the door crashed open. Cranston stood there, foul-faced and bleary-eyed.

'What's the bloody matter, monk?' he boomed. 'Where the...?' Cranston used an obscene word and glared at the knight. 'You still wish to challenge me, Sir Brian?'

Athelstan rose, grabbed Cranston by the arm and hustled him out of the room, closing the door behind him.

'Sir John,' he rasped, 'I am hearing this man's confession!'

Cranston tried to push Athelstan aside. 'By the sod!' he roared. 'I don't give a shit!'

'Sir John, this is nothing to do with you.'

Athelstan, using all his weight, pushed Sir John back and sent him tottering down the corridor. Cranston steadied himself, pulled his long, wicked-looking dagger from its sheath and walked slowly back, his red-rimmed eyes fixed on Athelstan. The friar leaned against the door.

'What are you going to do, John?' Athelstan asked softly. 'Are you, the Lord Coroner, going to slay a priest, a colleague and a friend?'

Sir John stopped and slouched against the wall, staring upwards at the great beams resting on their corbels of stone.

'God forgive me, Athelstan,' he whispered. 'My apologies to Sir Brian. I shall wait for you downstairs.'

The friar re-entered the room. Fitzormonde still sat, cradling his head in his hands. Athelstan touched him gently on the shoulder.

'Forget Cranston.' He smiled. 'A man whose bark is much worse than his bite. Sir Brian, you wanted me to hear your confession? So Burghgesh was murdered. Surely the blame rests squarely with Sir Ralph?'

Fitzormonde shook his head and looked up. 'Don't patronise me, Father. Ralph told us what he had done. We could have stopped it. We could have brought Sir Ralph to justice. We could have searched the seas to see if Bartholomew had survived.'

'Was that possible?'

'Perhaps. Sometimes the Moors sell prisoners in the slave markets. But we didn't look there for him. We could have looked after Bartholomew's widow and his little son, but we failed to do that.' Fitzormonde drove one of his fists into the palm of his hand. 'We should have executed Sir Ralph. Instead, we became his accomplices and shared out his ill-gotten wealth.'

'What happened to Bartholomew's widow?'

'I don't know. We went our separate ways. Eventually guilt caught up with Mowbray and myself, so we joined the hospitallers, handing over what wealth we had left to the Order. Horne came back to the city and grew powerful on his riches. Whitton entered the service of John of Gaunt.' Fitzormonde placed the goblet on the ground before him. 'Do you know, Father, it wasn't until Whitton was dead that I realised how he had held us in his evil thrall.' Fitzormonde paused. 'You have seen the great bear in the Tower bailey?'

'Yes.'

'Every afternoon I am here,' Fitzormonde continued, 'I go to stare at it. The beast is a killer, but I'm fascinated by it. Whitton was like that. Sir Ralph made his guilt a bond between us all. As the years passed, we became more confident that our crime had been forgotten and began the custom of every year meeting to celebrate Christmas. We never discussed Bartholomew.'

Athelstan nodded. 'That's the terrible thing about sin, Sir Brian. We let it become part of us, like a rotting tooth which we tolerate and forget.'

Fitzormonde rubbed his face with his hands.

'But what happened,' Athelstan asked, 'three years ago?'

'I don't know. We came to the Tower as Ralph's guests for Yuletide, supping as usual at the Golden Mitre in Petty Wales, but when we met Sir Ralph that particular time, he looked as if he had seen a ghost. In fact, he said he had, and that's all he would say.'

Athelstan seized the man's wrist and forced him to look up. 'Have you confessed all, Sir Brian?'

'Everything I know.'

'And the piece of parchment?'

'A reminder of the ship Bartholomew was sailing on.'

'And the four crosses?'

'They represent Bartholomew's four companions.'

'And the seed cake?'

Fitzormonde sighed and blew his cheeks out. 'A reminder of how Bartholomew saved us from the assassins, and a warning of our own deaths.'

'Do you know who murdered Sir Ralph and Sir Gerard?'

'Before God, I do not!'

'Could Bartholomew have survived?'

'He may have.'

Athelstan stared at the lime-washed walls. 'What about Bartholomew's son? He would be a young man now.'

Fitzormonde shrugged. 'I thought of that, but I have made some enquiries. Young Burghgesh was killed in France. Now, Father, my penance?'

Athelstan raised his hand and pronounced absolution, making the broad sweep of the sign of the cross above Fitzormonde's bowed head. Sir Brian looked up.

'My penance, Father?' he repeated.

'Your penance is the guilt you have borne. You are to pray for Burghgesh's soul and for those of Sir Gerard and Sir Ralph. And one more thing!'

'Yes, Father?'

'You are to go downstairs and repeat your confession to Sir John.'

'He'll arrest me for murder.'

Athelstan grinned. 'Sir John is an old soldier and, when sober, a keen student of the human heart. He has more compassion in his little finger than many a priest. He'll hear you out and probably roar for a cup of sack.'

Chapter 8

Fitzormonde left, closing the door quietly behind him. Athelstan went to gaze out of the window, staring absent-mindedly at the great tocsin bell which hung so silently on its icy rope above the snow-covered green. The sun, now beginning to set, made the bell shimmer like a piece of silver. Athelstan turned and glimpsed Fitzormonde talking quietly to Cranston. The coroner was nodding, listening intently to the hospitaller's confession.

Athelstan wandered back to Philippa's chamber but it was deserted. He stayed for a while reflecting on what Fitzormonde had told him. First, both Sir Ralph and Mowbray's murders were connected to that terrible act of betrayal in Cyprus so many years earlier. Secondly, and Athelstan shivered, there would be other murders. He packed his writing tray away whilst speculating on other possibilities. First, Burghgesh could have survived and come back to wreak vengeance. Secondly, someone else, possibly Burghgesh's son, had returned to make his father's murderers atone for the death. But, if it had been either of these, how would they get into the Tower, mysteriously ring a tocsin bell and then arrange for Mowbray's fall? Athelstan sighed. Sir Ralph Whitton's murder was simple compared to the complexities surrounding Mowbray's.

Athelstan rubbed his chin with the palm of his hand and remembered he'd promised Benedicta to meet her at the Fleet prison where Simon the carpenter would spend his last evening on earth. The thought of Benedicta made him smile. Their relationship had become calmer, more gentle. Then he remembered Doctor Vincentius and hoped the physician would not ensnare her with his subtle charm. Athelstan's smile broadened. Here he was, a friar, a priest, a man sworn to chastity, feeling twinges of jealousy about someone he could only claim as a friend.

He shook himself free from his reverie and looked around the chamber. The murders... what other possibilities existed? Was it one of the group? Not Fitzormonde, but perhaps Horne the merchant? Or could it be Colebrooke, who had discovered Sir Ralph's murky past and was promoting his own ambitions under the guise of revenge for past misdeeds? Athelstan swung his cloak around him, picked up his writing tray and examined the beautiful embroidery of the dorsar draped over the back of one of the chairs. Of course, terrible though it might be to imagine, Mistress Philippa had the cool nerve and composure to be a murderess, and Parchmeiner might well be her accomplice. Hammond the chaplain had the spite, whilst Sir Fulke had everything to gain.

Athelstan heard Cranston bellowing his name so left the chamber and went downstairs where the coroner stood kicking absentmindedly at the snow.

'You feel better, Sir John?'

Cranston grunted.

'And Fitzormonde told you all?'

The coroner glanced up.

'Yes, I believe he did, Athelstan. You think the same as I do?'

He nodded. 'Our sins,' he murmured, 'always catch up with us. The Greeks call them the Furies. We Christians call it God's anger.'

Cranston was about to reply when Colebrooke came striding across the green. The lieutenant looked white-faced and tense.

'My Lord Coroner!' he called out. 'You are finished here?'

'In other words,' Cranston half whispered to Athelstan, 'the fellow is asking us when we are going to bugger off!'

'We will leave soon, Master Lieutenant, but may I ask one favour first?'

Colebrooke hid his distaste behind a false smile. 'Of course, Brother.'

'You have messengers here. Will you send one to the widow Benedicta at St Erconwald's in Southwark? Ask her to meet Sir John and me at the Three Cranes tavern in Cheapside. And, Master Lieutenant?'

'Yes!'

'Sir Ralph's corpse – was it cold and the blood congealing?'

'I'm a soldier, Brother, not a physician. But, yes, I think it was. Why?'

'Nothing,' Athelstan murmured. 'I thank you.'

Colebrooke nodded and strode off. Cranston stretched lazily.

'A pretty mess, Brother.'

'Hush, Sir John, not here. I think these walls do have ears, and our boon companion Red Hand wishes an audience.'

Cranston turned and quietly cursed as the madman scampered across the snow to greet them, yelping like an affectionate dog.

'Lots of blood! Lots of blood!' he screamed. 'Many deaths, dark secrets! Three dungeons but only two doors. Dark passages. Red Hand sees them all! Red Hand sees the shadows creak!' The madman danced in the snow before them. 'Up and down! Up and down, the body falls! What do you think? What do you think?'

'Sod off, Red Hand!' Cranston muttered and, taking Athelstan by the arm, guided him past the great hall towards the gateway under Wakefield Tower. Athelstan suddenly remembered the bear, stopped and walked back to where the animal sat chained in the corner where curtain wall met Bell Tower. The friar was fascinated. He stared and hid a smile, hoping Sir John would not notice, for there was a close affinity between the shaggy beast and the corpulent coroner.

'It smells like a death house,' Cranston moaned.

The bear turned and Athelstan glimpsed the fury in its small, red eyes. The great beast lumbered to his feet, straining at the chain around its neck.

'I don't know which is the madder,' Cranston muttered, 'the bear or Red Hand!'

The animal seemed to understand Sir John's words for it lunged towards him with a strangled growl; its top lip curled, showing teeth as sharp as a row of daggers.

'I think you are right, Sir John,' Athelstan observed.

'Perhaps we should go.'

The friar watched with alarm the way the chain around the bear's neck creaked and shook the iron clasp nailed to the wall. They turned left to collect their horses from the stables.

'We could leave them here,' Athelstan remarked, 'and take a boat downriver.'

'God forbid, Brother,' Cranston snapped. 'Have you no sense? The bloody ice is still moving, and I never fancy shooting under London Bridge even on the fairest day!'

They left the Tower and rode up Eastcheap, turning into Gracechurch, past the Cornmarket where St Peter on Cornhill stood, and into Cheapside. The roar from that great thoroughfare was deafening: traders, merchants and apprentices shouted themselves hoarse as they tried to make up for their previous loss of trade. The bailiffs and beadles were also busy: two drunkards, barrels placed over their heads, were being led through the marketplace, followed by a stream of dirty, ragged urchins who pelted the unfortunates with ice and snowballs. A beggar had died on the corner of Threadneedle Street. The corpse, now stiff, had turned blue with the cold. A small boy armed with a stick tried to beat off two hungry-looking dogs which sniffed suspiciously at the dead beggar's bloody feet. Cranston tossed him a penny and, standing on an overturned barrel, bellowed for half the market to hear how he was Coroner of the city, and would no one help the poor lad have the corpse removed?

'I don't care if you're the bloody mayor himself,' one of the traders shouted back. 'Piss off and leave us alone!'

Athelstan drew his cowl over his head and pulled his sleeves down. He knew what was coming next. Cranston, true to his nature, jumped down from the barrel and grasped the unfortunate trader by the throat.

'I arrest you, sir!' he roared. 'For treason! That is the crime you have committed. I am the King's Coroner. Mock me and you mock the crown!'

The man's face paled and his eyes bulged.

'Now, sir,' Cranston continued quietly as the other traders slunk back, 'I can ask the wardsman to convene a jury of your peers or we can settle on a fine?'

'A fine! A fine!' the man gasped, his face turning puce.

Sir John tightened his grip. 'Two shillings!' he announced, and shook the fellow so hard Athelstan became alarmed and took a step forward, but the coroner waved him back.

'Two shillings, payable now!' Cranston repeated.

The man dug into his purse and slapped the coins into the coroner's hand. Sir John released him and the fellow slumped down on all fours, retching and coughing.

'Was that necessary, Sir John?' Athelstan whispered.

'Yes, Brother, it was!' Cranston snapped. 'This city is ruled by fear. If a trader can mock me, in a week every bastard in London will follow suit.'

Cranston scowled as two beadles, summoned by the commotion, approached. The self-important looks on their smug faces faded as they recognised Sir John.

'My Lord Coroner!' one of them gasped. 'What is it you want?'

Cranston pointed to the beggar's corpse. 'Have that removed!' he bellowed. 'You know your job. God knows how long the poor bastard has been lying there. Now move it before I kick both your arses!'

The beadles backed off, bowing and scraping as if the coroner was the Regent himself. Cranston turned and flicked his fingers at the urchin. The boy, arms and legs as thin as sticks, his eyes dark and round in a long, white face, came over, his thumb stuck in his mouth.

'Here, lad!' Cranston pushed the two shillings into an emaciated hand. 'Now, go to Greyfriars. You know it?

Between Newgate and St Martin's Lane. Ask for Brother Ambrose. Tell him Sir John sent you.'

The boy, the money clenched tightly in his fist, stared back, spat neatly between Cranston's boots and scampered off.

The coroner watched him go. 'The preacher Ball is correct,' he murmured. 'Very soon this city will burn with the fires of revolt if the rich do not get off their fat arses and do more to help!' He turned, his face now grave and serious. 'Believe me, Brother, God's angel stands at the threshold, the flailing rod of divine retribution in his hand. When that day comes,' Cranston rasped, 'there will be more violent deaths than there are people in this marketplace!'

Athelstan nodded in agreement and stared around. Oh, the marketplace was full of wealthy traders, merchants draped in furs, the wealthy artisans in jackets of rabbit and moleskin. Most looked well fed, plump even, but in the alleyways off the markets, Athelstan saw the poor; not like those in his parish but the landless men driven from their farms, flocking into the city to look for work though none was to be had. The Guilds controlled everything and soon these vagrants would be turned out, forced across London Bridge to swell the slums and violent underworld of Southwark.

'Come on, Sir John,' he murmured.

They pushed on up the Mercery, standing aside as a group of debtors from the Marshalsea, linked by chains, moved through the crowd, begging for alms both for themselves and other inmates. They found the Three Cranes tavern at the corner of an alleyway just opposite St Mary Le Bow. Benedicta was waiting for them, seated before a roaring fire; beside her on the ground, crouched like a little dog, sat Orme, one of Watkin the dung-collector's sons. Athelstan slipped him a penny, patted him lightly on the head, and the boy scampered off.

'Well, Benedicta, you left my church in good order?'

The widow smiled and unloosed the clasp of her cloak. Athelstan suddenly wondered what she would look like in a bright dress of scarlet taffeta rather than the dark browns, greens and blues she always wore.

'All is well?' he repeated hastily.

Benedicta grinned. 'Cecily the courtesan and Watkin's wife were screaming abuse at each other, but apart from that, you will be sorry to hear, the church still stands. Sir John, you are well?' She twisted her head to catch the coroner's eye as he scowled across at the innkeeper who was busy gossiping to the other customers around the great wine barrels.

'My Lady,' Cranston retorted, 'I would feel better—' he raised his voice to a bellow '—I would feel better if I got some custom, and the attention due to a King's officer!'

The landlord kept chatting so Cranston strode across, roaring for a cup of sack and wine for his companions.

'What's wrong with Sir John?' Benedicta whispered.

'I don't know. I think the Lady Maude has upset him. She is being mysterious and secretive.'

'Strange,' Benedicta mused. 'I meant to tell you, Brother, Lady Maude was seen in Southwark over a week ago. She is so memorable, so petite and sweet-faced.' Benedicta screwed up her eyes. 'Yes, I am sure they told me she was coming out of Doctor Vincentius' house.'

'Is he a ladies' man?' Athelstan asked hastily, and wished he could have bitten his tongue out the moment he spoke. Benedicta stared coolly back.

'Brother Athelstan,' she replied, 'can you show me a man who isn't?'

Cranston's return saved Athelstan from further embarrassment. The coroner swept his beaver hat from his head, scratched his balding pate, winked lecherously at Benedicta and turned to watch a now frightened taverner bring across a deep pewter bowl of sack and cups of wine for his companions.

'You are not eating, Sir John?'

'No,' Cranston muttered. 'I don't feel hungry and I suspect the innkeeper, after my blunt speech with him, would poison the bloody dish!'

Benedicta laughed merrily. 'Sir John, you must calm yourself!'

'No,' Cranston replied, lifting the goblet. 'I'll find serenity at the bottom of this cup.'

Benedicta watched in disbelief as Cranston drained his drink in one large gulp and boomed for more, smacking his lips, gently burping and belching. Benedicta bit her lower lip to stifle her laughter.

'Well, Brother.' Cranston patted his broad girth. 'With apologies to the Lady Benedicta, what do you make of Mowbray's death?' Cranston licked his lips. 'Or Sir Ralph's?'

Athelstan leaned against the table and ran his finger round the rim of the wine goblet. 'First, we have found that Sir Ralph was probably murdered by someone who entered the Tower by crossing an ice-bound moat. Secondly, Mowbray was lured to his death by the tocsin sounding. Thirdly, both murders are certainly linked with Sir Ralph's dreadful betrayal of Bartholomew Burghgesh in Cyprus so many years ago.' Athelstan smiled at Benedicta's quizzical face. 'You are puzzled, My Lady. Well, so are we. First, how can someone enter the Tower, murder Sir Ralph, then leave the fortress without being noticed? Secondly, why did Sir Ralph just lie there and allow his throat to be cut so savagely that his head was almost hacked from his body? You saw the corpse, Sir John, and the chamber? There was no sign of any struggle nor did the guards hear anything. Thirdly, who rang the tocsin bell and, at the same time, so subtly arranged for Mowbray to fall from the parapet?'

The coroner's face grew longer at Athelstan's every word.

'And the list of suspects,' the friar continued remorselessly, 'still stands. We may have met the murderer, yet it may equally be someone in the Tower or the city about whom we know nothing.'

'I do not know the full story,' Benedicta interrupted, 'but there is rejoicing in Southwark at Sir Ralph's death.' She lowered her voice. 'Pike the ditcher says it is the work of the Great Community. The secret peasant leaders wish to weaken the city before they organise their great revolt.'

'Nonsense!' Cranston slurred, now on his third cup of sack. 'Pike the ditcher, with all due respect, My Lady Benedicta, should keep his mouth shut and his neck safe! Sir Ralph was not murdered by any peasant.'

Athelstan sipped from his wine cup and made a face at the sourness of the drink. 'One person we have not met, My Lord Coroner, is the merchant Adam Horne. Benedicta, before we go on to meet Simon in the Fleet prison, there are certain enquiries to make. You will accompany us?'

Benedicta agreed, so they rose and left, Cranston bawling abuse at the hapless taverner. Outside it was growing dark, and only a red glow showed where the sun had set.

Cranston steadied himself carefully on the icy cobbles and stared at the sky.

'Why is it always red at night?'

'Some say,' Athelstan replied, 'it's because the sun slips into hell, but I think that's an old wives' tale. Come on, Sir John.'

Athelstan slipped round the coroner, tactfully linked one arm through his and, with Benedicta on the other side, crossed the now deserted Cheapside. The stalls were being packed away, the last iron-rimmed carts crashed along to Newgate or east to Aldgate. Weary apprentices and traders locked their shutters and put out lantern horns. The bell of St Mary Le Bow began to toll the curfew, the sign that all trading should cease, as four urchins pulled a huge yule log up to the door of one of the great merchants' houses. Cranston stopped to enquire directions of one of the market stewards who sat in his little toll booth on the corner of Wood Street. The fellow pointed down to the corner of the Mercery and Lawrence Street.

'You will find the Horne house there,' he said. 'A fine place, with a huge, black-timbered door and a coat of arms above it.'

They turned, staying in the centre of Cheapside as the melting snow began to slide from the sloping tiled roofs. The Horne house stood deserted, no lantern above the door, only a tired-looking Christmas wreath. Cranston stepped back and looked up at the lead-paned windows.

'No candlelight,' he murmured.

Athelstan pulled Benedicta closer into the side of the house to protect her from any snow falling from the small canopied hood of the doorway. He lifted the great brass knocker, cast in the shape of a dragon's head and brought it crashing down. There was no answer, so he knocked again. They heard the patter of footsteps and a whey-faced maid answered the door.

'Is Alderman Horne here?' Cranston slurred.

The young girl shook her head wordlessly.

'Who is it?' a voice asked from the darkness beyond.

'Lady Horne?' Cranston queried. 'I am Sir John Cranston, Coroner. You sent a message earlier today to the sheriffs at the Guildhall?'

The woman stepped out of the darkness, her drawn face bathed even whiter by the light of the candle she carried. Her cheeks were tear-stained, her eyes dark-shadowed and sad, whilst her steel-grey hair hung in untidy tresses beneath a white veil.

'Sir John.' She forced a smile. 'You had best come in. Girl, light the torches in the solar! Bring candles!'

Lady Horne led them up a stone-vaulted passageway into a comfortable but cold solar. A weak fire flickered in the hearth. Lady Horne told them to sit whilst behind them the girl lit candles. Athelstan gazed round. The room was positively luxurious with bright-hued tapestries on the walls, and exquisitely embroidered linen cloths placed on tables, chests and over the backs of chairs. Nevertheless, he could almost smell the stench of fear. The house was too quiet. He looked at Lady Horne who sat on the other side of the fireplace, an ivory and pearl rosary entwined around her fingers.

'You wish some refreshment?' she murmured.

Cranston was about to reply but Athelstan intervened.

'No, My Lady. This matter is urgent. Where is your husband?'

'I don't know,' she whispered. 'That terrible message arrived this morning and Sir Adam left immediately afterwards. He said he was going upriver to the warehouses.'

She clenched her hands tightly. 'I have sent messages there, but the boy returned and said my husband had already left. Sir John, what is the matter?' Her tired eyes pleaded with the coroner. 'What does this all mean?'

'I don't know,' he lied. 'But your husband, Lady Horne, is in terrible danger. Does anyone know where he has gone?'

The woman bowed her head, her shoulders shaking with sobs. Benedicta rose and crouched beside her, stroking her hands gently.

'Lady Horne, please,' Athelstan persisted. 'Do you know anything about the message or why your husband was so frightened?'

The woman shook her head. 'No, but Adam was never at peace.' She looked up. 'Oh, he was a man of great wealth but at night he would awake screaming about foul, bloody murder, his body coated in sweat. Sometimes he would tremble for at least an hour, but never once did he confide in me.'

Cranston stared across at Athelstan and made a face. The friar looked at the hour candle which stood on the table behind him.

'Sir John,' he whispered, getting up, 'it's almost seven o'clock. We must go!'

'Lady Horne.' The merchant's wife was about to rise but Cranston gently touched her on the shoulder. 'Stay and keep warm, the maid will see us out. If your husband returns, tell him to come to my house. It's not far. You promise?'

The woman nodded before looking away into the dying embers of the fire.

Outside Cranston stamped his feet, clapping his hands together. 'That woman,' he observed, 'is terrified. I suspect she knows the source of her husband's wealth, but what can we do? Horne could be anywhere in the city.'

Athelstan shrugged. 'Sir John, Benedicta and I must go to Fleet prison. We promised the parish we would visit Simon the carpenter.'

'Ah, yes,' Cranston replied tartly. 'The murderer.'

'You will go home?'

Sir John stared into the gathering darkness. He would have loved to but what was the use? All he'd do was sit and drink himself stupid.

'Sir John,' Athelstan repeated, 'the Lady Maude will be waiting for you.'

'No,' Cranston answered stubbornly. 'I'll go to the Fleet with you. Perhaps I can help.'

Athelstan glanced at Benedicta and raised his eyes heavenwards. The friar wanted Sir John to go; he was tired of the coroner's constant bad temper and sudden bouts of fury. He loved the fat knight, but on this occasion, dearly wished to see the back of him. Nevertheless, he agreed. They walked through the blood-stained slush of the Shambles, holding their noses against the sickening putrid smells from the slaughterhouses, and turned left into Old Deans Lane, a narrow alleyway ankle-deep in muck which ran between dark, overhanging houses. Somewhere in the distance a dog barked mournfully. At the corner of Bowyers Row, they stood aside as a huge, wooden wagon rolled by, pulled by four horses, their manes hogged, eyes blinkered and nostrils flaring at the corrupting smell of death. The horses' hooves and the wheels of the cart were muffled in straw so that it seemed to glide like a terrible phantasm. On one corner of the cart a torch flared, throwing the driver into ghastly relief as he sat cloaked and hooded, a grim death mask over his face.

'What is it?' Benedicta asked.

She brought up the hem of her cloak to cover her nose. Athelstan sketched a sign of the cross in the air and prayed the cart would continue, but it stopped alongside them. The driver tried to quieten the horses as two screeching cats, fighting over some vermin, scurried out of the shadows. Cranston knew what was in the cart. He had recognised the driver as the hangman from Tyburn.

'Don't look,' he whispered.

But Benedicta, her curiosity aroused, leaned on Athelstan's arm and, standing on tiptoe, peered over the rim of the cart. She stared in horror at the whitened, frozen cadavers which lay there under a tattered, canvas sheet. Their limbs hung all awry but round the neck of each was a thick, purple line, while the purple-red faces were contorted, swollen tongues held fast between ice-cold lips, eyes rolled back in the sockets.

'Oh, sweet Lord!' she breathed, and leaned against the wall as the driver cracked his whip and the cart rolled on.

'What was that?'

'The hanged from the Elms,' Cranston answered. 'At night the corpses are cut down and taken to the great lime pits near Charterhouse.' He glared at the widow. 'I told you not to look!'

Benedicta retched before, resting on Athelstan's arm, following Cranston through Ludgate and up towards the Fleet.

The prison did little to lighten their mood: grey frowning walls with a few sombre buildings peeping above them, and a black gateway with an arch which yawned as if it wished to devour any unfortunate who approached it. Cranston pulled at the bell and they were allowed through a wicket gate built into the ponderous door. A gaoler led them into the porter's lodge, the fellow bowing and scraping as he recognised Sir John. Athelstan was pleased then that the coroner had accompanied them. They went through a large hall where the debtors were jailed, furnished with side benches of oak and two long tables of the same wood, all covered in greasy filth. The people gathered around them were dirty and foul-smelling, men and women wearing threadbare jerkins and tattered cloaks. They pushed their way through the hall and up a stone-flagged passageway, past grated windows where poor debtors shook their begging bowls through the bars and whined for alms.

At last they went down slimy, cracked steps into the Hall of the Damned, the condemned hold, a massive, vaulted cellar with dungeons in the far wall.

'Who is it you wish to see?' the porter snapped.

'Simon the carpenter.'

The porter hurried across, chose a key and unlocked one of the doors.

'Come on, Simon!' he bawled. 'A rare treat! London's own coroner, a friar and a fair lady. Who could ask for more?'

Simon crept from the cell. Athelstan hardly recognised him: his face was a mass of sores, his hair long and matted with filth and vermin. The man's clothing had been reduced to rags and he was loaded with fetters. Simon shuffled awkwardly towards them, lifting his manacled hands to push his hair back. His lips were blue with the cold and his eyes, above sallow sunken cheeks, bright with fever.

'Father, you have brought a pardon?' he asked hopefully.

Athelstan shook his head. 'No, I am sorry. I just came to visit you, Simon. Is there anything I can do?'

The carpenter looked at him, then at Benedicta and, throwing back his head, laughed hysterically until the porter struck him across the face. The condemned man slumped to the floor, crouching like a beaten dog. Athelstan knelt beside him.

'Simon!' he murmured. 'Simon!'

The carpenter raised his head.

'Do you wish to be shriven? I will hear your confession.'

The man looked up despairingly.

'There's nothing left,' Athelstan whispered. 'This time tomorrow, Simon, you will be with God.'

The carpenter nodded and began to cry like a child. Athelstan turned. 'Sir John, Benedicta, please, give me a moment.'

They withdrew. The coroner bawled at the porter to follow them and, for the second time that day, Athelstan heard the confession of a man about to meet Death. At first, Simon spoke slowly and Athelstan had to fight hard to keep his composure as the chill of the dungeons seeped through his robe, turning his legs to blocks of ice, but then Simon allowed his emotions full rein. He talked of everything, a miserable litany of failure culminating in the rape of a child. Athelstan heard him out, pronounced absolution and rose, rubbing his stiff legs to make the warmth return. The porter came back.

'Tomorrow, Simon,' Athelstan whispered, 'I shall remember you. And, Simon?'

The condemned man looked up.

'You remember me before the throne of God.'

The carpenter nodded. 'I didn't mean to do it, Father. I was lonely, I'd drunk too much.'

'I know,' Athelstan murmured. 'God help you and her!' Athelstan turned to the porter and tossed him a silver coin. 'One good meal, sir.'

The porter caught the coin and nodded.

'One good meal,' Athelstan warned. 'I shall check on that.'

He was about to leave when Simon called out: 'Father!'

'Yes, Simon?'

'Ranulf the rat-catcher came to see me earlier today. He had been hired by a butcher in the Shambles. He said you were at the Tower because of Sir Ralph Whitton's death.' The carpenter grinned. 'Even though I have been shriven, it is good to know that bastard went before me. A strange place, the Tower, Father.'

Athelstan nodded. He felt Simon was only trying to prolong the visit. 'I worked there once,' the carpenter called out. 'A strange place, worse than this!'

'Why is that, Simon?'

'Well, at least here the cells have doors. In the Tower there are rooms, dungeons, where you go in, the doors are removed, and you remain until death behind a bricked wall.'

'Is that so?' Athelstan smiled. 'God be with you, Simon.'

Athelstan went back up the steps to rejoin Cranston and Benedicta. They never spoke until they were out of the prison, the wicket gate slamming shut behind them.

'The antechamber of Hell,' Athelstan murmured as they made their way down Bowyers Row under the dark mass of St Paul's. At Friday Street, Sir John made to leave.

Athelstan took him aside and stared into the bleary-eyed face.

'I thank you for coming, Sir John. Be at peace. Go home and talk to the Lady Maude. I am sure all will be well.'

Cranston scratched his head. 'God knows, Brother, but I feel the only good I did today was to listen to Fitzormonde and help that child. You know, the one who stood over the beggar man?'

'You came with us to the Fleet.'

'Aye,' Cranston muttered. 'I could not get a pardon for Simon, you know that, Brother, but I showed him one last mercy.'

'What's that, Sir John?'

'I left a coin for the executioner. Simon won't dance. He will be taken far up the ladder.' Cranston snapped his fingers. 'His neck will snap and it will all be over quickly.' The coroner stamped his feet and looked up at the star-filled sky. 'You had best hurry home, Brother. The stars await you.' He turned and tramped up the street. 'I only wish,' he called out 'we'd found Alderman Horne!'

Chapter 9

As Athelstan and Benedicta rode slowly back across the dark, choppy waters of the Thames, Adam Horne left the Crutched Friars monastery near Mark Lane just north of the Tower. He'd arrived just after Vespers to collect the message he had been told would be waiting for him. The grizzle-haired lay brother had smiled toothlessly and waved Horne into the door-keeper's lodge.

'It's been here all afternoon,' the lay brother murmured, handing him a thin roll of vellum. Horne anxiously unfolded the parchment and, begging the brother to bring a candle, hastily read the contents.

'Oh, my God!' he groaned as his hopes were dashed. Earlier in the morning he had received a piece of parchment with a sketch of a crudely drawn ship, and a flat sesame seed cake. He had tried to hide his fears from his poor wife and gone down to his warehouse, where another message had been awaiting him: he was not to return home, the short letter instructed, but to go to the House of the Crutched Friars where his anxieties would be resolved. He should fear nothing but put his hopes in the sender who wished him well. Now this short note cruelly dashed his hopes: the mysterious writer apologised for not meeting him but asked him to wait amongst the ancient ruins to the north-west of the Tower. Horne shredded the note, left the friary and made his way through the dark, ice-covered country lanes which cut round farms and smallholdings. He stared up at the starlit sky and shivered, not only from the biting cold but his own sombre fear of what might await him. Horne's common sense told him to run but he had waited too long. The threat had hung like a sword over his head for years and he wanted to confront it once and for all. A self-confident merchant, Horne also believed the meeting might end his fears for good. He could then go home, absolved from his part in that terrible crime committed so many years ago.

The line of trees ended and Horne stood on the edge of the common, in the far distance the lowering mass of the Tower. Perhaps he should go there? He sighed despairingly. Who could help him? Sir Ralph was dead and the surviving hospitaller would have no time for him. Horne gulped quickly at the realisation of his own guilt. Should he go on? He stared at the ice-covered ground and half listened to the cold wind moaning gently amongst the trees. Above him a raven cawed as it flew to hunt over the mudflats along the river. A fox barked. The sound was strident and made the hair curl on the back of his neck. Horne felt uneasy. He turned and stared back down the muddy track. Was someone there? Had he been followed?

Horne's face twisted into a snarl. He might be a fat, wealthy merchant now but fifteen years ago, he had fought as a knight, shoulder to shoulder with men who feared nothing on earth. Yes, he had been guilty. Even as much as Whitton, Fitzormonde and Mowbray had always been soft, they could whine and moan that they had not been to blame, but Horne had agreed to Whitton's plan and built a thriving business on the proceeds.

He fondled the long dagger he'd pushed through his wallet, drawing comfort from its metal-coiled handle. If there was an assassin about, he reassured himself, best to confront him now rather than be taken in the dead of night. An owl hooted. Horne snarled. 'Let all the hell hounds come from Satan's dark abyss! I will match blow for blow!' His empty words comforted him as he walked across to the ruins, a collection of snow-covered boulders. The old ones said the great Caesar once had a palace there. Horne, deeply agitated by a mixture of fear, terror and forced bravado, went and sat in the middle. He felt safer; despite the darkness, the white, snow-covered common and brittle ice would give him warning of any assassin's approach.

The merchant stared round the ruined Roman villa. A few yards away was a half-raised wall. Horne glared at it contemptuously. If any murderer lurked there, they would have to cover the ground and he had brought something special. A small arbalest, or miniature crossbow, swung from his belt, a bolt already in place. The darkness grew deeper. Horne studied the lights of the city. The wine he had drunk earlier in the day, his exertions and fear, made him feel warm and sleepy. A short stab of icy wind made him huddle deeper into his cloak and he stirred to keep the hot blood flowing through his veins. The merchant stared around into the gathering darkness and his courage began to ebb as he wondered who his strange benefactor might be. Horne closed his eyes, half sleeping, dozing. That's what Bartholomew Burghgesh had always told him to do.

'Rest whenever you can, my dear Adam. A true soldier always eats, drinks, sleeps and takes a wench whenever the opportunity presents itself.'

Horne smiled to himself. Brave, redoubtable man! A veritable paladin! Horne had liked him, but Ralph

Whitton had always been jealous of Bartholomew for being a better soldier than he. But surely there had been more than that?

Something about Whitton's wife being rather sweet on the young Bartholomew when he had, for a time, served as a knight banneret in the Tower. Horne sniggered to himself. Strange coincidence, the same place where Whitton had met his death. Horne looked up. Was that a sound he had heard? He sat still, his ears straining, but only the cawing of the ravens and the distant bark of some farm dog broke the chilling silence. Horne moved his feet restlessly. He would wait a few more minutes and then he'd go. He stared at the ground. Who was the murderer? he wondered. Could it be the hospitaller, Fitzormonde? Or Fulke, Sir Ralph's brother? He'd known Burghgesh quite well. Or someone else who believed he was God's vicar on earth to dispense justice and retribution? Or had Burghgesh survived, been taken prisoner, and then years later slipped back into England to reap bloody havoc on his foes? Or perhaps his son and heir? Had he really died in France, or else learnt about his father's terrible fate and secretly returned to stalk his sire's killers?

Horne chewed on his lip. He had to face the fact that he was a killer. He had been party to Burghgesh's murder. Sometimes at night this thought would rouse him screaming from his sleep. And was that why God had given him no son or heir? Was his wife's barrenness due to divine justice? Horne heard a sound, jumped up in terror and stared at the apparition just next to the old wall.

A man clothed in knight's armour, on his breast the red cross of the crusaders, his face hidden by that helmet! The same steel, conical shell with eagle's wings on either side and blue tufted crest on top. A chilling terror gripped

Horne's heart. 'My God!' he whispered. 'It's Burghgesh!' Or was it an apparition from hell? The armoured, visored figure just stood there, feet slightly apart, mailed, gauntleted fists gripping the handle of the great, two-edged sword with the blade resting on one shoulder.

'You are Burghgesh?' Horne hissed.

The apparition moved closer. Only the crunch of mailed feet on the hard ice broke the silence.

'Adam! Adam!' The voice was Burghgesh's, though it sounded sombre and hollow. 'Adam!' the voice repeated. 'I have returned! I come for vengeance! You, my comrade in arms, my friend for whom I would have given my life.' One mailed hand shot out. 'You betrayed me! You, Whitton and the rest!'

Horne moved suddenly, his hand going to the small arbalest which swung from his belt.

'You're no phantasm,' the merchant snarled. 'And, if you are, go back to Hell where you belong!'

He brought up the arbalest but, even as he did, the great two-edged sword scythed the air, neatly slicing the merchant's head from his shoulders. The decapitated head spun like a ball in the air, lips still moving; his trunk stood for a few seconds in its own fountain of hot red gore before crashing on to the blood-stained ice. Horne's mailed executioner carefully cleaned the sword, drew his knife and knelt beside the blood-gushing torso of his victim.

Some hours later, Sir John Cranston, muttering and cursing to himself, made his way from Blind Basket Alley up Mincing Lane into Fenchurch Street. Dawn had just broken and Sir John, unable to sleep, had risen early to confer with Alderman Venables about the continued disappearance of Roger Droxford, still wanted for the murder of his master, whose decapitated corpse Cranston had found. Sir John had spent a restless night tossing from side to side in his great double bed. He had tried to remain calm but still seethed with fury at Maude's continued intransigence in the face of his pleadings and questions: her only answer would be to bite her lip, shake her head and turn away in floods of tears. At last Cranston had risen and gone to his personal chancery but, finding himself unable to concentrate, had finished dressing and gone to rouse Venables. Cranston grinned wickedly. He'd enjoyed that, letting the good alderman know what it was like to be awoken just before dawn. The sleepy-eyed alderman, however, could give him no further information on Droxford.

'He can't have fled far, Sir John,' Venables murmured sleepily. 'God knows, in this weather only a fool would try to flee the city limits, and both the description and the reward have been circulated.' Venables had grinned. 'After all, Sir John, he's a man you would remember.'

'What do you mean?'

'Well, he had two fingers missing from one hand and his face was covered in hairy warts.' The alderman pulled his fur-lined bed robe around him, moving restlessly on the stone-flagged corridor and making it obvious the coroner should leave. 'What's so special about Droxford, anyway, Sir John?'

'He's special, Master Venables, because he's a murderer, a felon who has stolen over two hundred pounds of his master's monies, and it looks as if he has got away scot-free!'

Venables took one look at Cranston's angry face and agreed. Sir John had then stamped off, muttering curses about public officials who didn't seem to care. Yet, in his heart, Cranston knew he was a hypocrite. The business at the Tower was still shrouded in mystery. The fugitive Droxford, not to mention the easy-going alderman, were the nearest butts for Sir John's foul temper.

He turned into the still-deserted Lombard Street and up to the great stocks just before the Poultry. A group of beadles were standing around a beggar who sat imprisoned there, feet and hands tightly clamped, face frozen, eyes open.

'What's the matter?' Cranston bellowed.

The beadles shuffled their feet.

'Someone forgot to release him last night,' one of them shouted. 'The poor bastard's frozen to death!'

'Then some bastard will pay!' Sir John bellowed back, and continued up the wide thoroughfare, past a group of nightbirds, whores and petty felons now manacled together and being led down to the great iron cage on top of the Conduit. A frightened-looking maid let him in. Sir John suddenly stopped, eyes narrowing. Hadn't he glimpsed a shadow in the alleyway beside the house? He went back. Nothing. Cranston shook his head and, vowing he would drink less sack, brushed past the anxious-looking maid, down the passageway and into the stone-flagged kitchen. He thanked God Maude wasn't there. He was tired of their encounters.

'Any messages?' he barked at a subdued-looking Leif, still sitting in his favourite place in the inglenook of the great fireplace. The one-legged beggar lifted his head from his bowl of vegetables and spiced meat and shook his head.

'No, Sir John,' he replied. 'But I have polished the pewter pots.'

'Good,' he growled. 'At least someone in this city is working.'

Cranston poured himself a generous goblet of wine and seized a small white loaf the cook had left to cool on the kitchen table. The coroner stood snatching mouthfuls of bread and gulping noisily from a goblet whilst he stared angrily at the fire. What should he do? he wondered.

Whitton's and Mowbray's deaths at the Tower were still as unfathomable as ever. He had also failed to find Horne. Sir John knew it would only be a matter of time before his masters at the Guildhall or, worse still, the Regent at the Savoy Palace, asked for an account of his stewardship. He heard a sharp knock at the door.

'Go on, Leif,' he growled. 'I'm too bloody cold to answer it.'

Leif looked self-pityingly at him.

'Go on, you idle bugger!' Cranston roared. 'There's more to this house than sitting on your arse and stuffing your mouth with every bit of food you can lay your sticky little fingers on!'

Leif sighed, put down the bowl and hobbled out of the kitchen. Cranston heard the front door open and the man limping slowly back.

'What is it?' Cranston asked, winking good-humouredly at the maid who had also hurried down to see who was at the door. The girl smiled anxiously back and Cranston quietly cursed himself. He was frightening everyone with his foul temper. He must take a grip on himself. Perhaps he should ask Athelstan to intervene? 'Well, man?' he repeated. 'Who was there?'

'No one, Sir John.'

'What do you mean?'

'Well, there was no one there.' Leif steadied himself against the lintel of the door. 'Only this.' He held up a battered, leather bag tied at the neck and stained with watery dark marks around the base. 'I answered the door,' Leif ponderously repeated, 'no one was there, only this bag.'

'Then open it, man!' Cranston said testily.

The coroner turned away to refill his wine cup. He whirled around at Leif s horrified cry and the bump as the maid fell in a dead faint to the floor. The beggar man just stood there, eyes wide in horror, mouth slack; in his upraised hand he held by the hair the decapitated head of Adam Horne, alderman and merchant.

Now Cranston had seen decapitated heads, be they of murdered taverner or some lord executed on Tower Hill, but this was truly gruesome; it was not so much the half-closed eyes and still blood-dripping neck but the mouth forced open and, thrust inside, the mangled remains of the dead merchant's genitals.

Cranston grabbed the head from the horror-struck beggar's hand, thrust it back into the bag, stepped over the still prostrate maid and, roaring for Maude, dashed down the passageway to the door. He flung it open, rushing like an angry bull down Cheapside, but the snow-covered thoroughfare was still deserted, with no trace or sign of their mysterious, grisly visitor. Cranston stopped and, half crouching, retched violently as the true horror of what he had seen seized his mind and wrung his stomach as if it was a wet rag.

'Oh, the bastard!' he whispered. 'Oh, Lord help us!'

He staggered back inside the house. Maude, white-faced, stood at the foot of the stairs.

'Sir John, what is it?'

'Go back to your room, woman!' Cranston roared. 'Stay there!'

He turned to the grooms and servants now huddled together near the kitchen door.

'You,' Cranston barked at one, 'go for a physician! You,' he pointed to the cook and her assistant, 'take the maid into the solar!'

The poor, half-unconscious girl was hustled to her feet. Cranston walked back into the kitchen. Leif sat on the stool like a man pole-axed. The bag and its gruesome contents still lay where Cranston had dropped it. The coroner busied himself around the house. He shaved, changed his doublet, put on his sword belt and took his heaviest cloak from its hook outside the buttery. He found a heavy flour sack in one of the outhouses and placed the battered leather bag carefully in it.

'Leif,' he ordered, 'tell Lady Maude I am going to the Guildhall, then on to Southwark.'

The beggar, usually so garrulous but still dumbstruck at what he had seen, just stared and nodded, open-mouthed. Cranston swung the sack over his shoulder.

'Oh, Leif.' Cranston turned and grinned evilly at the beggar. 'There's more of that rich stew if you want it.'

Leif turned away, retching, whilst Cranston stalked out of his house muttering vengeance against all and sundry.

–

In St Erconwald's church, Athelstan had just finished the Mass for the dead and was now blessing the corpse of Tosspot, an old drunkard who'd lived in the cellars of the Piebald Horse tavern. Tosspot had been found dead the previous afternoon. Pike the ditcher and Watkin the dung-collector had, in the absence of any relatives, sewn the body into a canvas sack, placed it on a wooden trellis and brought it to lie in front of the chancel screen. Athelstan had always given strict instructions on this: any poor man or woman found dead in his parish was to be given honourable burial, so this included Tosspot. Athelstan sketched the sign of the cross above the corpse and sprinkled it with the Asperges rod. Around him the usual Mass-goers, Benedicta included, watched fascinated as Athelstan urged the soul to go out to meet his Christ whilst he, Athelstan, priest of that church, summoned God's army to meet this unfortunate man's soul; they were to lead it into Paradise and ensure it did not fall into the hands of Satan. Athelstan paused. And what about the body? he thought. Would that be safe? He looked down at his fingers and noted the chalk dust on their tips. Where had that come from? he wondered. It had not been there during Mass.

'Father,' Crim the altar boy whispered.

Athelstan, startled, looked up.

'Father,' the boy repeated, his face creased in a mischievous grin, 'you've suddenly stopped praying!'

Athelstan shook himself free from his reverie.

'We beg thee, Michael the Archangel,' he intoned the final prayer, 'to take the soul of this our brother.' He paused. What could he call him? Tosspot? What would the angels think of such a name? 'Take the soul of this our brother Tosspot,' he continued defiantly, 'into the bosom of Abraham.'

The friar glared at the congregation, but they all knelt, heads wisely bowed to hide their grins. Athelstan, trying to conceal his embarrassment, signalled at Watkin and Pike to lift the bier and follow him and Crim, bearing a lighted taper, into the cemetery. Outside the cold wind snuffed the taper out. Crim slipped on the ice and fell on his backside, cursing so loudly Athelstan had to bite his lip to keep his face straight. They crossed the lonely, haunted cemetery to the shallow grave Pike had dug in the ground. Athelstan caught a glimpse of the two lepers, shrouded in their hoods near the charnel house. He suddenly remembered the twig he had used to push the Hosts through the leper's squint for these two unfortunates to swallow. Athelstan smiled to himself. That's where the chalk had come from. They reached the grave. Pike and Watkin unceremoniously rolled old Tosspot into the shallow hole and, whilst Athelstan muttered some prayers, hastily covered it with icy lumps of clay. Athelstan then blessed the grave and with Watkin darkly hoping the body would stay there, they all trooped back into the church. Athelstan chose to ignore the dung-collector's dire speculation. The grave robbers, whoever they were, seemed to have disappeared. Perhaps moved on to vex some other unfortunate priest. He swept up the nave under the chancel screen and into the small, icy sacristy. Athelstan jumped as a large figure loomed out of the shadows.

'Sir John!' he snapped. 'Must you lurk like some thief in the night?'

Cranston grinned slyly. 'I must have words with you, Brother, and not here.'

Athelstan looked at him carefully. 'You've been drinking, Sir John?'

Cranston smirked. 'Yes and no. Quick! I'll wait whilst you divest.'

Athelstan hid his irritation. He doffed his chasuble, stole and cope, hastily hung them in the cupboard, gave a wide-eyed Crim a penny for his help then bustled Sir John back into the church. He beckoned to Benedicta who was standing near the baptismal font.

'Lock the sacristy, please,' he whispered to her. 'And then clear the church.' Athelstan looked around. 'Watkin!' he shouted. The dung-collector ambled slowly over, one eye on Sir John. 'Watkin,' Athelstan confided, 'I will be gone for some time. You are to ensure the candles are doused and the church is kept safe and, if you are so concerned about the cemetery, keep a watch there yourself.'

The sexton looked hurt and Athelstan could have bitten out his tongue. He had not intended to be so sharp, but Cranston's secretive arrival had unnerved him. The friar led the coroner out of the church. Cranston saw Bonaventure fairly skipping along to greet him but he had no desire to have that bloody cat rubbing up against his leg, so hustled Athelstan out to collect their horses.

'Follow me, my Mephistopheles,' he murmured. 'To a place of warmth and security.'

They crossed the beaten track, dodging between the heavy-wheeled carts, and led their horses down to London Bridge and into the welcoming warmth of the Piebald Horse tavern. Cranston loved this place, a veritable den of iniquity but one which sold good ales, fine wine and delicious food. Of course, the coroner personally knew Joscelyn, the tapster.

'A real sinner,' he had once described him as, 'who will get into heaven because he has stolen the gates.'

Athelstan agreed; the landlord of the Piebald Horse was a one-armed, reformed sea pirate who had confidentially explained to the friar how he would love to go to church but the smell of incense always made him feel ill. Athelstan smiled to himself. He found it strange that he had just buried Tosspot who used to clean the platters and tankards in this very tavern. The friar gazed round. The place looked cleaner; fresh plaster on the wall, the beams newly painted, whilst the rushes underfoot were fresh and sweet-smelling. Joscelyn waddled towards them. The old rogue's vein-streaked face was wreathed in smiles, his good hand scratching his chin as he relished the prospect of a fine profit. Sir John was a prodigious drinker and was well loved by the city's taverners.

'My Lord Coroner,' Joscelyn gave a mock bow, 'you are most welcome to my humble abode.'

'By the sod, you old bastard!' Cranston roared. 'Have you gone back to your old, wicked ways? Where did you get the sustenance to clean this sewer of iniquity?'

Joscelyn shrugged and spread his one good hand, fingers splayed out. 'I have a new partner,' he announced proudly, 'who sold his own tavern near the Barbican and moved across the river to be free from the prying of certain coroners!'

Cranston roared with laughter and led Athelstan over to the far corner where a table and stools were set apart from the rest of the customers. Athelstan felt rather embarrassed. Near the wine tuns, he noticed Pike the ditcher, the clay of the cemetery still fresh on his hands, deep in hushed conversation with a group of strangers. The Great Community, Athelstan thought, peasants from the snow-covered fields outside the city, slipping in to talk sedition, plan treason and plot rebellion. Pike noticed him and, eyes guarded, raised his tankard. Athelstan smiled back but watched as, a few minutes later, Pike rose and led the rest of his companions out of the tavern.

Cranston squatted down with his back to the wall, smacked his lips and gazed hungrily up at the hams and other meats hanging from ropes on the rafters to be cured. He watched a pot boy broach a new cask and through an open door glimpsed the kitchen with its huge oven where Joscelyn baked his own bread. A dusty-faced boy was now raking the coal and wood from this into a tidy, white pile of ash. The bread would then be slipped in, the oven door sealed, and when the oven cooled, the bread would be baked. A curious place, Sir John reflected, at the heart of Southwark's squalor, yet the ales and wine were always fresh and the food delicious. He glimpsed a table at the far end of the tavern with a huge silver nef, or spice ship. Cranston scratched his head. So much new wealth. He idly wondered if Joscelyn had returned to his old ways and was engaged in some petty smuggling.

Athelstan studied Cranston out of the corner of his eye. Sir John's temper had improved but Athelstan dreaded spending a day watching him guzzle one goblet of wine after another. The landlord waddled over.

'My Lord Coroner, you are ready to order?'

Cranston gazed speculatively at the ceiling.

'No fish!' he barked. 'Some pheasant or quail, cooked to a golden brown and stuffed with spices. I want the sauce thick. And some fresh bread!'

'And the Reverend Father?' Joscelyn asked sardonic-ally.

'The Reverend Father,' Athelstan replied smoothly, 'would like a bowl of thick leek soup, some bread, and a cup of wine with more water than claret.'

They waited until Joscelyn had walked away, roaring their order into the kitchen.

'Well, My Lord Coroner?' Athelstan asked. 'What has happened?'

Cranston outlined in sharp, succinct phrases the grisly events which had taken place earlier in the day. 'I have also been to the Guildhall,' he mournfully concluded. 'The mayor told me in no uncertain terms how displeased His Grace the Regent Duke of Lancaster is at our lack of progress. Adam Horne was apparently a member of his retinue.'

'And what was your reply?'

'I told him that I didn't give a rat's arse, and that I was doing the best I could.'

'I suppose,' the friar answered, 'the mayor accepted your eloquent reply?'

Cranston slouched back against the wall. 'Oh, we had a quarrel, but I have more sense than to seek a confrontation. I explained we had searched for Horne but could not find him.' He glanced across at Athelstan, his face full of self-pity. 'I must resolve the matter with the Lady Maude,' he whispered. 'It's clouding my mind.'

Athelstan waited until the slattern had served them with goblets of wine.

'Look, Sir John, let us take these events from the beginning.' Athelstan raised a hand. 'No, it is necessary. And, if you'll accept my apologies, we must for the time being put the matter of Lady Maude to one side.'

Cranston nodded glumly.

'Sir Ralph Whitton,' Athelstan began, 'received a warning that he was going to die because of a terrible act of betrayal committed in Outremer some years ago. I know,' Athelstan quietly continued, 'Sir Ralph was guilty of such an act. That's why in the back of his Book of Hours, he scribbled those prayers to Julian the Hospitaller.'

'Who was he?'

'A knight who committed terrible murders and spent his life in making reparation. Anyway,' Athelstan continued, 'Sir Ralph moves from his own chamber to the so-called security of the North Bastion tower. He is frightened and even refuses to take his Moorish servant, Rastani, with him. He drinks heavily the night before his death and retires to his bed chamber. What happened then?' Athelstan asked, trying to draw Cranston from his own dark thoughts.

The coroner slurped noisily from his cup. 'Well, my dear friar, according to all the evidence we have, Sir Ralph went to bed, and locked the door behind him, keeping the key with him. The door leading to the gallery on which his chamber stands was locked by the guards, whilst the other end of the passage is blocked by fallen masonry. The guards are on duty all night just inside the entrance to the North Bastion. They are both trusted men and the key to both the gallery door and another for Sir Ralph's chamber hang on a hook beside them. We have established, on good authority, that neither sentry left his post nor did they see or hear anything untoward.'

'And now the murder?' Athelstan prompted.

'Young Geoffrey,' Cranston continued, 'whom Sir Ralph apparently doted upon, comes across early the next morning. The guards search him for weapons and open the door to the gallery. The same door is then locked, apparently on Sir Ralph's orders, and Geoffrey goes to rouse him. The guards hear him knocking and shouting but then our young hero comes back. He announces his inability to arouse Sir Ralph, is about to return and unlock Whitton's chamber himself, then changes his mind and goes for Colebrooke the lieutenant. They both return to Sir Ralph's chamber and open it. The room is undisturbed, but Whitton is lying on his bed, his throat slashed, the corpse icy cold, and the shuttered windows wide open. That, my dear friar, is where our problem begins.'

'Not if we accept our conclusion,' Athelstan replied. 'That someone crossed the frozen moat and, using the steps in the wall, climbed up to Sir Ralph's chamber. The assassin prised open the lever on the shutters, entered and committed the crime. Nevertheless,' he persisted, 'our conclusion has its own problems. Why did Sir Ralph just lie there and allow his throat to be cut? He was a soldier, a warrior.' The friar shook his head. 'All we do know,' he concluded, 'is that the assassin must have been a member of the community at the Tower who knew Sir Ralph had changed his bed chamber, and he or she either committed the murder or hired a professional assassin to do it for them.' Athelstan stared across at a group of dicers who sat playing noisily on the other side of the tavern.

'And Sir Gerard Mowbray's murder,' Cranston observed, 'is no clearer. Who rang the bell? How did Mowbray fall? Of course Horne's murder,' he continued, 'was relatively easy. The assassin played upon his guilt and fear and probably lured the hapless man to his grisly death in that lonely place.'

'Where did he die?' Athelstan queried.

'In the old ruins to the north of the Tower. And, before you ask, his murderer left no trace.'

'And the suspects?' Athelstan asked wearily. He leaned across and tapped Sir John on the arm. 'Come on, My Lord Coroner, apply that sharp brain of yours!'

Cranston shrugged.

'Well, it could be Sir Fulke. His buckle was found on the ice and he stands to gain from his brother's death. Sir Ralph's servant Rastani was lithe and able enough to climb up that wall.' Cranston made a face at Athelstan. 'By the way, I checked on their story for the night Sir Ralph died; both Sir Fulke and Rastani were absent from the Tower and there are people who can guarantee their whereabouts.'

'Master Geoffrey could be the felon,' Athelstan remarked. 'But on the night Sir Ralph died he was in Philippa's bed, and on the night Sir Gerard died, in his lady's chamber. True, he went to rouse Sir Ralph, but he was searched for any weapons, he had no key, and even if he had entered the room, favoured son or not, Sir Ralph would scarcely have offered his throat to be cut.' Athelstan rubbed his face. 'The possibilities are endless,' he said. 'Hammond, the felonious chaplain. Colebrooke, the envious Lieutenant. The gracious Mistress Philippa. Not to mention our hospitaller who may have told us a pack of lies.' The friar narrowed his eyes. 'We must check on them all,' he murmured.

'Or Red Hand,' Cranston observed. 'The mad man who may not be as insane as he appears.'

Athelstan looked up and smiled. 'But we have made some progress, Sir John. If Fitzormonde is to be believed, we know the reason for the murders: Burghgesh's death on that unfortunate ship in the Middle Sea so many years ago. The picture on the parchment is to remind his murderers of their foul act and the sesame seed cake a warning of their impending doom.'

'And that—' Cranston almost shouted, glaring across at the landlord to bring his food, for his stomach was growling with hunger '—leads us to another mystery. Did Burghgesh really die? Or is he back, hiding in London, even the Tower? Or is there someone else? Perhaps his son or some other friend?'

Cranston leaned back as Joscelyn brought across the steaming platters of food. The landlord served Sir John himself, cutting thick slices of pheasant breast and laying them deftly with his one hand on the pewter platter whilst a maid scurried up with a jug of steaming gravy in which the bird had been cooked. Sir John grinned his thanks, took his own pewter spoon from his wallet, drew his dagger and set to as if he hadn't eaten for days. Athelstan watched in astonishment: Sir John's permanent hunger always fascinated him. A slattern brought his own meal, a thickly spiced bowl of soup. Athelstan asked to borrow a pewter spoon and ate slowly.

'They've forgotten the bread,' Sir John grumbled.

Athelstan called the girl back and small, fresh white loaves, wrapped in a linen cloth, were immediately served. Whilst he ate, Athelstan reflected on what they had discussed. He waited a while until Sir John had taken the edge off his appetite.

'There is one matter we have overlooked.'

'What's that?' Cranston mumbled, his mouth full of food.

'Horne's murderer means the assassin knows us or why should he send such a grisly trophy to your house?'

'Because the bastard's mad!'

'No, no, Sir John. It's meant as a warning. This murderer sees himself as doing God's work. He is sending a message: keep well away until my work is done. Don't interfere.' Athelstan lowered his spoon. 'Such a terrible thing,' he whispered. 'A man's genitals hacked off and stuffed into the mouth of his decapitated head. Of course,' he continued, 'Fitzormonde mentioned that.'

'What?'

'Well, how the Caliph of Egypt would punish in such a way anybody who transgressed his command. The head and genitals hacked off and both exposed above the city gates in Alexandria. It's obvious, Sir John,' he continued, 'our murderer must be someone who has lived in Outremer, someone who knows about the Hashishoni – the flat sesame seed cake, and that awful way of humiliating the corpse of an executed criminal.'

Cranston lowered his knife. 'But who is the murderer, Brother?'

'I don't know, Sir John, but I think we should re-visit the Tower and speak to our group of suspects.'

'And then?'

'We go to Woodforde.'

Cranston groaned.

'Sir John,' Athelstan persisted, 'it's not far – a few miles through Aldgate and down the Mile End Road. We must find out if Burghgesh ever returned and what happened to his son. Moreover,' he continued, 'perhaps it may give you some time to reflect on the Lady Maude.'

Cranston jabbed the point of his knife into a piece of soft meat, mumbled his assent and continued to eat as if his very life depended upon it.

Chapter 10

Athelstan and Cranston finished their meal and crossed London Bridge. Beneath them the water moved black and sluggish and they heard chunks of ice crashing against the starlings which protected the wooden arches from the fury of the Thames. They passed through Billingsgate. The air stank with the odour from the stalls, now freshly stocked with herring, cod, tench and even pike as the fishing fleets took advantage of a break in the weather.

The Tower was all abustle when they arrived. Like any good soldier, Colebrooke had the garrison working to break the tedium caused by the freezing weather, as well as to take his own mind off the recent murders. The lieutenant was standing on Tower Green, shouting orders at workmen who were refurbishing mangonels, scorpions and the great battering rams. A number of archers stood ankle-deep in the slush, practising at the butts, whilst others were being mercilessly drilled by the serjeants. Athelstan vaguely remembered rumours about how, in the spring, the French might attack the Channel ports and even force their way up the Thames to plunder and burn the city.

Colebrooke's displeasure at seeing Cranston and Athelstan was more than apparent.

'You have found the murderers?' he yelled.

'No, Master Lieutenant!' Cranston bellowed back. 'But we will. And, when we do, you can build the gallows.'

Cranston stepped aside as a butcher and two fletchers rolled barrels of salted pork down to the store house. The coroner wrinkled his nose. Despite the heavy spices and thick white salt, the pork smelt rancid and his gorge rose as he saw insects crawling out from under the rim of the barrel. He quietly vowed not to accept any food from the Tower buttery or kitchens. Colebrooke, seeing his visitors would not be deterred, turned away to issue further orders. Athelstan took advantage of the delay to walk over to where the bear, squatting in its own filth, was busy plundering a mound of refuse piled high before him. The madman, Red Hand, sat like an elf fascinated by the great beast.

'You are content, Red Hand?' Athelstan asked softly.

The man grimaced, waving his hands in the air as if mimicking the bear. Athelstan crouched down beside him.

'You like the bear, Red Hand?'

The fellow nodded, his eyes intent on the bear.

'So does the knight,' Red Hand slurred and Athelstan caught the stench of wine fumes on his breath.

'Which knight?'

'The one with the cross.'

'You mean Fitzormonde?'

'Yes, yes, Fitzormonde. He often comes to stare. Red Hand likes Fitzormonde. Red Hand likes the bear. Red Hand does not like Colebrooke. Colebrooke would kill Red Hand.'

'Did you like Burghgesh?' Athelstan asked quickly. He caught the gleam of recognition in the madman's eyes.

'You knew him,' Athelstan continued. 'As a young soldier, he once served here.'

Red Hand looked away.

'Surely you remember?' Athelstan persisted.

The madman shook his head and stared at the bear, but Athelstan saw him blink away the tears which pricked his madcap eyes. The friar sighed and rose, dusting the wet ice from his robe.

'Brother Athelstan!' Cranston barked. 'Master Colebrooke is a busy man. He says he cannot waste the day whilst you converse with a madman.'

'Master Colebrooke should realise,' Athelstan replied, 'that it is a matter of opinion, as well as the judgment of God, who is sane and who is mad.'

'Father, I mean no offence,' Colebrooke answered, taking off his conical helmet and cradling it in his arms. 'But I have a garrison to command. I will do what you want.'

Athelstan smiled. 'Good! Mowbray's body, where does it lie?'

Colebrooke pointed to the Chapel of St Peter ad Vincula. 'Before the chancel screen. Tomorrow it will be buried in the cemetery of All Hallows church.'

'Is it coffined?'

'No, no.'

'Good, I wish to see the corpse, and after that My Lord Coroner and I would like to speak with all those affected by Sir Ralph's death.'

Colebrooke groaned.

'We are here on the Regent's authority,' Athelstan interrupted. 'When these matters are finished, Master Lieutenant, we shall report on the support, or lack of it, we have had in our investigation. We will meet the group in St John's Chapel.'

Colebrooke forced a smile and hurried off, shouting at his soldiers to search out Sir Fulke and others. Cranston and Athelstan walked over to St Peter's. The church was a dour, sombre place, cold and dank. The nave was shaped like a box, with rounded pillars guarding darkened aisles.

At the top a small rose window afforded some light. The chancel screen was of polished oak and before it, surrounded by a ring of candles, lay the corpses of Sir Ralph Whitton and Sir Gerard Mowbray. The embalmers had done what they could but, even as they walked up the nave, both Cranston and Athelstan caught the whiff of putrefaction. The two bodies lay under canvas sheets on wickerwork mats supported by wooden trestles. Cranston stood away, waving Athelstan on.

'I've eaten too richly, Brother,' he murmured. 'Look for what you want and let's get out.'

Athelstan was only too happy to oblige. He ignored Sir Ralph's corpse but lifted back the insignia over the hospitaller's and the canvas sheet which lay underneath. He did not wish to look at Mowbray's face. Athelstan had seen enough of death. Instead he examined the white, scabrous legs of the hospitaller, picking up one of the candles to study the purple-yellow bruise just above the shin on the corpse's right leg. Satisfied, he pulled back the canvas sheet, replaced the tallow candle, genuflected towards the sanctuary and left the church, Cranston following as quickly as possible. They stood on the porch steps and eagerly drank in the invigorating cold air.

'Good Lord, Sir John,' Athelstan murmured, 'I always thought St Erconwald's was bad but, if ever I moan about it again, remind me of this church and I'll keep my mouth shut.'

Cranston grinned. 'It will be my pleasure, Brother. You found what you are looking for?'

'Yes, I did, Sir John. I believe Sir Gerard was not pushed from the parapet. Someone laid a spear or a piece of wood at the top of the steps whilst the hospitaller was at his usual place at the far end of the parapet walk, near Salt Tower.' Athelstan pursed his lips. 'Yes, it could be done under cover of darkness whilst Sir Gerard was lost in his own thoughts.' He narrowed his eyes and stared at the distant wall of the Tower. 'The tocsin sounded. Mowbray hurried along the parapet. In the dark he would not see the obstacle. His leg struck it, he slipped and fell to his death.'

'But we don't know who rang the bell or placed the pole on the parapet. Remember,' Cranston continued, 'apart from Fitzormonde and Colebrooke, everybody was in Mistress Philippa's chamber.'

'Colebrooke might have done it,' the friar replied. 'He might have seen the knight standing on the parapet, crept up, placed the pole there, and somehow or other arranged for the tocsin to be sounded.'

'But we have no proof?'

'No, Sir John, we do not. But we are collecting it. In bits and pieces.' He sighed. Only time will tell if we are successful.

They found Colebrooke and the rest of the group sitting on benches in the Chapel of St John. Their displeasure at being summoned was more than apparent. Hammond kept his back half-turned. Fulke slouched, staring up at the ceiling; Rastani seemed more confident and Athelstan caught the sardonic mocking look in his dark, brilliant eyes. Colebrooke marched up and down as if he was on parade whilst Mistress Philippa leaned against the wall, looking sorrowfully down at Tower Green.

'Where is Geoffrey?' Athelstan asked.

'Geoffrey Parchmeiner,' Fulke replied, 'being a rather frightened, silly young man, may have many vices.' The knight ignored his niece's furious look. 'But he works hard. He has better things to do than hang around the Tower answering idle questions whilst good men are killed and the murderer walks scot-free.'

'Thank you for that speech, Sir Fulke,' Cranston replied, beaming falsely around. 'We have only one question and I apologise to you, Sir Brian, but it's a name, that's all. Bartholomew Burghgesh – does it mean anything to any of you?'

Athelstan was amazed at the transformation caused by Cranston's words. The coroner's smile widened.

'Good,' he announced. 'Now we have your attention.' He glanced quickly at the hospitaller's angry face. 'Sir Brian, you must not answer, and if you are patient, you will see why we ask. Well,' the coroner clapped his hands, 'Bartholomew Burghgesh?'

'Hell's teeth!' Sir Fulke snarled and walked into the centre of the room. 'Don't play games, Sir John. Burghgesh was one name my brother, Sir Ralph, would never have mentioned in his presence.'

'Why?' Athelstan asked innocently.

'My brother could not stand the man.'

'But they were comrades-in-arms.'

'Were,' Fulke emphasised. 'They quarrelled in Outremer. Bartholomew was later killed on a ship taken in the Middle Sea by Moorish pirates.'

'Why?' Cranston barked.

'Why what?'

'Why did your brother dislike Burghgesh so much?'

Fulke stepped closer and lowered his eyes. 'It was a matter of honour,' he murmured. He licked his lips and glanced nervously towards Philippa. 'Sir Ralph once accused Bartholomew of paying too much attention to your mother, Sir Ralph's wife.'

'Were the allegations true?' Athelstan asked.

Fulke's face softened. 'No,' he stammered. 'I'll be honest – I liked Bartholomew. He was funny, always thought the best of people. He was both gentle and courteous.'

Athelstan suddenly glimpsed the steel in Sir Fulke's character.

'You really did like him, didn't you?'

'Yes, yes, I did. I was much distressed at the news of his death.' Fulke shuffled his feet and looked down at the floor. 'I'll be honest,' he continued. 'When I was younger, I used to wish Bartholomew was my brother because, God forgive me, I did not like Ralph.' He looked up, his eyes sad. 'Years ago, he and Bartholomew served as officers here in the Tower.' Fulke coughed and cleared his throat. 'My brother was treacherous. He was cruel. He ill-treated Red Hand. He even beat the priest here when he was only a young clerk.'

The chaplain blushed with embarrassment.

'Come on, tell the truth!' Fulke now glared round, snarling like a dog. 'Sir Ralph was hated!'

Mistress Philippa stepped forward, her face white with fury. 'My father is sheeted, waiting for burial, and you speak ill of him!'

'God forgive me, Philippa, I only tell the truth!' Fulke flung out his hand. 'Ask Rastani! When he was a boy, who plucked his tongue out?'

The Moor just stared back. His eyes never flickered.

'It's true!' Fitzormonde intervened. 'It was over the Moor that the bad blood first surfaced between Burghgesh and Whitton.'

Fulke slumped back on the bench. 'I've said enough,' he snarled. 'But I'm tired of these questions. Mistress Philippa, your father was a bastard and no one here will gainsay me.'

Cranston and Athelstan just stood amazed at this sudden outburst of hatred and animosity. Good Lord, Athelstan thought, anyone here could be Sir Ralph's murderer. Burghgesh had been well loved. Did someone in this room believe he was God's executioner to avenge a good man's death? Athelstan looked around.

'Master Parchmeiner will not be here today?' he asked, taking advantage of the sudden lull.

'No,' Sir Fulke replied wearily. 'For pity's sake, Father, who would want to stay here? So many memories, so much hatred.'

Mistress Philippa sat huddled on one of the benches, her face in her hands. Sir Fulke went over to her and patted her gently on the shoulder. Cranston caught a smirk on Rastani's face. Was he the murderer? the coroner wondered. He recalled Athelstan's words, how the slayer of Adam Horne used a method practised in Moorish countries to desecrate the body of a criminal and traitor.

'We have seen enough,' Athelstan whispered. 'We should go.'

'Just one more thing,' Cranston announced. 'You knew Adam Horne the merchant?'

'Another bastard!' Sir Fulke hissed. 'Yes, yes, Sir John. Horne was my brother's friend.'

'Well, he's dead.' Cranston proclaimed flatly. 'Found murdered last night in the ruins just north of here.'

Fitzormonde swore quietly. The others looked up in alarm.

'I wonder where you all were?' Cranston asked.

'Hell's teeth, Sir John!' Colebrooke snapped. 'Now the thaw's come, anyone could slip in and out of a postern gate.'

Cranston smiled wanly. The lieutenant was right: it would be nigh impossible to make everyone account for their movements. Horne could have been murdered any time between dusk and dawn.

'Come, Sir John,' Athelstan murmured.

They took their leave unceremoniously, Cranston waving Colebrooke aside. They hardly spoke a word until they had collected their horses and left the Tower, going up towards Eastcheap.

'Oh, Lord save us!' Cranston suddenly broke the silence. 'What hatred exists in the human heart, eh, Brother?'

'Aye,' Athelstan replied, gently guiding Philomel away from the snow-covered sewer which ran down the middle of the street. 'Perhaps we should all remember that, Sir John. Minor jealousies and misunderstandings can fan the petty flames of bickering into the roaring fires of hatred.'

Cranston glanced at Athelstan out of the corner of his eye and smiled at the barbed reminder of what was true of Fulke and others in the Tower was also true of his relationship with the Lady Maude.

'Where to now, Brother?' he asked.

'To Master Parchmeiner's shop opposite Chancellor's Inn near St Paul's.'

'Why?' Cranston asked.

'Because, my dear Cranston, he was not present with the rest in the Tower and we must interrogate everyone.'

They rode up Candlewick Street and into Trinity, a prosperous part of the city Athelstan rarely frequented. The houses were spacious and grand; their lower storeys were built of solid timber, the projecting gables above were a framework of black beams and white plaster. The roofs were tiled, unlike the houses of many of Athelstan's parishioners who had to be content with reeds and straw. Many of the windows had pure glass and were protected by wood and iron. Servants from these houses regularly flushed out the sewers with the water they used to wash clothes so the streets did not reek as they did in Southwark. Before several of the imposing entrances stood armed retainers wearing the gaudy escutcheons of their patrons: bears, swans, wyverns, dragons, lions, and even stranger beasts. Stocky, well-fed merchants walked arm-in-arm with their plump wives, clad in garments of silk and satin, decorated with miniature pearls of exquisite delicacy. Two canons swaggered by from the cathedral, clad in thick woollen robes lined with miniver. A group of lawyers in gowns of red, violet and scarlet, trimmed with lambswool, sauntered arrogantly by, their cloaks pulled back to display decorated, low-slung girdles.

Pigs wandered here with bells slung round their necks to show they were the property of the Hospital of St Anthony and couldn't be slaughtered. Beadles armed with steel-pointed staffs dispersed fowl or curbed the yapping of fierce yellow-haired dogs, whilst bailiffs tried to move on a strange creature dressed like a magpie in black and white rags. The fellow loudly claimed he had in his battered, leather coffer some of the most marvellous relics of Christendom: 'One of Charlemagne's teeth!' he yelled. 'Two legs of the donkey that carried Mary! The skull of

Herod's servant and some of the stones Christ turned into bread!'

Athelstan stopped and restrained the beadles who were harassing the poor fellow.

'You say you have one of the stones Christ turned into a loaf of bread?' the friar queried, trying hard to hide his laughter.

'Yes, Brother.' The relic-seller's eyes brightened at the prospect of profit.

'But Christ didn't change stones into bread. The devil asked him to, but Christ refused.'

Cranston, also grinning, drew close to watch the charlatan's reaction. The relic-seller licked dry lips.

'Of course he did, Brother,' he replied in a half-whisper. 'I have it on good authority that when Satan left, Christ did it but then changed them back to show he would not be tempted to eat. It will only cost you a penny.'

Athelstan dipped into his purse and drew out a coin.

'Here.' He pressed it into the fellow's grimy paw. 'This is not for your stone. Keep it. It's your ingenuity I am rewarding.'

The man gaped, open-mouthed, and Athelstan and Cranston walked on, quietly laughing at the relic-seller's quick response. They passed the Littlegate of St Paul's where a lay brother was feeding a group of lepers with mouldy bread and rancid pork slices, as laid down by the city fathers who judged such food actually helped them. Cranston glared across in disgust.

'Do you really think it does?' he asked Athelstan abruptly.

'What, Sir John?'

'Such food, does it really help lepers?'

Athelstan gazed at the grey cowled figures with their staffs and bowls for alms. 'I don't know,' he murmured. 'Perhaps.'

The lepers made him think about the two who lurked in the cemetery of St Erconwald. A memory stirred but he could not place it, so pushed the matter to one side. They turned into an alleyway off Friday Street and Cranston began to bellow at passersby for the whereabouts of Parchmeiner's shop. They found it on the corner of Bread Street, a narrow, two-storeyed tenement with a shop below and living quarters above. There was a stall in front, but because of the inclement weather, this was now bare so they opened the door and went inside. Athelstan immediately closed his eyes and sniffed the sweet odour of fresh scrubbed parchment and vellum. The smell reminded him vividly of the well-stocked library and quiet chancery of his novice days at Blackfriars. The shop itself was a small, white-washed room with shelves along the walls stacked with sheets of parchment, ink horns, pumice stones, quills, and everything else one would need in a library or chancery.

Geoffrey himself was sitting at a small desk. He smiled and rose to greet them.

'Sir John!' he cried. 'Brother Athelstan, you are most welcome!' He went into the darkness beyond to bring back two stools. 'Please sit. Do you want some wine?'

Surprisingly, Cranston shook his head.

'I only drink when Sir John does,' Athelstan mockingly replied.

The parchment-seller grinned and sat down behind his desk.

'Well, what can I do for you? I doubt you want to buy parchment or vellum – though, Brother, I have the best the city can offer. I am a Guild member and everything I sell carries their hallmark.' Geoffrey's good-natured face creased into a smile. He shook his head. 'But I don't think you come to buy.' His face became grave. 'It's the business at the Tower, isn't it?'

'Just one thing,' Cranston answered, moving uncomfortably on the small stool. 'Does the name Bartholomew Burghgesh mean anything to you?'

'Yes and no,' Geoffrey replied. 'I never met him, but I heard Sir Fulke talk of him, and once Philippa repeated the name in her father's presence. Sir Ralph became very angry and stormed out. Of course, I asked Philippa why. She just shook her head and said he was an old enemy of her father's, and refused to be drawn any further.'

Athelstan watched the young man intently. Could this languid, rather effete fop be the Red Slayer? The terrible murderer who stalked his victims in the Tower?

'Geoffrey?' he asked.

'Yes, Brother.'

'You have known Philippa how long?'

'About two years.'

'And Sir Ralph liked you?'

The parchment-seller grinned. 'Yes, though God knows why. I can hardly ride a horse and the call of arms does not appeal to me.'

'You were with him the night he died?'

'Yes, as I have said, I was with him in the great hall. Sir Ralph was morose and became maudlin in his cups.'

'He was drunk?'

'Very.'

'You helped him across to his chamber?'

'Well, again, yes and no. Master Colebrooke assisted me. I took Sir Ralph to the top of the stairs into the

North Bastion tower but the passageway was so narrow Colebrooke helped him the rest of the way.'

'And you stayed with Mistress Philippa that night?'

The young man looked embarrassed and his eyes dropped. 'Yes. If Sir Ralph had known, he would have been most angry.'

'But,' Athelstan intervened, 'he favoured your court-ship of his only daughter?'

'Yes, I think he did.'

'Why?' Cranston barked. 'I mean, as you have said, you're no soldier.'

'No, I am not. I am not a lord or a knight but a merchant, Sir John, and a very good one. I am one of those who lends money so the King can hire his knights.' The parchment-seller gestured round his well-stocked shop. 'It may not look much but my profits are high. I am a wealthy man, Sir John.'

'One other matter.' Athelstan smiled. 'We have touched upon it before. You went to rouse Sir Ralph. What happened?'

'The guards opened the passageway door and locked it behind me as Sir Ralph had ordered. I went down and tried to rouse the constable. There was no answer, so I went back. I told the guards and took the key to Whitton's chamber. I was going to open it myself but changed my mind and went for Colebrooke.'

'Why did you do that?'

Geoffrey pulled a face. 'I knew something was wrong by the silence, not to mention the cold draught under the door of Whitton's chamber.'

Athelstan remembered the gap under Sir Ralph's door and nodded. Someone standing outside the room would have felt the powerful draught and know something was wrong.

'Why didn't you open the door yourself?' Cranston asked.

The young man smiled weakly. 'Sir John, I was frightened. Sir Ralph was not a popular man. Looking back, I suppose I was worried someone might be in the chamber.'

'And the night Mowbray died?'

'I was with Mistress Philippa, drunk as a lord. Ask the others.'

'And you never left?'

Geoffrey grimaced. 'Like the rest, I went to use the privy along the corridor. When the tocsin sounded, I lurched out with the others to see what was wrong. I didn't do much. I was drunk and I hate those parapet steps. I wandered around, looking busy, and found Fitzormonde and Colebrooke standing over Mowbray's body.' The young man paused and looked sharply at Athelstan. 'I know why you are here. There's been another death in the Tower, hasn't there?'

'Yes, yes,' Athelstan murmured and gave Parchmeiner the details of Horne's death.

Geoffrey leaned back in his chair and whistled softly. 'I suppose,' he said wearily, 'you wish to question me about that?'

'It would,' Cranston observed, 'be helpful to know where you were last night.'

Parchmeiner shrugged. 'I worked in my shop, then I got drunk as a bishop in a nearby tavern, the Golden Griffin. You could ask there.'

Athelstan smiled. What would be the use? the friar thought. Horne could have been killed at any hour.

209

He studied Parchmeiner's girlish face. 'You are London-born?' he queried, trying to look at the parchment lying on Geoffrey's desk.

'No, Brother, I am not. My family are Welsh, hence my colouring. They moved to Bristol. My father traded in parchments and vellum in a shop just beneath the cathedral there. When he died I moved to London.' Geoffrey picked up the piece of parchment. 'My sister, now married, still lives there; she has just written inviting herself to town for the Yuletide season. She, her husband,' his face grew mock solemn, 'and their large brood of children will bring some life to the Tower.' He turned to Sir John. 'My Lord Coroner, you have more questions?'

Sir John shook his head. 'No, sir, we have not.'

They rose, made their farewells, and stepped out into the cold, icy street.

'What do you think, Brother?'

'A young man who will go far in his trade, Sir John. He has his roots.' The friar grinned. 'Yes, Sir John, like you I wondered if he could be Burghgesh's son. But I am sure he is not.' Athelstan stopped and stared hard at the coroner. 'We are looking for a killer without ties, Sir John. Someone who is pretending to be something he or she is not. Someone who knows about the great act of betrayal so many years ago. The question is, who?'

'Well!' Cranston clapped his hands together. 'We'll not find it here, Brother, but perhaps in Woodforde...' The coroner wiped his nose on the back of his hand and stared up at the sky. 'I don't want to stay in London,' he murmured. 'The Lady Maude needs a rest from me. And you, Brother?'

'My parish,' Athelstan drily replied, 'will, I think, survive the continued absence of their pastor a little longer.'

They separated at the corner of Friday and Fish Streets, agreeing to meet within two hours at a tavern outside Aldgate on the Mile End Road. Sir John stamped off, leading his horse, whilst Athelstan continued down Trinity into Walbrook, along Ropery to London Bridge. Thankfully, he found St Erconwald's fairly deserted except for Watkin, to whom he gave strict instructions about the custody of the church, and Ranulf the rat-catcher who had come to remind him of his promise that if a Guild of Rat-Catchers were founded, St Erconwald's could be their chantry church.

'I promise you, Ranulf, I will think on the matter,' Athelstan replied, trying to hide his amusement at the thought of St Erconwald's full of tarry-hooded rat-catchers, all looking like Ranulf. The fellow's yellow, wizened face broke into a sharp-toothed smile. He skipped down the steps as happily as any boy.

'Brother,' Watkin mournfully moaned.

'What is it?'

'Well—' The dung-collector turned on the top step of the church and pointed towards the frozen cemetery. 'We still haven't set a watch.'

'Why should we, Watkin? The grave robbers have moved on.'

The dung-collector shook his head. 'I don't think so, Brother, and I am afeared worse might happen.'

Athelstan forced a smile. 'Nonsense. Now look, Watkin, I will be back late tomorrow evening. Take a message to Father Luke at St Olave's. Ask him to be so kind as to come here and say Mass tomorrow morning. You will know where everything is? And tell the widow Benedicta to help you. You'll do that?'

Watkin nodded and stumped off, muttering under his breath about priests who didn't listen to tales of the dark shapes which did dreadful things in city churchyards. Athelstan watched him go and sighed. How could he deal with the cemetery when there was no evidence of any danger threatening? He checked the door of the church was locked and stood engrossed in his own thoughts about Cranston. The Lord Coroner was proving to be as difficult a problem as the dreadful deaths they were investigating. What was wrong with the Lady Maude? Athelstan wondered. Why didn't Cranston ask her outright?

Athelstan smiled as he went across to his own house. Strange, he concluded. Cranston, who was frightened of nothing on two legs, seemed terrified of his little lady wife. Athelstan checked that the windows and doors of the priest's house were locked, slung his saddle bags over a protesting Philomel, and both horse and rider wearily made their way along the icy track. He stopped at an ale-house to leave further messages with Tab the tinker for Benedicta and Watkin; they were to lock the church after morning Mass and, if the widow felt so inclined, she should take Bonaventura back to her own house. The friar then made his way back on to the main highway, past the Priory of St Mary Overy and across London Bridge. He stopped midway to say a prayer in the Chapel of St Thomas for the safety of their journey and then continued on his way.

Cranston was waiting for him at the small tavern just outside Aldgate in the Portsoken overlooking the stinking city ditch. The coroner seemed in good spirits. Athelstan concluded it was due to the large empty wine bowl in front of Sir John but Cranston, winking and burping, staunchly kept his hidden resolve not to vex Athelstan further with his own worries and anxieties. The friar joined Sir John in one last cup of mulled wine, heated with a red-hot poker and spiced with cinnamon, before they reclaimed their horses from the stable and made their way along the darkening highway towards Mile End. Cranston remained full of good cheer, aided and abetted by an apparently miraculous wineskin which never seemed to empty. Athelstan, tired and saddle sore, prayed and cursed whilst Cranston, farting and swaying in the saddle, chattered about this or that. Finally Athelstan reined in Philomel and grasped the coroner by the wrists.

'Sir John,' he asked wearily, 'this business at the Tower – we are making no headway. How long can we spend on the matter?'

'Until we finish.' Cranston's eyes gleamed back. 'By the sod, Brother! Orders are orders, and I don't give a rat's fart about mumbling monks, icy roads or cold journeys. Now, have I told you of the Lady Maude's preparations for Christmas?'

Athelstan groaned, shook his head and kicked Philomel forward as Cranston regaled him with Lady Maude's intended banquet of boar's head, cygnet, venison, quince tarts and junkets of apple-flavoured cream. The coroner chattered like a magpie as the weak daylight died and dusk fell like a grey powder, shrouding the wide waste stretches of snow. The distant forest became obscured by a misty darkness which closed in round them, broken by the odd pinprick of light as they passed some hamlet or village. No wind blew but it was deathly still and bitterly cold.

'I am sure,' Athelstan mumbled to himself, 'the very birds will freeze on the trees and even the hares on the hill will remain underground.'

Cranston, the wineskin now surprisingly empty, only replied with a short stream of belches. They passed a crossroads where a cadaver hung, black and frozen, its head twisted to one side, face unrecognisable after the crows had feasted there. Cranston stopped and pointed down a track to a light blinking in the distance.

'We'll stop there for the night, Brother. A good, snug tavern, The Gallow's Friend.' He leaned over and smiled at Athelstan. 'Despite its name, you'll like it.'

Athelstan did. It was a clean, well-swept establishment with secure stables, a fresh herb-smelling tap room, and a large roaring fire with the logs piled high – though he baulked at the huge four-poster bed he'd have to share with Sir John.

'No, no, My Lord Coroner,' Athelstan murmured. 'I insist you sleep alone.'

'Why, monk?'

'Because, coroner, if you rolled over in your sleep, you'd crush me to death!'

Laughing and joking, they left their bags there and made their way down to the tap room where the landlord's wife served them huge fish pies, the crust, golden and crisp, hiding a savoury sauce which dulled the flavour of the rancid fish. Athelstan tactfully asked the landlord for a pallet bed to be placed in their chamber and sat down to eat almost as heartily as Cranston. Of course, the coroner drank as if there was no tomorrow and when he had had his fill, leaned back against the pillar of the huge fireplace, belched, and pronounced himself satisfied. Athelstan stared into the flames, half listening to a wind which had suddenly sprung up, now whining and clattering against the tightly secured shutters.

'Brother?'

'Yes, Sir John?'

'This business at the Tower, could it be black magic?'

'What do you mean?'

'Well, the head that was sent to me.'

Athelstan stretched his hand out to the flames. 'No, no, Sir John. As I have said, we are not dealing with a demon but something worse, a soul steeped in mortal sin. But whose?' He looked up at Sir John, who had his fiery red nose deep in a wine cup again. 'What's puzzling,' Athelstan continued, 'is why now? Why has the murderer chosen this moment? And how can they know about the dreadful events surrounding Burghgesh's death?'

'What do you mean?' Cranston slurred.

'Well,' Athelstan replied, 'we should be looking for a man or woman with no background, someone who has suddenly appeared on the scene, but everyone we have talked to has their own little niche.'

Cranston burped. 'I don't know,' he slurred. 'It could still be black magic because I'm damned if I can find a way through the tangle. Now, as I have said to Lady Maude…' The coroner suddenly stopped and stared into his wine cup, and the good humour drained from his face.

'Come, Sir John,' Athelstan said quietly. 'It's time we slept.'

Surprisingly, Cranston agreed, drained the cup and slammed it down on the table. He stood up, swaying and smiled benevolently down at his companion.

'But do you believe, Brother?'

'What, Sir John?'

'In the black arts? I mean, the business in your cemetery?'

Athelstan grinned. 'To be perfectly honest, Sir John, I am more frightened of the human heart than any mischievous demon. Now, come. Let's rest.'

Athelstan was pleased he had judged the moment right because, by the time they reached the top of the rickety wooden staircase, Cranston was half-asleep and beginning to mumble piteously about how he missed Lady Maude. Athelstan led him down the cold, darkened passageway and into the small chamber. He gently lowered Cranston on to the bed, pulled off the coroner's boots and made his companion as comfortable as possible. The coroner turned, belched, and quietly began to snore. Athelstan grinned and covered the huge frame with a coverlet. Sleeping, Cranston reminded the friar more than ever of the huge bear in the bailey of the Tower. Athelstan went over and knelt beneath the small, horn-glazed window, crossed himself and gently mouthed the words of David's psalm.

'Out of the depths have I called to thee, O Lord. Lord, hear my voice.'

By the time he had reached the fourth verse, Athelstan was already distracted. Was Sir John right? he wondered. Did the great demon, the Red Slayer, haunt both his cemetery and the Tower of London? He closed his eyes, finished the psalm and made his way to the pallet bed. For a while Athelstan lay listening to Cranston's heavy snoring and fell asleep almost at the very instant when, back in the darkened cemetery outside St Erconwald's, shadows flitted across the graveyard to crouch over a freshly dug grave.

Chapter 11

In his dream, Athelstan stood on a darkened ship. The bowsprit, mast and sails were covered in black crepe. Above him on the poop, a skeleton, its face a white, leering mask, held the wheel and grinned wickedly down at him. The sea was smooth and clear as thick, dark glass. The sky overhead was empty of stars and hung like a purple-blue cloth around the ship as it drifted towards the horizon where a fiery red glow lit the gateway to Hell. On one end of the mast a figure jerked spasmodically. Athelstan glimpsed the blackened, twisted face of Pike the ditcher hanging by the neck. The friar turned as someone tapped him on the shoulder. His brother Francis stood there: his face was blueish-white under a shock of black hair. A thin red snake of blood trickled out of the corner of his mouth; his chest was an open, bubbling mass of blood where he had received his death wound.

'You ran away from your monastery, Brother?' His voice sounded hollow.

Athelstan stretched out his hand. 'I am sorry, Francis,' he murmured. Athelstan stared around. Was Cranston here? He was sure he could hear the coroner's voice.

Athelstan walked to the entrance of the hold and gazed down. A naked woman squatted there, her face hidden behind a black veil; from her mouth came a foul toad and round her neck curled an amber snake, its red-slit eyes flashing like diamonds. A fat-bellied rat crouched beside her. Athelstan walked down the steps. Behind the woman, kneeling stern and impassive, was a knight in full armour, gauntleted hands resting on the hilt of his great two-handled sword. The hold stank of death and Athelstan could feel someone pressing close behind him. He squirmed violently as a hand seized his shoulder.

'Athelstan! Athelstan! Brother, for God's sake!'

The friar opened his eyes. Cranston, his fat face wrinkled with concern, stared down at him.

'Brother, what is the matter?'

Athelstan stared back. 'Good Sir John, I was dreaming.' He raised a clammy hand and rubbed his face. 'I was dreaming,' he repeated.

'And not a pleasant one!'

'No, Sir John. Some succubus of the night with the power of a thousand scorpions seized my mind.'

Cranston gazed quizzically back and Athelstan grinned.

'I am only joking. I think my nightmare was due more to the table than the grave. We dined too well last night.'

'Yesterday is gone and today is today,' Cranston pompously replied. 'Come on, Brother, it's daybreak.'

Athelstan rose quickly, said a hasty prayer and washed himself in the freezing water from a cracked pewter jug. They gathered their possessions and moved down to the cold, deserted taproom. The fire was not lit and the room didn't seem as cheerful and welcoming as it had the night before; they broke their fast quickly on warm oat cakes and mulled wine, saddled their horses and rode back along the track to the highway.

The day looked as if it would be a fine one. A weak sun was about to rise, turning the darkness to a dusty grey:

their horses plodded along the frozen track, both riders taking special care against the potholes, some as deep as a man, which could bring down and even kill both the unwary rider and his horse. The countryside was empty and silent. Athelstan shivered as he remembered his nightmare and the eerie stillness of that terrible dream. The hedgerows on either side were still thickly covered with snow and, beyond them, the fields lay iron hard under sheets of ice. A circle of hungry crows soared noisily above a clump of oak trees, branches black against the lightening sky.

'I wish I was back in London,' Cranston moaned. 'I hate the bloody countryside. I hate the silence!'

Athelstan caught a blur of colour in a ditch on the side of the track and pulled his horse over to look closer. The corpse which lay there was frozen hard, that of an old man covered from head to knee in a loose, threadbare gown. Athelstan closed his eyes and breathed a prayer as he glimpsed the blue-black holes where the hungry ravens had pecked at the scrawny, whitening flesh.

'God rest him!' Cranston murmured. 'Brother, there is nothing we can do.'

They moved on through a silent, sleeping village, only a few plumes of black smoke giving any sign of life. After an hour's ride they approached the village of Leighton. At the crossroads they glimpsed a group of villagers huddled round the blackened scaffold. Thankfully, the iron gibbet which swung from its hook was empty. The villagers were gathered round a corpse whilst beside it two burly labourers hacked the iron ground at the foot of the scaffold. Then hoes and mattocks cleared a shallow hole while their breath hung heavy in the frost air. Athelstan looked at Cranston. The coroner shrugged though his hand went beneath his cloak to ensure his dagger was loose in its sheath. The villagers turned at the riders' approach. An old woman, her face yellow and lined with age, scrawny body covered in the battered hide of a cow, shuffled towards them.

'Morrow! Morrow!' she cried. 'Travellers on a road like this?' Her milky eyes grinned slyly up at Athelstan. 'Good morning, Father. 'Tis rare to see a priest up so early.'

'Mother!' Cranston bellowed back, loosening the muffler round his mouth. 'It's good to see anyone in such Godforsaken weather. What are you doing?'

'Burying Eadwig.'

'Here?' Athelstan asked. 'You have no church, no cemetery?'

The old hag lifted her skinny hand. 'Come and see! Come and see!'

Reluctantly they pushed their horses nearer. Cranston's mount became skittish and even Philomel showed a lively interest in the group round the scaffold. The villagers parted as the coroner and his companion approached. Athelstan glimpsed red, dirty faces, greasy, matted hair, and the occasional glare of hatred at their well-fed horses and warm, woollen cloaks. Cranston took one look at Eadwig's body, closed his eyes and drew away. The peasant had been hanged. His face was black, tongue half-bitten off but still clenched tightly between yellow teeth, whilst one eye had popped from its socket and lay grotesquely against the bruised cheek.

'Good God!' Athelstan breathed. 'What happened?'

'He killed himself,' the old hag cackled. 'And you know the law, Father?'

'Oh, yes, Mother, I know the law.' He looked at the small, wooden stake leaning against the scaffold. 'Sir John, I suggest we ride on.'

The coroner needed no second bidding. They turned their horses, ignoring the soft cackles of laughter behind them. Athelstan closed his eyes, praying from whatever psalm he could remember to fend off the awful terrors which clung to the world of men. Behind him he heard the faint sounds of a wooden mallet driving the stake through the suicide's heart.

'Good God!' Cranston murmured. 'You priests, Athelstan, should change all that. Only the Good Lord knows why the poor bastard killed himself, but must a suicide be buried near a gibbet at the crossroads with a stake driven through his heart?'

'The bishops have tried to stop it,' Athelstan replied. 'But Christ's teaching, Sir John, in certain parts and over certain hearts, lies as thin and as loose as a spider's web.'

They rode through Leighton, following the track which skirted the dark mass of Epping Forest and into Woodforde just as the church bell tolled for Nones. The village was an unprepossessing one: a few villagers, hooded and cloaked against the cold, scurried about shooing scrawny chickens away from the horses. Some boys were bringing battered wooden buckets up from the well and the occasional housewife emptied the slops from the night jars out into the middle of the street. Even the alehouse was still shuttered and locked.

'Like a village of the dead,' Athelstan murmured.

'Aye, it might as well be, Brother,' Cranston replied through his muffler. 'The cold will stop all work in the fields.'

A young urchin, his face pinched white by the cold, suddenly appeared and walked solemnly alongside them, a dirty canvas bag clutched in one bony hand. Athelstan reined in Philomel.

'What's the matter, boy?'

The urchin just stared, round-eyed, at Philomel's tail.

'Come on, lad, what do you want?'

'Mother told me to follow. Told me to wait for the horse to lift its tail.'

Cranston chuckled. 'He is waiting for our horses to shit!' he exclaimed. 'It's good manure and, if dried, burns well and cheerily.'

Athelstan grinned, pulled back his hood, dug into his purse and threw the boy a penny. 'You can have everything our horses will drop, boy,' he announced solemnly. 'And there's a penny for your trouble. You know the Burghgesh family? They have a manor house here.'

'Oh, all gone,' the lad replied, his eyes still fixed on Philomel's tail. 'The house lies beyond the village near Buxfield but it is deserted and closed up. Father Peter will tell you that.' He pointed to where the tiled-roofed church with its grey, ragstone tower peeped above the treetops.

'Then,' Athelstan said, kicking Philomel into a trot, 'that's where we'll stop!'

They rode through the wicket gate of the church, following the pathway which snaked between the trees and overgrown graves to the Norman church which stood on the brow of a small hillock. Beside it was a modest, two-storeyed house, its roof made of yellowing thatch, the windows nothing more than wooden shutters. Athelstan looked back. The young boy still stood behind him, one hand gripping the bag, the other balled into a tight fist, guarding Athelstan's penny as if it was the key to heaven itself.

'Father Peter's in?'

'He will be there,' the boy replied. 'And, for another penny, I'll look after your horses.'

Athelstan nodded and another coin was tossed in the air.

'That young man will advance far,' Cranston murmured as they dismounted and knocked on the door. They heard bolts being pulled back, the door swung open and a clean-shaven, cheery-faced Father Peter peered out.

'Travellers in this weather?' His voice was burred by a thick country accent but, despite the snow-white hair and slight stoop of the shoulders, Father Peter was an active, cheerful man. He hardly waited for their introductions but ushered them into the warm, sweet-smelling room, chattering and asking questions like a magpie. He took their cloaks and told them to sit on a bench which he pushed towards the heat of the fire.

'A coroner and a Dominican come to visit me,' he announced in mock wonderment, and squatted down beside them on a stool. Father Peter took three earthenware bowls from a small cupboard near the inglenook and served them generous portions of soup from a black bowl which hung perilously from an iron hook above the flames. 'Bits of fish, some herbs, what's left of my vegetables.' The priest screwed up his eyes. 'Ah, yes, and some onions.'

Both Athelstan and Cranston gripped the warm bowls and sipped at the rich stew which scalded their mouths and lips but put some warmth into their frozen bellies. Father Peter watched, even as he sipped from his own bowl. Athelstan smiled back and put his bowl down.

'At the moment it's too hot to eat, Father,' he murmured apologetically. 'Even to hold.'

Cranston, however, had no such difficulty. He slurped as noisily as a ravenous dog, mopping up what was left with hard crusts of bread which Father Peter shoved before him on a wooden platter. At last Cranston burped, smacked his lips and handed the bowl back.

'The best meal in many a day, Father. We thank you for your hospitality.' The coroner stretched his great hands out towards the flames. 'We will not keep you long. You know the Burghgesh family?'

Father Peter's eyes narrowed. 'Aye,' he replied. 'I know of them.'

Athelstan began to sip carefully at his now cooling bowl of soup.

'Will you tell us, Father?'

The priest shrugged. 'What is there to say? Bartholomew Burghgesh and his wife lived in a manor house near Buxfield. Bartholomew was always a restless man, born to the sword and the horse rather than the plough and the bailiff's accounts. He went to London and served in the retinues of the great ones. In the old King's time, he was in the garrison of the Tower, then he went abroad with others to fight in Outremer.'

'And his wife?'

Father Peter made a moue. 'She was a quiet, sickly woman. They had one boy... what was his name? Ah, yes, Mark.' Father Peter sighed. 'Oh, they were well looked after. A steward administered the manor, and Bartholomew always sent gold. Then about – oh, some fourteen or fifteen years ago – news came of Bartholomew's death. He had been killed on board a ship taken by the Moors in the Middle Seas. By that time Mark was a young man. He

224

took his father's death with little show of regret, but the mother became ill and died within a year of her husband.'

'And Mark Burghgesh?'

'He was like his father, his head full of stories about Roland and Oliver and performing marvellous feats of arms. For a while he was Lord of the Manor. After the old King's victories in France, he raised money from the bankers, bought a destrier, and armour, and formed a small retinue of archers of like-minded men from the village.' The priest paused and stared into the flames. 'I remember the morning they left,' he continued dreamily. 'A beautiful summer's day. Sir Mark on his black warhorse, his dark red hair oiled and combed; before him went his squire carrying a banner with the Burghgesh arms, and marching behind were six archers with steel caps, quilted jerkins, long bows and quivers full of goose-quilled arrows. A brave sight.' The priest rocked himself gently. 'None of them came back,' he murmured. 'They all died in the blood and muck.'

Athelstan caught his breath. So like his own story. He and Francis had joined such a retinue. Athelstan had returned but his brother's body still lay mouldering in some forgotten field in France.

'None of them came back?' Cranston repeated, fighting hard to control the excitement in his voice. 'So Mark Burghgesh could still be alive?'

The priest stared at him and shook his head. 'Oh, no, Sir John. I spoke wrongly. No one came back alive. Come, I'll show you where Mark is.'

They rose. Father Peter handed them their cloaks, taking his own from a wooden peg, and they followed him out into the cold. The young boy still stood like a soldier, holding the reins of the horses, his eyes looking eagerly at the piles of steaming dung obligingly dropped by both Philomel and Cranston's mount. Father Peter stopped.

'Boy, take the horses round to the stable. You'll find some oats there. Then go in and take some soup. Don't worry, the horses won't wander off.'

The urchin stared at Athelstan.

'Go on, lad,' the friar ordered. 'You'll freeze to death standing there. And, I promise, the horse dung's yours.'

They reached the church door. Father Peter unlocked it and they entered the darkened nave. It was cold, the air icy. Athelstan gazed at the square, squat pillars decorated with greenery like his own in Southwark, though not as beautiful. He hasn't got a painter, Athelstan thought. Father Peter caught his eye and Athelstan felt guilty at his petty pride.

'A fine church, Father,' he murmured.

Father Peter grinned. 'We try, Brother. But I would give a king's ransom for a good painter and craftsman.'

They went beneath the simple chancel screen, across the sanctuary into a small lady chapel which lay in the far corner of the church. A large wooden statue of the Virgin and Child stood on a stone plinth whilst around the walls were raised tombs, simple and square, lacking any effigy or ornamentation. Father Peter went across and gently tapped one.

'Sir Mark Burghgesh lies here,' he announced quietly. 'His body was sent back for burial.'

Cranston stared in disappointment at the grey ragstone tomb. 'Are you sure, Father Peter?'

'Yes,' the priest said. 'The embalmers did their best to dress the corpse: before the coffin was lowered, I looked once more at the face. Sir Mark had received a terrible death wound on the side of his head, caused by a battle axe or mace, but I am certain it was he.'

Athelstan hid his disappointment and gazed despondently at Cranston. Their cold journey through the bitter Essex landscape had been fruitless.

'Why do you want to know all this?' Father Peter asked as he led them out of the church.

'There's been a murder, Father, in London,' Cranston answered, chewing his lip. 'We hoped our journey here would yield fresh evidence. Have you noticed anything untoward in the village?'

'Such as?'

'Anything,' Athelstan pleaded. 'Any news or gossip about the Burghgesh family?'

The priest shook his head. Athelstan and Cranston looked at each other despondently as they left the church and re-entered the priest's house where the boy was lapping a second bowl of soup as hungrily as a starving dog. At their approach he scurried into a corner. Father Peter waved them back to their seats and went across and poured them generous stoups of ale from the jar just outside the small buttery door.

'No,' he repeated, sitting down on the stool and cradling the blackjack of ale in his hands, 'Woodforde is a quiet place. Even quieter now the Burghgeshes have left.'

'What happened to their manor house?'

'The King's Commissioners sealed it off. No one has been there since.' The priest coughed. 'I should know. The Sheriff of Essex pays me a small stipend to ensure the seals on the doors and windows are not broken.' He looked at Cranston. 'And they are still sealed. After all, there's nothing there. All the moveables have been removed, the roof has fallen in, the surrounding meadows and ploughlands been sold off.'

'There was no other heir?'

'None that I know of.' Father Peter suddenly took the tankard away from his lips. 'In heaven's name!' he exclaimed. 'There was something. Yes,' he murmured excitedly, 'about three or four years ago, something very strange. It was like a dream. Now, when was it? Yes, it was at the beginning of Advent. I forget the actual year. I had said morning Mass, gone across to the house to break my fast then went back to clear the altar.' Father Peter stared into the flames. 'I went up the nave and was surprised to see a man, cowled and hooded, kneeling at the entrance to the Lady Chapel.'

'Where Mark Burghgesh is buried?'

'Yes, yes. Now I trod softly, and at first the man didn't hear me. But when he did, he rose very quickly, pulled his cowl close about his head, and brushing by me, left the church, ignoring my salutation. All I glimpsed were a few strands of grey hair and a white, neatly barbered beard.' Father Peter picked up his tankard and sipped from it. 'Now, it had been years since I had seen Bartholomew Burghgesh and I considered him long dead, yet I am sure that man I glimpsed that cold December morning was Sir Bartholomew himself. He had his walk, the gait and stance of a professional soldier.'

Athelstan leaned forward excitedly. Was Sir Bartholomew alive? he wondered. Was he the bloody-handed slayer stalking his victims? 'Continue, Father,' he whispered.

'Well, I didn't mention it to anyone. The villagers would think I had been drinking or wandering in my wits.'

He grinned at Athelstan. 'You can appreciate, Brother, how the sheep like to gossip about their shepherd.'

Athelstan smiled back and stole a sideways glance at Cranston who was sitting, open-mouthed, at Father Peter's revelation.

'A year later,' the priest continued, 'on the Feast of All Hallows, I was in the village ale-house. Autumn was here, the countryside was fading under the colder, harsher weather. We were talking about death and exchanging gruesome ghost stories. The landlord, God rest him – the fellow has since died – suddenly spoke up, declaring that he had seen the ghost of Sir Bartholomew Burghgesh. Of course, the others laughed at him but he insisted and said that at about the same time I thought I'd seen Sir Bartholomew, a stranger had arrived in the village late at night and stopped at the ale-house for food and drink. The man had been cloaked and hooded and hardly ever spoke except to buy his meal.' Father Peter closed his eyes. 'The landlord said the fellow made it obvious he wanted to be left to himself. After all, Woodforde's on the highway into the city. We have many people who like to keep their business to themselves. Anyway, the stranger was about to leave when a slattern dropped a tankard. The man whirled round and for a few seconds the landlord saw his face. He swore it was Bartholomew Burghgesh.'

Father Peter sighed. 'Of course, I kept quiet about what I had seen, but I was intrigued. I journeyed out to the old manor house near Buxfield. If it was Burghgesh, I thought, surely he would have returned to his former home? Yet I discovered that nothing had been disturbed.' He shrugged and spread his hands. 'That's all I can tell you. Only God knows if the man I and the landlord glimpsed was Sir Bartholomew. I heard no other rumours about his sudden return, either from abroad or beyond the grave, so I let the matter rest.'

'Father,' Athelstan persisted, 'please, when was this? Three or four years ago?'

The priest stared into the fire.

'Yes, three years ago,' he replied. 'But,' he smiled, 'I can tell you no more.'

Cranston leaned forward and clasped Father Peter by the wrist.

'Father, your hospitality is only matched by the value of what you have told us.' The coroner glanced at Athelstan and smiled. 'Come, Brother, it's not yet noon. If we travel hard and fast, we can be back in the city before nightfall.' He looked across at Father Peter. 'I thank you for your hospitality, Father.' He turned and tossed a penny at the lad still squatting in the corner. 'You, boy, will either make a good squire or a merchant.'

They rose, gathered their cloaks, and within the hour were clear of Woodforde. They journeyed through Leighton, past the grisly scaffold with the freshly dug makeshift grave still visible at its foot, and back on to the Mile End Road. Cranston, who had stopped at a local tavern to refill his miraculous wineskin, was full of chatter and speculation.

'It's possible, Brother,' he boomed for the umpteenth time, his bewhiskered lips red from the juice of the grape, 'quite possible that Sir Bartholomew is still alive and hiding in or near the Tower to carry out his silent war of revenge.'

'Sir John,' Athelstan replied, 'I would agree, but where would Burghgesh hide? Is he a member of the garrison? A kitchen scullion? Some tradesman who has the right of access?'

Cranston made a rude noise with his lips.

'Or,' Athelstan continued, 'does Sir Bartholomew squat like some dark spider in the city whilst others carry out his dreadful commands?'

Cranston reined in his horse.

'Strange, mind you,' he murmured.

'What?'

'Well, three years ago Whitton was disturbed, agitated, as if he had seen a ghost. At the same time, Brother, a cowled and hooded figure was seen in the tavern near the Tower, and the same person, probably Burghgesh, also seen in Woodforde.'

'You're saying Whitton's agitation was caused by Burghgesh's reappearance?'

'Of course.'

'But, if that is so, what has happened to Burghgesh since?'

He and Cranston were still arguing rival theories when they reached Aldgate long after dark and made their way through a small postern door in the city gate. Cranston, full of wine and his own theories, was now certain they had grasped the truth. Athelstan did not demur. At least, he concluded, their journey to Woodforde had diverted the coroner's mind from his constant agonising over the Lady Maude's mysterious conduct.

–

As Athelstan and Cranston made their way back into the city, the hospitaller, Fitzormonde, was standing in the bailey of the Tower, staring at the huge bear now stuffing its cruel mouth with scraps from the Tower kitchen. Like Athelstan, Fitzormonde was fascinated by the beast and secretly admired the madcap Red Hand who was the only man who dared approach the animal. Fitzormonde, despite his travels, had never seen such a huge beast. Most bears were small and black, sometimes no higher than a man, but this great, shaggy-furred animal reminded him of stories he had heard from knights who had served with the Teutonic Orders in the wild black forests of the north. How they had seen deer twice the size of anything in England and bears such as this one, which would crush a horse in its huge, muscular arms.

The bear suddenly stopped eating and glared at the knight, its small, piggy eyes red with hatred. It opened its mouth, growling deep in its throat in a display of wickedly sharp teeth. The huge beast strained at the great iron chain clasped to the collar round its neck. Fitzormonde stepped away and the bear went back to its meal, shuffling its food into a dirty untidy pile as if it suspected Fitzormonde would like to take it away. The knight stamped his feet to keep warm. Tomorrow, he thought, he would leave the Tower. He had already said as much to Mistress Philippa when he had met her and her rather effeminate betrothed.

Fitzormonde gazed up at the cruel gargoyle faces on the Chapel of St Peter ad Vincula. Yes, he thought, tomorrow, he would pay the chaplain to sing one last Mass for his fallen comrades then go back into the city and request from his superiors some mission or task well away from this benighted fortress.

He started as he heard a whirring noise in the air. He looked up. A raven? No, what was it? The hospitaller suddenly stepped back in panic as the bear sprang into life, towering above him, its great paws clawing the air. The bear roared at him with fury, its black muzzle and huge jaws covered in a thick white froth. Fitzormonde's hand went to his dagger as the bear danced like a demon, pulling at the great chain clasped in the wall. What was wrong with the animal? What had happened?

Fitzormonde made to run but, even as he turned, heard the great iron chain spring loose and saw the bear rush towards him. He tugged at his knife but had it only half-drawn when the huge taloned paw of the bear smashed his head as if it was a rotten apple. Roaring with fury, the bear dug his claws into the dying knight's unprotected back and dragged him across the cobbles, bellows of rage proclaiming its triumph.

Chapter 12

Athelstan was furious. He felt the anger burn his innards until his heart pounded and the blood throbbed in his head. For a moment, the friar didn't give a damn about anything – the teaching of his Order to be gentle or the precepts of the gospels about kindness. All that mattered was the anger raging within him as he stood in the cemetery outside St Erconwald's church. The snow had now turned into an icy, grey slush which dripped off graves, trees, bushes and the low cemetery wall as the thaw continued under clear skies and a weak wintry sun. Athelstan cursed, using every filthy oath he had learnt from Cranston. He beat the staff he held against the loose brick, furious enough to grind the rock into sand.

Oh, he had found everything in order on his return: Bonaventura, asleep and well, curled up in the church like some fat bishop as Cecily cleaned and swept the nave. Benedicta and Watkin had set up the crib in one of the aisles, using figures carved by Huddle. The painter had also finished a vivid picture of Christ in the manger, just above the baptismal font inside the church door. Even Ursula's pig had resisted its usual forays into his garden, and Pike the ditcher had cleared the gravel-strewn path in front of the church.

Athelstan had pronounced himself satisfied and chattered about parochial matters as he stabled, watered and fed Philomel. But even then, he had sensed the anxiety in the faces of those who had come to welcome him: Benedicta, Pike, Watkin, Cecily, and Tab the tinker. They had followed him around the church, answering his questions whilst exchanging secretive, anxious glances.

At first Athelstan dismissed their concern as some petty matter. Had Cecily been flirting again, or one of Pike the ditcher's sons peed in the church? Perhaps Ranulf borrowed Bonaventure or Watkin's children had been drinking from the holy water stoup? The members of his parish council had fussed round him like noisy chickens. At last, just before he locked the church, Athelstan tired of their secrecy.

'Come on!' he demanded, confronting them. 'What has happened?'

They shuffled their feet and looked away. Benedicta suddenly became concerned about an apparent spot on her gown.

'It's the cemetery, Father!' Watkin blurted out. 'Tosspot's grave has been disturbed.'

'When?'

'The night you left.'

Athelstan had been so angry he'd used language which made even Pike the ditcher's face blanch.

'Perhaps Sir John will do something now,' Benedicta tactfully intervened. 'Or maybe if we make an appeal to the Alderman of the Ward?'

'Aye!' Athelstan rasped. 'And perhaps pigs will fly and we'll find pork in the trees tomorrow morning. The people who do this terrible thing are bastards! They are wicked and fear neither God nor man. Even the pagans honour the corpse of a dead man. Not even a dog would do this!'

His parishioners had withdrawn, more frightened of their gentle parish priest's terrible rage than the dreadful news they had brought. Athelstan had stormed off to his house and drunk a cup of wine with a speed Cranston would have admired. He slept fitfully that night, not even thinking of climbing the tower steps to study the stars. He'd tossed and turned on his pallet bed, fuming with rage at the sinful desecration of his cemetery. The next morning he rose early, opened the church, perfunctorily fed Bonaventura, skipped through the morning office and tried hard to concentrate whilst he celebrated Mass. Bonaventura, like the cunning cat he was, seemed to sense his patron's change of mood and quietly stole away. At the end of the Mass, before he gave the final benediction, Athelstan spoke in sharp, terse tones.

'Our cemetery has been violated once again,' he declared. 'I, Athelstan, priest of this parish, say this, as God is my witness – no further burials will take place until the ground has been re-consecrated and this problem resolved!' He glared round at his small congregation. 'I will go to the highest in the land, be it the young King himself or the Archbishop of Canterbury. Guards will be set and, God forgive me, I shall see these villains hang!'

His parishioners had quietly left and Athelstan, now calming, felt a twinge of guilt as he glared down at Tosspot's ravaged grave.

'Your fiery temper, priest,' he muttered to himself, 'is no more curbed than it was twenty years ago. And your tongue is as sharp as ever.'

He breathed deeply. Yes, he had been too hard, he reflected, far too brusque with Benedicta and the others, but especially with the widow. She had stayed for a few seconds after Mass, not to gossip but simply to say that the chief bailiff of the ward, Master Bladdersniff, had accosted her on her way to church. He wished to see Athelstan on an urgent matter.

'Oh, yes,' Athelstan muttered. 'Master Bladdersniff, as usual, closing the stable door after the horse has bolted!' Athelstan felt a fresh surge of rage. If St Erconwald's had been one of the wealthy city churches, guards would have been set immediately and this would never have happened. Even Cranston, that fat-arsed coroner, hadn't helped, wrapped up like some mewling maid in his own concerns. Athelstan stared once more round the cemetery, it was so cold, so bleak. He remembered Father Peter and envied the Woodforde priest's quiet domesticity. 'Bloody Cranston!' Athelstan muttered. 'Bloody murder! Bloody Tower! The bloody hearts of men and their evil doings!' He kicked the icy mud. 'I am a priest,' he hissed to himself. 'Not some sheriff's man.'

'Father? Father Athelstan?'

The friar turned and glared at the young pursuivant who stood, cloaked and hooded, behind him. 'Yes, man, what is it?'

'I have been sent from the Tower by Sir John Cranston. He wants to see you in the Holy Lamb tavern off Cheapside.'

'Tell My Lord Coroner,' Athelstan retorted, 'that I'll be there when I'm there, and he'd better be sober!'

The young man looked surprised and hurt. Athelstan grimaced and spread his hands.

'Lord, man, I'm sorry. Look, tell Sir John I'll be there when I can.'

He took a step closer and saw the fellow's white, pinched face and dripping nose. 'You are freezing,' the friar muttered. 'Go across to my house, there's a jug of wine on the table. Fill a goblet. You'll find one on a shelf above the fire hearth. Drink some mulled wine, and get some warmth in your belly before you return.'

The pursuivant turned and scurried off like a whippet.

'Oh, by the way,' Athelstan yelled after him, 'I did mean what I said. Sir John is not to drink too much!'

Athelstan walked slowly back to his church, up the steps and into the porch.

'Father?'

Athelstan jumped as Master Luke Bladdersniff, chief bailiff of the ward, stepped out of the darkness, his lean sallow face and wispy blond hair almost hidden under a tattered beaver hat.

'Good morrow, Master Bailiff.'

Athelstan studied the ward man: his close-set eyes were dark-rimmed and looked even more like the piss-holes in the snow, as Cranston so aptly described them. Athelstan had always been fascinated by the man's nose. Broken and slightly twisted, it gave Bladdersniff a rather comical look which sat awkwardly with the fellow's usual air of bombastic self-importance. Athelstan wearily waved him into the church.

'Master Bladdersniff, I suppose you have come to discuss why my cemetery is violated and its graves robbed whilst you and the ward council do nothing about it?'

Bladdersniff shook his head, while peering over his shoulder, back into the darkness of the church porch.

'What is it, man? What's over there?'

The bailiff's mouth opened and shut like a landed carp. Athelstan stared more closely. The fellow looked as if he was going to vomit. His white face had a greenish tinge and the dark eyes were watery, as if Bladdersniff had been violently retching.

'For God's sake, man, what is it?'

Again the bailiff looked back into the darkness. 'It's Tosspot!' he mumbled.

'What?'

'Tosspot! Or, at least, part of him,' Bladdersniff replied, beckoning the priest to follow him.

Athelstan took a taper and went to where the bailiff stood over a dirty piece of canvas in a dark corner of the church porch. Bladdersniff pulled this open and Athelstan turned away in disgust. A man's leg lay there, or at least part of it, cut above the knee as neatly and as sharply as a piece of cloth by an expert tailor. Athelstan stared at the bloody stump and mottle-hued skin.

'Good God!' he breathed, and caught the stench of corruption from the slightly puffed flesh. 'Cover it up, man! Cover it up!'

Athelstan doused the taper, walked out of the church and stood on the top step, drawing in deep breaths of fresh morning air. He heard Bladdersniff come up behind him.

'What makes you think it was Tosspot?'

'Oh, you remember, Father. Tosspot was always regaling his customers at the tavern with tales of his old war wound, an arrow in the leg. He was continually showing his scar as if it was some sacred relic.'

Athelstan nodded.

'Aye,' he replied. 'Old Tosspot would do that whenever he became drunk.' The friar looked at the bailiff. 'And that leg bears the same scar?'

'Yes, Father, just above the shin.'

'Where was it found?'

'Do you want to see?'

'Yes, I do.'

Bladdersniff led him down Bridge Street, across Jerwald and into Longfish Alley, which led down to Broken Wharf on the riverside. As he walked, Athelstan never spoke a word and the people who knew him stepped aside at the fierce, determined expression on the usually gentle priest's face.

Athelstan noticed little except the dirty, filthy slush of the streets they crossed. He ignored greetings and seemed totally unaware of the traders and hucksters behind their battered stalls and booths shouting for custom. Even the felons fastened tightly in the stocks failed to provoke his usual compassion, whilst he treated Bladdersniff as if the bailiff hardly existed. Athelstan felt sick at heart. Who would do that to poor Tosspot's corpse? he wondered. How would it profit them? They reached Broken Wharf above the riverside. Bladdersniff took the friar by the arm and pointed down to the dirty mudflats where gulls and crows fought over the rubbish left on the riverside. Athelstan looked out across the Thames. The water looked as dirty and dark as his own mood. He noticed the great chunks of ice still floating, crashing together as they swirled down to thunder against the arches of London Bridge.

'Where did you find it?'

'Down there, Father,' Bladdersniff brusquely replied. 'On the mud, wrapped in that piece of canvas. An urchin looking for sea coal found it and brought it to one of the traders who recognised old Tosspot's wound.' The bailiff coughed nervously. 'I have heard about the raids on your cemetery.'

'Oh, you have? That's good.' Athelstan smiled falsely at him. 'You think the limb was washed in by the river?'

'Yes, I do. Now, at any other time, Father, the river would have swept it away, but the heavy ice has interfered with the current and the canvas bag was pushed back to the bank.'

'So you are saying it must have been thrown in here?'

'Yes, Father, either here or some place very close.'

Athelstan looked to his left, along the mud flats and walls which stretched down to London Bridge. Too open, he reflected. No felon would dream of committing such a terrible act in a place where he could be seen. He looked to his right and the long row of great houses whose gardens stretched down to the riverside. A recent memory stirred. 'I wonder,' he murmured to himself. 'I really do wonder...'

'What, Father?'

'Nothing, Master Bladdersniff. Go back to my church. Collect what is left of poor Tosspot and bury it as you think fit.'

'Father, it's not my...'

'Do it!' Athelstan snarled. 'Do it now or answer to the City Coroner, Sir John Cranston!'

'He has no jurisdiction here.'

'Yes, but he can get it!' Athelstan retorted. 'Oh, for God's sake, man, do it for me. Do it for poor Tosspot, please?'

Bladdersniff stared, nodded, and strode away.

Athelstan walked back to St Erconwald's. He had recognised one of the houses down near the riverside and remembered how cleanly and sharply the limb had been cut. This stirred memories of his own military experience in the makeshift hospitals of the old King's armies in France. Athelstan thought of the cemetery. Where were the lepers? Why hadn't they noticed anything? Athelstan remembered the lepers he had seen near St Paul's the day he and Cranston had visited Geoffrey Parchmeiner. Their begging dishes!

Athelstan stopped in the middle of Lad Alley. 'Oh, my God!' he whispered. 'Oh, sweet pity's sake!' The white chalk he had found on his fingers after Mass when he and young Crim had pushed the sacred host through the leper's squint... The friar suddenly felt weak and leaned against the urine-stained wall. Other memories flooded back. 'Of course!' he whispered to himself. 'That's why the cemetery wasn't disturbed for a while. The thaw! But when the river was frozen, they couldn't get rid of what they'd stolen.' Athelstan's face contorted into a sudden snarl. 'The bastards!' he hissed. 'The evil bastards!'

He strode back down Lad Alley into one of the busy thoroughfares which ran parallel to the riverbank. A young urchin, running after a ball, bumped into him, slipping and sliding on the icy slush. Athelstan seized him tightly by the shoulder until the boy winced.

'Father, Father, I didn't mean to! Honest, I didn't!'

Athelstan looked at the urchin's pallid face.

'I am sorry,' he replied gently. 'No hurt was intended. But here, lad. For a penny, take me to Doctor Vincentius' house. You know the physician?'

The boy didn't know Vincentius and shook his head, but ran to a local stall-holder who provided clear instructions. The urchin then led Athelstan through an alleyway and into a quiet street of houses, grand, half-timbered affairs, though their paint was now peeling and their unwashed façades gave sad, mute witness to grander, more prosperous days. The boy pointed to the third one down with its windows shuttered, though the huge front door was freshly painted and reinforced with shining bands of steel. Athelstan handed the penny over, went across and pounded on the door until he heard the patter of quick footsteps and the bolts drawn back. A lank-haired young man opened the door, dressed in a blue cotehardie fringed with squirrel fur. His eyes widened in alarm when he saw the friar.

'Brother Athelstan!'

'How do you know my name, you bastard?' the friar shouted, and pushed him back against the wall. 'Where is Doctor Vincentius?'

'He's in his chamber.'

Athelstan didn't wait for the fellow to usher him in but strode along the lime-washed stone corridor and threw open the door at the far end. Vincentius was sitting behind a great oaken desk in his warm, dark, panelled chamber. Athelstan was aware of shelves stuffed full of parchments, a zodiac chart on the wall, the smell of herbs and spices, and a small log fire crackling merrily in the hearth. The doctor rose, his dark eyes guarded, tawny face creased into a smile.

'Brother Athelstan! What is the matter? What can I do…?'

'This for a start!' Athelstan punched the doctor as hard as he could, sending Vincentius sprawling against the wall, knocking over a small table and sending a yellowing skull crashing on to the map-strewn floor. The doctor got up and dabbed at the cut at the corner of his mouth with the back of his hand. His dark eyes now mocked the priest.

'You seem in a temper, Father?'

Athelstan heard the young man come up behind him. 'It's all right, Gidaut,' Vincentius murmured. 'But perhaps we'd better start to pack once again.'

Athelstan glared at the doctor as the door closed softly behind him.

'You are a bastard, Doctor! A heretic! A despoiler of graves! I have just seen what's left of poor Tosspot's corpse. If the wardsman had any sense, he would be here with the city guard. Only a skilled physician could cut a leg so cleanly.' He walked closer to the desk. 'And don't lie! You and your creature out there—' Athelstan indicated the door with a toss of his head. 'A clever pair. Dressed like lepers, your faces masked by skins covered with white chalk, you lived in my cemetery by day, or at least part of it, finding out what happened. And who would dream of approaching a leper? And, even if they did, you were well prepared. Your face was covered in a cloth mask, the skin of your hands discoloured. Then of course, you would come back at night and take whatever you wanted!' Athelstan breathed heavily. 'God forgive me,' he muttered. 'I'm no better than other men. Do you know, when a man is declared a leper, he attends his own requiem? We think of him as already dead, and so did I. The lepers in my cemetery were just shadows to me, walking bundles of rags. Only one thing was missing: I never saw them with begging dishes, and didn't realise that till this morning.' He glared at the physician. 'You really should have been more careful, Vincentius. You took those corpses and, when you were finished, ditched what was left into the Thames. But the river was sluggish. This morning the grisly remains of your macabre activities floated back to the riverbank.'

The doctor still kept his back to the wall and watched the priest guardedly. 'You are most observant, friar. Benedicta told me that.'

Athelstan flinched at the look in the doctor's eyes. 'Aye,' the friar replied, slumping down on a stool. 'But I should have been *more* observant. I found chalk on my fingers after I had passed the Host through the leper's squint.' He glared at the doctor. 'That's sacrilege, you know? To take the Eucharist as a cover for your blasphemous doings.' Athelstan glared around him. 'Yes,' he rasped, 'I should have been more observant. I never saw you with a begging bowl, nor could I remember you in the streets around the church.' He rose. 'You broke God's law as well as the King's. I am leaving now but I will be back with the city guard. Tonight you will be in Newgate getting ready to stand trial before King's Bench at Westminster!'

'Benedicta also said you were a tolerant priest. Aren't you going to ask me why, Father?' Vincentius replied softly.

The physician suddenly had a wary, frightened look in his eyes. 'I did wrong,' he muttered, slumping into his chair. 'But what real harm did I do? No, no!' He waved his hand at Athelstan. 'Listen to me! I have studied medicine in Bologna, with the Arabs in Spain and North Africa, and at the great school of physic in Salerno. But we doctors know nothing, Father, except how to apply leeches and bleed a man dry.' Vincentius laced his fingers together and rested his elbows on the desk. 'The only way we can learn about the human body is to open it up. Dissect each part; study the position of the heart, or the coursing of the blood, or the composition of the stomach. But the church forbids that.' He held up a beringed hand. 'I swear I meant no disrespect, but my hunger for medical knowledge, Father, is as great as yours for saving souls. And where could I go? To the execution yards or battlefields where the corpses are so mauled they are beyond recognition? So

I came to Southwark, outside the jurisdiction of the city. Yes, yes.' He saw the look of annoyance in Athelstan's eyes. 'To a poor parish where no one cared, just as they don't for the famished children who roam the streets near your church.' Vincentius played with a small knife. 'I took to imitating a leper to spy on the graveyard, taking only those corpses over whom no one had a claim.'

'I claimed them!' Athelstan yelled. 'God claimed them! The church claimed them!'

'Yes, I took the corpses,' Vincentius continued, 'and dissected them. Gidaut and I buried them at night in the river, but then we stopped because of the great frost.' He shook his head. 'I did wrong, but are you going to hound me for that? I did good work here, priest. Go out into the streets of Southwark, talk to the mother with the lanced cyst in her groin. To the urchin whose eyes are clean. To the labourer whose leg I set properly. And if I hang, what then, Brother? Who will give a damn? The poor will still die, and the physicians in Cheapside who milk their patients of both money and health will clap their hands to see me dance at the end of a rope.'

Athelstan sat down wearily on the stool. 'I don't want your death,' he replied. 'I want the dead in my cemetery to lie as God expects them to. I want you to go, doctor.' Athelstan rose and dusted down his robe. 'I am sorry I struck you.' He stared at Vincentius. 'But you must be gone from here. I don't know where to, and don't really care, but in a week, I want you out of the city!' Athelstan suddenly felt tired and weak, and realised he hadn't eaten for some time. 'I am sorry I struck you,' he repeated, 'but I was angry.' He suddenly remembered Cranston was waiting for him and looked back at the doctor. 'Oh,' he said, 'you owe me one favour.'

Vincentius sat back in his chair. 'What is that, Father?'

'Well, two to be exact. First, you had a visitor here – Lady Maude Cranston. Why did she come?'

Vincentius grinned. 'The Lady Maude, despite being in her thirtieth year, is now *enceinte.*'

Athelstan stared back in disbelief. 'She's with child!'

'Yes, priest. About two months gone. Both she and the child are healthy, but she is frightened of Sir John not believing her. She doesn't want to disappoint him. I believe they lost a child some years ago?'

Athelstan nodded and the doctor enjoyed the look of stupefaction on the priest's face.

'She told me about Sir John. I advised her most carefully against the pleasures of the flesh. I believe her husband is a mountain of a man?'

'Aye,' Athelstan answered, still dumbstruck at what he had discovered. 'Sir John is certainly that.'

'And the second favour, Father?'

'You served in Outremer?'

'Yes, I did. For a time I practised in hospitals in both Tyre and Sidon.'

'If you met someone there, how would you greet them?'

Now the physician looked surprised.

'*Shalom,*' he answered. 'The usual Semitic phrase for "peace be with you".'

Athelstan lifted his hand. 'Doctor Vincentius, I bid you farewell. I do not expect we will meet again.'

'Priest?'

'Yes, physician?'

'Are you pleased that I am going because of what I have done, or pleased that I am leaving and will not see the widow Benedicta again? You love her, don't you, priest? You, with your sharp accusations against others!'

'No, I don't love her!' Athelstan snapped. But even as he closed the door behind him, he knew that, like St Peter, he was denying the truth.

–

Sir John Cranston, Coroner of the City, squatted bleary-eyed in a corner of the Holy Lamb tavern and stared self-pityingly across Cheapside. He had drunk a good quart of ale. Athelstan had not arrived, so he'd decided to return home. He would deal with his wife like a man should, with abrupt accusations and sharp questions, but he wished the friar had come. He would have liked his advice on so many things.

Cranston leaned back against the wall and squinted across the tavern. The latest business at the Tower was dreadful. He had gone to see Fitzormonde's badly mauled corpse: half the face had been torn away and the man's body savaged almost beyond recognition. Cranston rubbed the side of his own face with his hand. At first Colebrooke had believed the death was an accident.

'It was just after dusk,' the lieutenant had informed him. 'Fitzormonde, as was customary with him, had gone to watch the bear. One second everything was peaceful, the next Satan himself seemed to sweep out of hell. The bear broke loose and mauled the hapless hospitaller. I ordered archers down and the bear was killed.' Colebrooke shrugged. 'Sir John, we had no choice.'

'Was it an accident?' Cranston asked. 'The bear breaking loose?'

'At first we thought so, but when we examined the beast, we found this in one of his hindquarters.' The lieutenant handed Cranston a small bolt from the type of crossbow a lady would use for hunting.

'Who was in the Tower at the time?'

'Everyone,' Colebrooke replied. 'Myself, Mistress Philippa, Rastani, Sir Fulke, Hammond the chaplain – everyone except Master Geoffrey who had returned to his shop in the city.'

Cranston had thanked the lieutenant and gone over to the shabby, dank death house near St Peter ad Vincula where Fitzormonde's mangled remains lay, waiting to be sewn into their canvas shroud. The corpse was hideous, nothing more than a scarred, bloody pile of flesh. Cranston had left as quickly as he could, questioned those he found, and concluded that the crossbow bolt had been loosed by some secret archer: this had goaded the bear to fury and, snapping its chain, it had attacked Fitzormonde.

Cranston gazed one more time round the tavern, sighed and closed his eyes. Was there no way of resolving this problem? he thought. And where the bloody hell was Athelstan?

'My Lord Coroner?'

Cranston opened his eyes. 'Where have you been, monk? And why are you grinning?'

Athelstan smiled and called over to the taverner. 'Two cups of your best Bordeaux. And I mean your finest.' He sat down, still beaming at Sir John. 'My Lord Coroner, I have some news for you.'

Chapter 13

Sir John Cranston sat in the high-backed chair in his spacious, stone-flagged kitchen and stared lovingly at Lady Maude, who was standing at the table filling jars with comfits. He couldn't believe Athelstan's news, not at first. The truth had only sunk in after three further goblets of Bordeaux and Athelstan's repetition of what he had learnt from Doctor Vincentius. At last, Cranston thought, it all makes sense...

He stole a glance at his wife's waist and realised Lady Maude's voluminous skirts would conceal any thickening of the waist; even her nightgowns were quilted, and of course the thought of another child had never occurred to him. After Matthew's death from plague so many years ago at the age of three, Cranston had given up all hope of an heir. He drummed his fingers on the arm of the chair. Lady Maude caught his glance and sniffed into a jar to hide her surprise at Sir John's sudden change of mood. Should she tell him now? she wondered. Or wait, as she had planned, till Christmas Day?

Lady Maude had been stunned by the realisation her monthly courses had ceased and a friend had recommended Doctor Vincentius. The physician had confirmed her hopes and given her sound advice on what to eat and drink and to be gentle with herself. She had to refuse Sir John's amorous embraces but could not tell him the reason. She had to be certain. Lady Maude bit her lip. There was another reason: once Sir John learnt the truth, she would know no peace. He would hang round her like a great shaggy guard dog, watch her every move and give her endless lectures about 'being safe and keeping well'. Lady Maude lowered her face. The child, she silently prayed, must be healthy. She would never forget Sir John when Matthew died. He, who had the courage of a lion, just sat like a little boy, with not a sound, not a moan, nothing save those streams of silent tears.

Sir John's thoughts followed a similar pattern; he had solemnly promised Athelstan not to broach the matter with his wife but wait for her to do so. He had also promised to allow Vincentius to leave London unscathed. However, Cranston narrowed his eyes, he would have to think again about that. Perhaps in the new year letters should be sent to every sheriff in England about Doctor Vincentius and his iniquitous activities in other people's graveyards? The coroner stirred and looked across at Athelstan, who was chatting merrily with Leif the beggar.

'Brother, you will stay for some dinner?'

'No, Sir John, I must go. Perhaps later?'

'And the business at the Tower?'

Athelstan rose from his chair. 'I don't know, Sir John. Perhaps it is best if you eat and reflect on what we have already learnt. We'll discuss it tomorrow, eh?' He looked admiringly at the jars Lady Maude was filling. 'You expect guests at Yuletide?'

'I thought so, Father,' she replied. 'My relatives from Tiverton in Devon.' Lady Maude threw a mock angry glance at Sir John's snort of displeasure. 'They were supposed to come but the roads are impassable, not even messengers can get through. I was talking to one of the aldermen's wives. She said her husband's trade had been badly hurt. All of his journeymen travelling to the south-west have had to turn back.'

Athelstan smiled and Lady Maude went back to her comfits. She strove to hide her agitation as Brother Athelstan informed Sir John that one of his parishioners, a Doctor Vincentius, was leaving Southwark and would not be returning. Lady Maude hid her face. She was sorry the doctor was going. He had been a most skilful man. She sighed and stared at the table. Now she would have to look around for a good physician, someone better than the usual leeches who lived round Cheapside.

Athelstan winked secretively at Cranston, made his farewells, and walked out into the darkening street. He collected Philomel from the stables of the Holy Lamb and rode back through the darkness, chuckling to himself at Sir John's reaction to his news. He hoped Lady Maude had heard his announcement about Vincentius' departure. Perhaps, the friar concluded, it was all for the best.

Philomel suddenly slipped on a strip of ice. Athelstan groaned in despair, dismounted and, gathering the reins in his hands, gently guided the old horse along the darkened pathway. Above him the houses rose sheer and sombre. Outside each of the great Cheapside mansions an oil lamp burned, but as Athelstan turned the corner at St Peter Cornhill and went down Gracechurch into Bridge Street, the tracks became darker. He had to pick his way carefully round the mounds of refuse, night soil and scraps of food where rats gnawed and scampered. Behind him a door slammed and a night bird nesting in the eaves of a house flew out in a burst of black feathers, making Athelstan jump. Beggars whined for alms. A whore stood on the corner, the orange wig straggling across her raddled face made all the more ghastly in the light of the candle she cradled in her hand.

She cackled at Athelstan and made a rude gesture. He sketched the sign of the cross in her direction. A city bully-boy leaning against the door of an ale-house saw the lonely figure and felt his wooden knife hilt. But when he glimpsed Athelstan's tonsure and the crucifix round his neck, he thought better of it.

Athelstan moved on, relieved to see the soldiers in the torchlight guarding London Bridge. Its gates were closed but the city archers recognised 'the coroner's chaplain', as they called Athelstan, and let him through.

The friar crossed the bridge, the sound of Philomel's hoof beats hollow on the wooden planks. It was an eerie experience. Usually the bridge was busy but now it was silent and shrouded in a thick river mist. Athelstan had the ghostly impression of walking across some chasm between heaven and hell. The gulls nesting in the wooden arches below flew out, shrieking in protest at this unexpected disturbance. Athelstan remembered the ravens in the Tower. Another death there, he thought, two if he included the bear. Athelstan felt sorry for the beast.

'Perhaps it was for the best,' he murmured to himself. 'Never have I seen so unhappy an animal.' He recalled the teaching of some of his Franciscan brethren who, following the preaching of their founder, maintained all animals were God's creation and should never be ill-treated or kept in captivity.

Athelstan passed the silent darkened Chapel of St Thomas of Canterbury in the centre of the bridge. The wardsmen on the Southwark bank shouted at him; some of them even wondered if he was a ghost. Athelstan sang out his name and they let him through, teasing him gently about his unexpected appearance.

The friar led Philomel through the dark alleyways of Southwark. He felt safer here. He was known and no one would dare accost him. He passed a tavern where a boy, to earn a few crusts, stood just within the doorway, sweetly singing a carol. Athelstan stopped and listened to words promising warmth and cheer. He patted Philomel on the neck. 'Where will we spend Christmas, eh, old friend?' he asked and walked on. 'Perhaps Lady Cranston might invite me, now her relatives are not coming from the West Country.'

He stopped abruptly. 'Lady Maude's relatives!' he murmured to the dark, quietened street, and felt a shiver go up his spine. 'Strange,' he murmured. 'Something so small, a mere froth on the day's happenings.' He rubbed the side of his face. Lady Maude's words stirred memories of something else he had heard.

He almost dragged Philomel back to St Erconwald's, so eagerly the destrier snickered angrily at him. Athelstan stabled the old war horse, ensured all was well in the church, and guiltily remembered his anger earlier in the day. Bonaventura was apparently out courting so Athelstan went across to the house, built up the fire and hastily ate a piece of bread. After a few bites he tossed it into the fire as the bread was stale, and poured himself a goblet of watered wine. He cleared the rough tabletop and began to list all he knew about the murders in or near the Tower.

The thought which had sparked his memory in the street outside might, he speculated, be the key to resolving the entire problem. He smiled as he remembered old Father Anselm's oft-repeated axiom in his lectures on logic. 'If a problem exists, a solution must exist. It's only a question of finding the path in. Sometimes it can be by the smallest chink of light.' Anselm would then cast a beady eye on Athelstan. 'Always remember that, young Athelstan. It applies as much in the realm of metaphysics as it does to a day's ordinary events.'

Athelstan closed his eyes. 'I still remember that, Father,' he murmured. 'God rest you.' He arranged his writing tray, marshalled his thoughts and dipped the grey goose quill into the ink, cursing when he found it was cold. He held the pot over the candle to warm it and hastily re-read the memoranda he had written when he was in the Tower. Once the ink was heated, he carefully listed his conclusions.

Primo – despite being well protected, Sir Ralph Whitton had been slain in the North Bastion tower. Sir Ralph had slept behind a locked door to which he held the key, as did the guards outside. The door to the passageway in which the chamber stood was also locked; again the keys were shared with his trusted bodyguard. Yet all these precautions had been brought to nothing. His assassin had apparently entered the chamber by crossing the frozen moat and, using footholds in the Tower wall, had climbed up, unlatched the window, entered and slain Sir Ralph.

Secundo – the assassin must have known the Tower well to use these footholds, yet why didn't the clamour of the shutters being opened, not to mention the assassin's entry into the chamber, arouse Sir Ralph? The buckle from Sir Fulke's boot had been found on the ice. Was this a clue to the possible murderer?

Tertio – the young man, Parchmeiner, had been the first person to try and rouse Sir Ralph but the chamber had only been opened by Master Colebrooke the lieutenant.

Did Sir Ralph's second-in-command have a role in this murder?

Athelstan gazed at what he had written, shook his head and smiled. 'No, no!' he whispered. 'All that must wait.'

Quarto – Mowbray had been killed by a fall from the parapet, but how had he slipped? Who had rung the tocsin bell? Who had been absent from Mistress Philippa's chamber? Only two: Fitzormonde and Colebrooke.

Again, Athelstan shook his head.

Quinto – Alderman Horne's death. Athelstan made a face. No clues there whatsoever.

Sexto – Fitzormonde's death? He and Cranston had seen that the bear's chain could have been clasped more securely, and Fitzormonde was in the habit of staring at the bear. But who had been the assassin who fired the bolt and roused the beast to such a murderous rage?

Septimo – Sir Ralph and others had died because of their terrible treachery towards Sir Bartholomew Burghgesh. Had Burghgesh died on that ship so many years ago or had he returned to England? The vicar of Woodforde claimed to have seen him, as had the land-lord of the ale-house there. Was this the same mysterious person the landlord at the Golden Mitre tavern had also glimpsed? If so, Burghgesh had been seen by at least three people around Advent three years ago, the same time Sir Ralph Whitton had been in such a state of deep distress. But if Burghgesh had survived and returned to England, how and where was he hiding now? One further problem: Sir Ralph's distress had apparently diminished. Surely this would not have happened if Burghgesh had survived? Sir Ralph would only have taken comfort had he appeared three years ago and died.

Octavo – whoever had sent the sinister notes to Whitton and the others must have access to the Tower. Did Burghgesh or his son, hidden in the city, send their messages and accomplices into the Tower?

Nono – who stood to profit from the murders? Colebrooke? He wanted promotion and knew the Tower well. He had been present in the Tower when all three had died. Sir Fulke? He, too, benefited from his brother's death; his buckle had been found on the ice outside the North Bastion tower. He also knew the Tower well and had been there when the two hospitallers perished. Rastani? A stealthy, subtle man who might have taken his own vow of vengeance against Sir Ralph and his companions. He knew the fortress well and had been present when the hospitallers died.

Athelstan shook his head. The same applied to Hammond, that rather sinister chaplain. Or was it Mistress Philippa in collusion with her lover? And what about Red Hand, the mad man who perhaps was more sane than he appeared?

Athelstan looked up and gasped. Red Hand! The hunchbacked albino had mentioned secret dungeons being bricked up, and Simon the carpenter had mumbled something similar.

Athelstan sat for a while, head in his hands. He picked up his pen, stared round the darkening kitchen and glimpsed a bunch of holly in the far corner. Christmas in a few days, he thought. He got up, warmed his fingers over the brazier and wished Benedicta was with him to share a cup of mulled wine. He recalled Doctor Vincentius' words about his affection for the widow, and stared into the fire. Was it so obvious? he wondered. Did the other parishioners recognise his feelings as well? He shook his head to clear his mind. No, he must concentrate on the problem in hand. A shutter clattered and Athelstan jumped as a dark shadow pounced on to the rush-strewn floor.

'Bonaventura!' he muttered. The cat padded over and brushed majestically against the friar's leg. 'Well, Master Cat, you have come for something to eat?'

The cat stretched, arching his back. Athelstan went into the buttery, filled a cracked, pewter bowl full of milk and watched the cat lap it up before going to stretch out in front of the fire. Athelstan went across and fastened the shutters: windows, doors and passageways, he thought, recalling once again Red Hand's mutterings and Simon the carpenter's dark warnings. Athelstan looked enviously at the cat. 'It's all right for some,' he grumbled and sat down before his parchments to continue his study. He took each name, building up a line of argument as if he was preparing some theological disputation.

The hours passed. Athelstan rubbed his eyes wearily. Only one path remained open: the one shown by Lady Maude's innocent remarks which had so abruptly startled him on his journey back to Southwark. Athelstan drew a rough plan of the Tower and continued to pursue the conclusions he had reached. Just before dawn he pronounced himself satisfied. He had found the assassin, though very little else. For that he would need Cranston.

-

The next morning Sir John rode like a young knight down Cheapside to the Golden Mitre tavern near the Tower. The coroner felt as if he was riding on air. Even the cold morning breeze felt as warm and soft as the caress of a young woman.

Cranston had embraced the Lady Maude most passionately before getting out of bed that morning. She had clung tearfully to his chest and muttered about speaking to him soon. He had murmured sweet nothings, patted her on the head, rose, dressed and, going downstairs, bellowed for a cup of sack whilst a groom saddled his horse. Sir John felt as proud as a peacock to know he would be a father again. He rewarded himself with a swig from his 'miraculous wineskin', as Athelstan called it, sucking the robust red juice into his mouth. He beamed around expansively. Oh, it was a fine day to be alive!

Sir John scattered pennies before a group of beggars shivering on the corner of the Mercery. He shouted cheerful abuse at the poulterers who were cleaning and gutting chickens and other fowl in their huge iron vats for the Christmas season. A whore was being led bare-shouldered through the streets, her head shaved close under a conical white cap. A bagpiper went before her whilst a scrawled notice, pinned to her dirty bodice, proclaimed her a public slut. Cranston stopped the procession and had her freed.

'Why, Sir John?' the rat-mouthed bailiff asked.

'Because it's Christmas!' he roared back. 'And Christ the beautiful boy of Bethlehem will be with us once again!'

The bailiff was going to object but Cranston's hand fell to his dagger, so the fellow cut the woman's bonds. She stuck out her tongue at the bailiff, made an obscene gesture at Cranston and scampered off up an alleyway. Sir John rode on into Petty Wales. He arrived at the tavern and, tossing the reins of his horse to a groom, swaggered into the sweet-smelling tap room.

'Monk, where the hell are you?' he bellowed, giving the other customers the fright of their lives and bringing a wide-eyed taverner scurrying to attend to him.

'Sir John, you are happy?'

'As a fly on a horse's arse in summer!' Sir John bawled back. He threw the miraculous wineskin at the taverner. 'Fill that! The friar told me to meet him here,' he muttered. He gazed through the smoke and gloom and glimpsed Athelstan, nodding half-asleep over a table.

'Bring a cup of sack for me,' Cranston ordered the landlord. 'Fresh oatcakes, and a strip of dry gammon!' He smacked his lips. 'Some eel stew for the Brother and, even though it's Advent, he'll take a jug of watered ale!'

The coroner swaggered across and tapped the half-sleeping friar on the shoulder. 'Arouse yourself, Brother!' he bawled. 'For, by the sod, the devil walks, roaring like a lion seeking whom he may devour!'

'I hope he's not as heavy-handed as you, Cranston,' Athelstan grumbled, opening his eyes and gazing wearily up.

Cranston crouched down beside him. 'Good morrow, monk.'

'I am a friar.'

'Good morrow, friar. And why are you not so full of the joys of Yuletide?'

'Because, Sir John, I am cold, tired and totally dispirited.' Athelstan was about to continue the litany of his woes when he caught the mischief dancing like devils in Cranston's eyes. 'It's good to see you happy, Sir John. I suppose you have ordered food?'

Cranston nodded, swept his great beaver hat off his head and slumped down on the bench opposite.

They had eaten their fill and Cranston downed two cups of claret before Athelstan had finished his story. The coroner shook his head, asked a few questions and whistled softly under his breath.

'By the sod, are you sure, Brother? So much from an innocent little remark by the Lady Maude?'

Athelstan shrugged. 'Lady Maude's little comments have caused a great deal of consternation in the last few days, Sir John.'

Cranston belched, rose, and bellowed for his wineskin, tossing coins at the taverner. 'You have carried out my instructions, Sir John?' Athelstan asked.

'Yes, friar, I have.' Sir John stretched and yawned. 'All our suspects are waiting in the Tower, though Parchmeiner will arrive late. You want to see Colebrooke first?'

'And Red Hand?'

'Ah, yes, Red Hand.'

'You have the warrant, Sir John?'

'I don't need any bloody warrants, monk! I am Cranston, the King's Coroner in the City, and they will either answer the question or face the consequences.'

They made their way out of the tavern where they left their horses, down some alleyways and through the great yawning entrance to the Tower. Colebrooke was waiting for them at the gatehouse. Athelstan noticed he was wearing hauberk, mailed shirt and leggings.

'You are expecting trouble, Master Lieutenant?'

'Sir John's instructions seem most stringent,' Colebrooke replied.

'Where's Red Hand?'

'What do you want that mad bugger for?'

'Because I ordered it,' Cranston replied.

They crossed the green, the sparse grass now visible beneath the wide swathes of grey slush. Two soldiers trailed behind. Colebrooke sent one across to the small door in the base of the White Tower. Athelstan stared sadly across at the far corner where the great bear had sat, now empty and forlorn, but the ground still showed the marks of its occupation and a few pathetic scraps of food still littered the icy cobblestones.

'God rest the bear's soul!' Athelstan murmured.

Cranston turned. 'Do bears have souls, friar? Do they go to heaven?'

Athelstan grinned. 'If your heaven needs bears, Sir John, then there will be bears! But, in your case, I suppose heaven will be miles and miles of taverns and spacious ale-houses!'

Cranston slapped his thigh with his gauntlet. 'Oh, I like you, Brother.' And he beamed at a surprised Colebrooke.

Suddenly the door of the White Tower was thrown open and the soldier re-emerged, dragging Red Hand by the scruff of the neck.

'Let him go!' Athelstan shouted. He went across, crouched and clasped the hunchback's hand in his. He stared into the madcap's milky eyes and saw the tear stains on his raddled cheeks. 'You mourn the bear, Red Hand?'

'Yes. Red Hand's friend has gone.'

Athelstan looked at the soldier and indicated he should move away. 'I know, Red Hand,' Athelstan whispered. 'The bear was a magnificent beast, but he will be happy now. His spirit's free.'

Red Hand's watery eyes caught Athelstan's. The madman smiled. 'You're Red Hand's friend?'

Athelstan studied the hunchback's face, his scrawny, white hair and grotesque mottled rags. He recalled Father

Anselm's other words of wisdom: 'Always remember, Athelstan, every man is in God's image. A flame burns as fiercely in a broken jar as it does in the most elaborately carved lamp.'

'I am your friend,' Athelstan replied. 'But I need your help.'

Red Hand's eyes became wary.

'I want you to show me your secrets.'

'What secrets, Master?'

'What the bloody hell are you doing, Brother?'

Athelstan threw a warning glance at the coroner.

'Look, Red Hand,' Athelstan whispered. 'You talked to me of chambers, dungeons, which were bricked up.'

Red Hand tried to prise his fingers free of Athelstan's, but the friar held firm.

'Please,' he murmured. 'Did Sir Ralph have such secret cells? If you tell me, Red Hand, I can trap the man responsible for the bear's death.'

The madman needed no further encouragement. He turned. 'Wait! Wait there!' he pleaded, and ran back through the small door of the White Tower. He re-emerged a few seconds later with a little bell which he tinkled. 'Follow Red Hand!' he shouted. 'Follow Red Hand!'

Cranston looked in disbelief at Athelstan. Colebrooke seemed angry.

'What's the little sod up to?' Cranston murmured as the scampering madcap led them across Tower Green to a door which had rusted firmly shut at the foot of Wakefield Tower. Red Hand stopped at the door, bowed three times and tinkled his bell.

'What's in there?'

Colebrooke shrugged. 'Some dungeons dug deep into the earth.'

'Open it!'

'I haven't got any keys.'

'Don't be obstructive,' Cranston barked. 'Open the bloody thing!'

Colebrooke turned, hands on hips, and yelled orders. Soldiers ran over. Under Colebrooke's instruction, they wheeled across a huge battering ram, swinging its iron head against the door until it buckled and swung off its hinges.

'Torches!' Cranston ordered.

Cressets were brought and hastily lit. Red Hand scampered down the slime-covered stairs, which fell away into icy cold darkness. At the bottom of the steps ran a small corridor, narrow, dank and evil-smelling. On the right nothing but mildewed walls; on the left two cell doors, their locks rusted shut. Athelstan stiffened as he heard squeaks and rustles and, spinning round, glimpsed a brown, greasy body slinking away into the darkness.

'Break the doors down!' Cranston bellowed.

The soldiers attacked the heavy but rotting wood, smashing open a huge hole. Athelstan took a torch and went in. There was nothing there except rats, squeaking and scampering on a rotting pile of straw in the far corner.

'Hell's teeth!' Cranston hissed. 'Nothing!'

They clambered out through the open door. Cranston held the torch up and examined the wall between the doors.

'Look, Athelstan!' he exclaimed.

The friar studied the wall carefully.

'There's another door,' Cranston continued. 'But it's been bricked up. Look, it bulges out and the plaster is fresher than the rest of the wall.'

'You found it! You found it! You found it!' Red Hand clapped his hands and jumped up and down like a child playing a game. 'They have found the secret door!' he sang out. 'They've won the game!' The madcap stopped shouting. 'I did that,' he announced proudly. 'Sir Ralph Whitton told me to do it. The door was locked and I bricked up the entrance.'

'When?' Athelstan asked.

'Oh, years ago. Years ago!'

Cranston snapped his fingers. 'Smash that wall down!'

The soldiers set to with iron-headed mallets and hammers. Soon the corridor was thick with a foul white dust.

'There's a door!' one of them exclaimed.

'And that too!' Cranston ordered.

In a few minutes the rotting wood behind the destroyed wall buckled and snapped, the soldiers creating a large enough hole for Cranston and Athelstan to crawl through. Torches were ordered and Cranston held one up.

'Oh, Good Lord!' Cranston whispered, staring at the decaying skeleton slumped on a bed of rotted muck. 'Who is that? And what terrible son of Satan ordered such a hideous death?'

'To answer your questions, Sir John, I suspect these are the mortal remains of Sir Bartholomew Burghgesh. And Whitton, a man steeped in murder, ordered it.'

'Look!' Sir John hissed, snatching the torch and holding it up against the wall just where the white skeletal arm rested. Athelstan peered at the crude drawing of the three-masted ship carved into the stone, the same as had been found on the letters sent to Sir Ralph and others. Cranston's eyes rounded in surprise.

'Brother, you are right.'

'Yes, Sir John. Now, let's see if the rest of my theory has substance.'

They told Colebrooke to leave guards near the cell and eagerly returned to the cold brisk air of Tower Green.

'What did you find?' the lieutenant asked anxiously, coming up behind them.

'Be patient, Master Lieutenant. But come, I have further favours to ask of you.'

Athelstan guided him by the elbow away from the rest. Cranston watched the friar and soldier talk quietly together.

'Is Red Hand needed?' The hunchback suddenly appeared, jumping up and down.

Cranston smiled, dug into his purse and pushed two silver pieces into the man's hand, patting him gently on the cheek.

'Not for the moment, Red Hand. But you have my thanks and that of the Regent, the Mayor, and the city of London.'

The hunchback's eyes danced with delight. He ran off, leaping with glee, cavorting and laughing at the dark ravens which cawed noisily above him.

'Red Hand's a champion! Red Hand's a champion!' he yelled.

Athelstan rejoined Sir John. 'The lieutenant has his orders,' he murmured. 'Come, My Lord Coroner, the drama is about to begin.'

The rest of the Tower household were waiting in Philippa's chamber. Sir Fulke was dressed most elegantly in a dark gown of gold-fringed murrey. Philippa, now wearing full mourning weeds and a black veil, sat in the window seat, head bowed over a piece of embroidery. Rastani crouched by the fireplace, the chaplain sat on a stool opposite. All except Philippa looked up and glowered as Athelstan and Cranston entered.

'We have been waiting for an hour,' Sir Fulke bellowed.

'Good!' Sir John replied. 'And, by the sod, you will wait another bloody hour if I want it! We are here on the King's business. Four men lie dead, one of them Sir Ralph Whitton, a high-ranking official, albeit a perfect bastard!'

Mistress Philippa looked up, her face a white mask of fury. Athelstan closed his eyes, even as Sir John gave the girl his most profuse apologies.

'So, shall we begin?' Sir Fulke shouted.

'In a while, in a while,' Athelstan murmured. 'We wait for Master Colebrooke and young Geoffrey, I believe.'

Cranston slumped on to a window seat next to Philippa but she turned her back. Athelstan brought a stool across and set out his writing tray, ink stand and pen on the table before him. Colebrooke, breathing heavily, pushed open the door.

'All is ready, Sir John.' The lieutenant went over to Athelstan. 'Here, Brother!'

Athelstan clasped his hand and hid up his voluminous sleeve what the lieutenant had given him. The friar stared round the silent chamber. It is here, he thought, we shall trap the murderer.

Chapter 14

Cranston twiddled his thumbs and beamed around. Athelstan noticed with quiet amusement that beneath his cloak Sir John was wearing doublet and hose of a deep bottle-green, with silver fringes and buttons to match. One of the coroner's best set of robes, a sure sign Cranston was in good fettle. The rest of the group, however, remained subdued: Hammond staring at the floor, Rastani gazing into the fire. Sir Fulke bit his lip and tapped his foot impatiently. Colebrooke fidgeted whilst Philippa stabbed furiously at a piece of embroidery. Footsteps sounded outside, the door swung open and Parchmeiner entered. Athelstan glimpsed the guards outside and was glad Colebrooke had the sense to have armed soldiers nearby. The young man was red-cheeked and breathless. He smiled at Philippa, crossed the room and kissed her gently on the lips before gazing round expectantly.

'Sir John! Brother Athelstan! Why the sudden affray?'

The friar rose. 'Shalom, Geoffrey!'

'Peace to you, Brother.' The young man's face was suddenly tinged a deep red.

Athelstan smiled. 'How do you know the Arabic word for peace?'

The young man shrugged. 'I buy and sell. I know more than one language.'

'Pull back your cuffs, Master Parchmeiner!'

The young man looked flustered. 'Why?'

'Pull them back!'

'I can't see...'

'Pull them back!' Cranston ordered. 'Now!'

Parchmeiner undid the embroidered cuffs and Athelstan gazed down at the white rings which broke the dark flesh of the man's wrists.

'How did you come by the marks of slave manacles?' Athelstan asked. 'Trading?' He moved quickly and suddenly pulled the man's knife from his belt and tossed it across to Cranston. 'And how are your relatives in Bristol? Have you heard from them?'

The young man's eyes narrowed and Athelstan noticed his determined mouth and chin. The veil was slipping. In future, Athelstan promised himself quietly, he would study faces more closely.

'Don't lie, Geoffrey. You have no relatives in Bristol. You sent no letters. The West Country has been cut off by snow. How could you be in communication with people in Bristol when the western roads have been impassable?' Athelstan smiled bleakly at Cranston. 'Isn't it strange how such an innocent remark brought all these matters to a head?' Athelstan stepped closer, aware of the sudden change of atmosphere in the room. Philippa now stood, her fist pressed to her mouth. The others were tense, immobile as statues.

'But your name's not Parchmeiner, is it?' Cranston barked.

Athelstan took a step nearer. 'Who are you?' he said quietly. 'Mark Burghgesh?'

A smile flickered across Parchmeiner's face as he tried to assert himself. 'What nonsense is this?' he snapped. 'Philippa, I have known you two years. I come from

Bristol. My sister lives there. She will be here in a few days.'

Athelstan shook his head. 'No, she won't, young man. That road is blocked, both literally and metaphorically. Moreover,' he continued, 'you still haven't told us about the rings round your wrists.'

The young man looked away. 'I used to wear bracelets,' he lied glibly.

'This is nonsense,' Philippa intervened. 'Are you going to accuse Geoffrey of my father's murder?'

'Yes, I am!' Athelstan announced.

'But someone climbed the North Bastion!'

'No, they didn't!' Athelstan looked at Colebrooke. 'Master Lieutenant, you have everything ready?'

Colebrooke blinked nervously and nodded.

'Then let us begin,' Cranston barked. 'Master Lieutenant, you have armed guards and archers, both in the corridor and downstairs?'

'Yes, Sir John.'

'Good. They will guard everyone here. If anyone attempts to escape, shoot them!'

With Cranston leading, they walked out of the chamber, down the stairs and out across Tower Green beyond the first curtain wall to where the lonely, bleak North Bastion stood. They entered the doorway and stood in the porch where the two soldiers stood expectantly on guard. On the far wall there was a wooden rack with metal hooks from which keys hung.

'Now,' Athelstan said to the guards, 'on the morning Sir Ralph was found dead… tell me again what happened.'

One of the soldiers grimaced. 'I takes young Parchmeiner upstairs,' he said. 'No, I take the key from the rack.

I takes him upstairs. I unlocks the door to the passageway, let him through, lock it and come down.'

'Then what?'

'Well,' the second soldier interrupted, 'we hear Master Geoffrey calling Sir Ralph.'

'What happened then?' Athelstan asked.

'He comes back and knocks on the door.' The fellow pointed to the top of the stairs. 'We unlock it, he comes down and sends for the lieutenant.'

'No,' Athelstan interrupted. 'Something else happened, or so you told us.'

One of the guards scratched his unshaven chin.

'Ah,' his companion spoke up. 'I knows what. Young Geoffrey said he would rouse Sir Ralph himself and we gives him the key. He then goes up the stairs, changes his mind, comes back, returns the key and goes for Master Colebrooke.'

'Good,' Athelstan smiled. 'Now, Sir John, I will retrace Parchmeiner's steps.' He glanced quickly at the young man, whose face was pale, eyes narrowed and watchful. Philippa was staring at him like a child who cannot explain the sudden, unexpected mood of a parent. Sir Fulke and the chaplain stood bemused but Athelstan noticed the mute Rastani had edged closer to Parchmeiner, his hand not far from the knife hilt stuck in his scabbard.

'My Lord Coroner,' Athelstan exclaimed, 'before we go any further, everyone should give up their arms except Lieutenant Colebrooke.'

There were mild protests, but Cranston repeated Athelstan's order and knives and swords clattered to the ground in an untidy heap.

'Now we shall begin,' Athelstan said. 'Sir John, you will start counting?'

The friar nodded to one of the guards. 'Unlock the door at the top!'

Cranston bellowed out the numbers as Athelstan went upstairs. The door swung open and was locked behind him. Cranston stopped for a few seconds at number twenty as he heard Athelstan call out Sir Ralph's name before continuing. He had just passed the number fifty when he heard Athelstan pounding on the door at the top of the steps. One of the guards ran up and opened the door. Athelstan emerged. He tripped down the steps behind the soldier.

'Now,' the friar exclaimed, 'I want the key to Sir Ralph's chamber!'

Athelstan took one of the keys from its hook and went halfway back up the stairs, shook his head and came down.

'On second thought,' he said, 'let us send for Master Colebrooke.' He handed the key back to the soldier. 'Tell me,' the friar asked, 'did I take any longer than young Geoffrey?'

'No, about the same. He was a little longer in the passageway, but not much.'

Sir Fulke pushed his way forward. 'What does this all mean?' he demanded.

Athelstan smiled. 'Now I will show you. Master lieutenant, re-open the door at the top of the stairs and let us all go up.'

The lieutenant ran to re-open the door and they all followed him down the cold, vaulted passageway. Colebrooke unlocked Whitton's chamber and they followed him in. Sir Fulke promptly cursed. Philippa gave a short scream. The chamber was icy cold, the shutters wide open, and the bolster on the dirty, grey mattress of the four-poster bed had been savagely slashed, the goose feathers trickling out in grisly reminder of Sir Ralph's murder.

'Who did this? What evil nonsense is this?' Hammond the chaplain spoke up.

Athelstan ignored him and confronted Parchmeiner.

'You know what I have done,' he said quietly. 'Exactly what you did on the morning you murdered Sir Ralph, and I'll tell you how. First, when Sir Ralph moved to the North Bastion, you acted the role of the obsequious future son-in-law. You helped him move a few possessions across. You see, the chamber was guarded when Sir Ralph moved in but not before, so you carefully oiled the hinges and the lock of the door, which explains the oil stains in the corridor outside. Secondly, the floor above is sealed off, and at the far end of the corridor outside is a pile of fallen masonry. You hid a dagger there amongst the rubble, as I asked Colebrooke to conceal Sir John's. After I slashed the bolster, I hid the dagger there again. On the night before Sir Ralph died, you sat with him at table. You helped him to drink deeply, aided probably by a fairly strong sleeping potion, enough to make him drowsy. Thirdly, you helped Sir Ralph to the foot of the steps, the guards took him up to his chamber, and it is probably then that you exchanged the keys. You took the one Sir Ralph left there for the use of the guards and slipped another on to the hook. I asked Colebrooke to do the same. He handed the real key to me when we were in Mistress Philippa's chamber.' Athelstan paused. 'The next morning you come across, the guards search you, but you have nothing except your own harmless possessions, which,' Athelstan touched the young man's side carefully, 'like any merchant, include a ring of keys. You climb the steps, the guards let you through, and you proceed to Sir Ralph's chamber. As you knock and shout, you open the door silently because the lock hinges are so well oiled. The rest was easy.'

'But—' Colebrooke intervened.

'Not yet,' Athelstan snapped back. He studied Parchmeiner's eyes carefully. 'Once inside, you move very quickly. The shutters are unlatched, the cold air streams in. You cross to Whitton's bed and yank his head back. Sir Ralph, still in a heavy stupor, may have opened his eyes for a brief few seconds as you slashed his throat. You wipe the knife on the bedclothes, lock the door, slip the knife back into its hiding place and stand knocking on the door at the far end of the corridor.'

Athelstan saw the faint look of amusement in Parchmeiner's eyes, though the young man's face remained cold and impassive.

'It was then,' Athelstan continued, 'that you slipped the key to Sir Ralph's chamber off your ring. You go downstairs, ask for the false key, go back up the steps and make the sudden change whilst your back is turned. You return the correct key to the guards. I have just proved two keys can look alike. You then go looking for Colebrooke.'

'Oh, no!' Philippa, her face now white and drawn, as she slumped against Sir Fulke, her eyes fixed on Geoffrey. 'Oh, please God, no!' she repeated.

'It happened that way,' Cranston airily declared. 'My clerk has proved it. The guards simply saw and heard what they were supposed to.'

'Brother Athelstan!'

'Yes, Sir Fulke?'

'My brother's body was cold when the lieutenant came up.'

'Of course it was,' Cranston snapped. 'The brazier and the fire had died, which makes me think Whitton was drugged. The murderer threw the shutters open and the icy air rushed in. Remember, it was a freezing cold morning, and of course Master Parchmeiner's delay in sending for Colebrooke would have helped matters.'

Athelstan suddenly caught a glimpse of colour from the corner of his eyes. 'Sir John! Rastani!'

The coroner, in spite of his bulk, moved quickly. He caught the mute even as the fellow sprang at his master's assassin. Cranston hoisted the struggling man by the front of his jerkin as easily as a baby.

'You, sir,' the coroner said quietly, 'will keep your place till these matters are finished!' He shook Rastani as if he was a rag doll. 'You understand?'

The mute threw one vicious glance at Parchmeiner.

'Do you understand?' Cranston's grip tightened.

The mute's mouth opened and shut, then he nodded slowly. Cranston gently lowered him and two of Colebrooke's guards now took up position on either side of the Moor.

'You will watch him!' Cranston ordered curtly. 'Well, come on, pull your swords!'

During this spectacle, Parchmeiner never turned a hair but looked coolly at the friar, who knew he was in the presence of a natural killer, someone who had seized his opportunity to wreak the most terrible vengeance.

'Master Colebrooke!' Athelstan called, not taking his eyes off the murderer. 'I want Master Parchmeiner's hands bound and a rope tied round his waist.'

Colebrooke rapped out commands and one of the guards forced Parchmeiner's arms behind his back, tying both wrists and thumbs together. Another soldier unloosed his belt and pushed one end through Parchmeiner's, wrapping the other end tightly round his own wrist guard. Athelstan relaxed. He gazed round the freezing death chamber.

'We need not stay here,' he declared. 'We may return to Mistress Philippa's chamber.'

The young girl hardly said a word but moaned softly as her uncle enfolded her in his arms. The group left the North Bastion. As they crossed Tower Green, Colebrooke, now aware of the danger, ordered a serjeant-at-arms to beat the tambour, calling the garrison to arms. Orders rang out, gates were closed, and as they went up the steps to Philippa's chamber, Athelstan heard men-at-arms and archers taking up positions below. He turned and smiled at Cranston.

'I must apologise. Your dagger is still in the pile of masonry in the North Bastion tower.'

'Don't worry,' he muttered. 'What I have seen is worth more than a thousand daggers.'

In the chamber, Parchmeiner stood between the two guards. Athelstan looked at him curiously for the young man was now smiling as if savouring some secret joke. The rest were a quiet, captive audience. Rastani, sullen and withdrawn, slumped on a stool between two burly serjeants-at-arms. Philippa moaned softly, lost in her own grief, flanked on either side by her uncle and the chaplain. Cranston filled himself a goblet of wine. Athelstan went and crouched near the fire, warming his hands over the flames.

'The other deaths were easy,' he continued evenly. 'The night Mowbray died, he went up on the parapet near the Salt Tower whilst the rest of you gathered here in Philippa's chamber for supper. I suspect Master Parchmeiner arrived last. You see Mowbray, like any soldier,' he turned and grinned at Colebrooke, 'was a creature of habit. Let us dismiss Master Parchmeiner's fear of heights as a lie. He knew Mowbray was on the far side of the parapet, standing in his usual spot, so he crept up and placed the butt of a spear or an axe pole at the top of the steps, wedging it neatly between the crenellations of the wall. He then comes to Mistress Philippa's chamber and the meal begins.'

'But he never left,' Sir Fulke interrupted. 'He never left to ring the tocsin bell!'

'Of course he didn't!' Cranston answered. 'Master Colebrooke, everything is ready? The garrison has been warned? Well,' Cranston slammed his wine goblet down on the table, 'I need to relieve myself. I understand there's a garderobe down the passage?'

Sir Fulke, a perplexed look on his face, nodded. Cranston went out of the side door. The rest of the group remained impassive like figures in a fresco. Suddenly everyone jumped as the great tocsin bell began to sound, followed by shouted orders, men's feet running, and then the bell stopped tolling. Cranston, grinning from ear to ear, sauntered back into the room.

'Who rang the bell?' the chaplain squeaked.

'I did,' Sir John replied.

'How?'

'What Sir John did,' Athelstan replied quietly, turning his back to the fire, 'was to go along to the garderobe. An archer, carrying a small arbalest, went with him. I noticed that the window above the privy overlooked Tower Green. The archer, standing behind the curtain which hides the privy, shot a bolt and hit the bell.' Athelstan shrugged. 'You know the mechanism. Once it is tilted slightly the bell begins to toll.'

'But it was dark,' Sir Fulke spoke up.

'No, Sir Fulke. As you may remember, at night there are torches around the bell.'

'But the bolt was never found!'

'Of course not. The snow around the tocsin was thick and undisturbed. The bolt would hit the bell and fall into the snow. When the soldiers from the garrison checked why the bell had been rung, they would be looking for footprints, not a crossbow bolt, no bigger than your hand, embedded deep in the snow and ice.'

'And the crossbow?' Parchmeiner spoke for the first time, his voice harsh and staccato.

Athelstan shook his head. 'Like the dagger, you could have left it in the corridor and, when finished, replaced it or dropped it down the privy hole. And who would notice? As you hastily left the garderobe and ran back to the chamber, everything was in uproar as the tocsin sounded. No one would see any connection between your leaving and the bell sounding. You had gone to the privy, not downstairs, and the guards had seen no one approach the bell. The rest was easy,' Athelstan murmured. 'In night-shrouded confusion, you ran up to the parapet and tossed the weapon over the wall into the ditch. If anyone saw you on the steps, you could always pass as a hero looking for the cause of poor Mowbray's death.' Athelstan looked at Cranston. 'When Sir John told me about the crossbow bolt found embedded in the bear, I suddenly realised how the tocsin bell could have been so mysteriously sounded.' Athelstan felt suddenly tired and rubbed his face with his hands.

'God knows,' the coroner boomed, going to stand legs apart in front of the prisoner, 'how you lured poor Horne to his death, though the man was so full of fears it would be easy enough to play on them.' Cranston clutched

Parchmeiner's face in his hand and squeezed it tightly. 'I saw the grisly remains of your work.'

Parchmeiner brought his head back, smiled, and spat full into Cranston's face. The coroner wiped the spittle from his cheek with the hem of his robe then, bringing his hand back, slapped Parchmeiner across the face. He turned and looked at Athelstan as the young man struggled between his guards.

'Don't worry,' Cranston said. 'I won't strike him again, but he deserved that for bringing his evil deeds into my house and under my roof.'

He went and refilled his wine goblet. He took it over and offered it to Philippa where she sat with her uncle, but she wouldn't even raise her head. Sir Fulke looked away so Cranston walked into the middle of the room, sipping from the cup. 'Finally, Fitzormonde's death.' He made a face. 'That was easy.' He gestured at Parchmeiner. 'Our young killer here pretends to leave the Tower, and with people milling about during the great thaw, no one would really notice him slipping back in again, perhaps wearing a different cloak or hood. There are enough shadowy corners in this fortress to hide an army. Every evening Fitzormonde always went to see the bear and Parchmeiner seized this opportunity. Once again armed with an arbalest, he fires. The beast, enraged, launches itself at Fitzormonde. The badly secured chain snaps and the hospitaller dies. Whilst Geoffrey exploits the chaos to slip through the main gate or one of the postern doors and be safe beyond reproach.'

'You have no proof!' Parchmeiner rasped. 'No proof at all!'

'No, but we can get it!' Athelstan answered. 'First, I can prove that a man may climb the North Bastion in the middle of the night and at the dead of winter. But could he climb down again? I can examine the rubble outside Sir Ralph's chamber for stains of blood from the dagger you hid there but undoubtedly collected later. Master Colebrooke can also make enquiries about who oiled the locks and doors of Sir Ralph's chambers. The tocsin can be examined for the mark of a crossbow bolt and the ground carefully searched, for it undoubtedly still lies hidden in the ice and snow. We could start making enquiries about who was where on the night Adam Horne died.' Athelstan walked up to the white-faced man. 'We can also hold you in a dungeon here until the snow melts, and make careful investigations after these friends and relatives of yours in Bristol.'

'But why? Why?' Philippa's gaunt face was anguished, dark shadows appearing under her reddened eyes. 'Why?' she screamed.

'Fifteen years ago,' Cranston replied, too full of pity to look at her, 'your father and the others whom Parchmeiner murdered served as knights in Outremer under the leadership of Sir Bartholomew Burghgesh. You have heard the name mentioned? Your father,' Cranston continued, not waiting for a reply, 'and the others cruelly betrayed Sir Bartholomew in order to seize certain treasure he had taken from the Caliph of Egypt. Now Sir Bartholomew left Cyprus for Genoa but the others, led by Sir Ralph, secretly informed the Caliph and the ship Sir Bartholomew was travelling on was attacked.' Cranston scratched his head. 'The accepted story is that Bartholomew died on that ship but, as we now know, three years ago, just before Christmas, Burghgesh came to see your father at the Tower. Sir Ralph, either by trickery or force, took Sir Bartholomew captive and imprisoned him in a dungeon beneath this very tower. He used the madcap Red Hand to block up the cell. After all, who would listen to the rantings of an idiot?' Cranston whirled round as the young man struggled between his guards.

'He is here?' Geoffrey shouted. 'Bartholomew's body is here?' Parchmeiner suddenly went limp. 'Oh, God!' he whispered. 'If only I had known!'

Athelstan crossed to his side. All the hatred and arrogance in the assassin's face had now fled and the friar felt a twinge of compassion at the tears brimming in the young man's eyes.

'Who are you?' Athelstan whispered. 'Tell me! You have my promise, you will see Bartholomew's last resting place.'

Parchmeiner looked down at the floor. 'Burghgesh was not my father,' he replied in a faraway voice. 'But I wish to God he had been. I was on the same ship as him when it was taken. I was only an orphan, so I clung to Sir Bartholomew.' Geoffrey smiled faintly. 'He protected me,' he whispered. 'He put me behind him and fought like a paladin until the Moors promised both of us our lives if he surrendered.' The young man looked up and blinked. 'They kept their word, but Bartholomew was beaten with the bastinado until the soles of his feet turned to raw flesh. Then we were sold as slaves to a merchant in Alexandria. Sir Bartholomew tended the garden and I was put to work in the scriptorium, curing and storing parchment. The years passed. Sir Bartholomew never gave up hope. He looked after me, treated me as a son, protected me against those who would have preferred to treat me like a woman. One night, Bartholomew cut our master's throat and rifled his treasure room. We fled across the desert to Damietta, bribed a merchant and took ship to Cyprus, thence to Genoa and across Europe to Southampton.'

'How long ago was this?'

'Three years ago. Sir Bartholomew had told me about Whitton and the treasure but,' the young man's voice almost broke, 'my master was good and true. He still couldn't accept that his comrades—' the words were spat out '—his *comrades* had betrayed him!' The young man shook his head, mouthing oaths quietly to himself. 'We travelled to London. Sir Bartholomew still had the treasure he had stolen from the merchant in Alexandria, gold and silver coins, so we lived like lords in a tavern near Barbican Street.' Geoffrey now stared at Athelstan. 'Can you believe that, Brother? He wouldn't accept he had been betrayed. He left me in the tavern and went to Woodforde, but returned disconsolate. His wife and son were both dead and the manor house in disrepair. We stayed for a while until Sir Bartholomew said his comrades would meet as planned near the Tower every Advent before Christmas.' The young man licked his lips. 'Sir Bartholomew made enquiries as to what had happened to each of his comrades. Two were hospitallers, one a merchant.' Geoffrey laughed. 'Sir Bartholomew, God bless him, was even pleased to hear that Whitton was now Constable of the Tower and told me all about this fortress, every nook and cranny.'

The murderer stirred restlessly between his captors, now lost in his own memories. 'Bartholomew went to meet Whitton. He said he would find out the truth, whatever it cost.' The young man made a grimace. 'But he didn't return and my own suspicions were proved correct. Whitton, who had betrayed him fifteen years ago, had now used his position to have Bartholomew killed.' He glared at Athelstan. 'I am glad I killed them! I gave them fair warning. I used the same sign Bartholomew always shared with me in our captivity – the three-masted ship which brought us together.'

'And me?' Philippa cried. 'What about me?'

'What about you?'

'Didn't you love me?'

The young man laughed. 'You need a heart to love, Philippa. I have no heart, no soul. Bartholomew was my life.' He dismissed the girl with a contemptuous glance. 'I used you,' he continued, ignoring her loud sobbing. 'I took Bartholomew's gold to plot Whitton's downfall. I knew about manuscripts and vellum, so I became Geoffrey Parchmeiner. Oh, by the way, Geoffrey is my Christian name. Geoffrey Burghgesh, you can call me. I sold the best parchment for a pittance to the Tower. I became friendly with the constable's daughter and wheedled my way into her affections.' The murderer smiled to himself.

'You studied the constable? His movements? His moods?'

'Oh, yes, Brother. I knew that each Advent he and the other murderers met to feast and glory in their sin. I became what he wanted me to be – a rich young merchant besotted with his rather plain daughter. You see, Brother, if you spend your youth as a prisoner of the Moors, you learn how to act. You have to in order to survive.'

'Why now?' Cranston barked. 'Why not a year ago?'

The young man shook his head. 'Sir John, I had to plan. I had to study my quarry, and when the Thames froze over, I struck. Oh, I enjoyed it. I would have been successful if it hadn't been for you, Brother. I sent Horne's head to Sir John to show justice had been done.'

The young man grinned at Cranston as if relating a good story, and Athelstan realised for the first time that Geoffrey's mind was disturbed.

'Of course,' he continued, 'my scheme might have gone awry, but if so, I would have plotted something else. After all, there's more than one road to Hell. And I waited because revenge, as you can all appreciate, is a dish best served cold.'

'You bastard!' Sir Fulke shouted.

'A limb of Satan!' Hammond cried.

'Perhaps,' Parchmeiner retorted. 'But they all deserved to die.'

'No, they didn't,' Athelstan said quietly. 'They did wrong but at least two of them were genuinely sorry. You could have brought an appeal against them at King's Bench. The very accusation would have destroyed Sir Ralph.'

'I am God's judgment!' Parchmeiner yelled, glaring round the room. 'I am their doom! Horne knew that when he saw me dressed in armour similar to that Sir Bartholomew had worn.' He turned and spat in Sir Fulke's direction. 'God damn you and all your family. I even took the buckle from your shoe and left it on the ice. It would have been a nice twist, eh? To be hanged for the murder of your own brother?'

Sir Fulke turned his back.

'The rest was so easy,' Geoffrey continued. 'The letters were sent. Sir Ralph moved to the North Bastion. I oiled both the hinges and lock of the chamber door, and hid a dagger in the rubble in the passageway. I changed the keys when I helped the drunken bastard to his last resting place.'

'And the rest?' Athelstan asked.

'Oh, Mowbray was easy, sulking in the darkness. I'd been up to the parapet before and he'd never noticed. I did place an arbalest in the corridor and hit the tocsin bell then threw it down the sewer hole.' Geoffrey giggled. 'Horne was a victim of his own fears, a veritable fool, and I did warn Fitzormonde about that bear.' The assassin bit his lip. 'I could have killed them by other means but, once Whitton accepted me, the game had to be played.'

Cranston walked up to face him. 'Geoffrey Parchmeiner,' he intoned, 'also known as Burghgesh, I arrest you for murder. You will be taken to Newgate prison and, at a fixed time, answer for your terrible crimes in the court of King's Bench.' He looked round and nodded at Colebrooke. 'Take him away.'

'I want to see Bartholomew's last resting place!'

'Yes, you may,' Athelstan replied. 'Master Lieutenant, let him look at what we discovered this morning, but bind him well!'

The murderer threw one ferocious look at Fulke before Colebrooke and his soldiers hustled him out of the door. Athelstan sighed and looked round.

'Sir Fulke, Mistress Philippa, I am sorry.'

Philippa buried her face in her uncle's shoulder and silently wept. Sir Fulke just looked away.

'Sir John,' Athelstan said, 'we are finished here.' He put his writing implements back into the canvas bag, bowed to Sir Fulke and followed Sir John down the now darkening steps.

Outside Cranston took a deep breath. 'Thank God that's over. Brother!'

They walked under the forbidding mass of Wakefield Tower where they waited whilst a servant scurried back to the North Bastion tower to collect Cranston's dagger.

'A true murderer,' Sir John said quietly.

'Aye!' Athelstan replied. 'Insane or possessed, driven by hatred and revenge.' He looked up at the ravens cawing noisily above them. 'I'll be glad to be free of here, Sir John. This place has the stink of death about it.'

'It is called The House of the Red Slayer.'

'It's well named,' Athelstan replied.

They stood aside as Colebrooke marched by, Parchmeiner now tightly bound, almost hidden in the middle of his guards. The servant came back with Cranston's dagger and they left for the nearest tavern.

Sir John, of course, demanded refreshment after what he called his 'arduous labours'. Athelstan matched him cup for cup until they separated. Sir John went back to continue his rejoicing whilst Athelstan led a protesting Philomel up Billingsgate and across London Bridge to the dark loneliness of St Erconwald's.

–

A few days later, on Christmas Eve, Athelstan sat at his bench just inside the chancel screen, cradling a purring, contented Bonaventura on his lap. The friar looked around the sanctuary. All was ready for Christmas. The altar had a fresh cloth trimmed in gold, the sanctuary had been swept, the altar decorated with holly and ivy, the greenery and blood-red berries shimmering in the candlelight. The children had rehearsed their mummers' play. Athelstan laughed softly remembering how Crim, who had played the role of Joseph, had disrupted the proceedings by a short fist fight with one of the angels. Cecily had swept the nave and dusted the ledgers, and tomorrow he would celebrate three Masses: one at dawn, one mid-morning and the other at noon. Athelstan closed his eyes. He would remember his dead, his parents and his brother Francis, the men killed so violently in the Tower, as well as young Parchmeiner, who would surely hang.

The bishop had given him permission to re-consecrate the cemetery and Pike the ditcher had announced that Doctor Vincentius had left. Benedicta had been upset and Athelstan still felt wracked by feelings of guilt. He absent-mindedly kissed Bonaventura between the ears. He had apologised to all concerned for his ill temper on the morning he had heard about Tosspot's grave being desecrated. Athelstan sighed. All seemed to be in order, but was it? Christmas would pass, the Feast of the Epiphany would come, and with it fresh problems. Perhaps he would arrange a feast, a banquet for the parish council, to thank them for their kindness? Watkin had given him a new spoon made of horn; Ursula the pig woman a flitch of bacon; Pike the ditcher a new hoe for the garden; Ranulf the rat-catcher a pair of moleskin gloves and Benedicta, God bless her, a thick woollen cloak against the rigours of winter. Yet tomorrow, after Mass, he would be alone. Athelstan stared at the candle flames. Did God hide behind the fire? he wondered. He closed his eyes.

'Oh, Lord of the hidden flame,' he prayed, 'why is it so terrible to be alone?' He jumped, then grinned as the church door was flung open. 'Good Lord,' Athelstan beamed. 'I have heard of the power of prayer, but this is truly miraculous!'

'Monk!' Cranston bellowed, standing like a Colossus swathed in robes at the back of the church. 'I know you are here, Athelstan. Where are you bloody well hiding? By the sod, it's too early for your damned stars!'

Athelstan rose and walked under the chancel screen. 'Sir John, you are most welcome.' He looked carefully at the coroner. 'Surely not another murder?'

'I bloody well hope not!' Cranston roared, walking up the church, beating his hands together. 'I need some refreshment, Brother. You will join me?'

'Of course, Sir John, but this time I pay.'

'A priest who pays for what he drinks,' Cranston mocked. 'Yes, it must be Christmas.'

Athelstan collected his cloak from where he had flung it over the baptismal font and they walked out into the cold afternoon air.

'Let us go to the Piebald Horse!' Cranston suggested. 'A good cup of claret and some hot stew will do us both body and soul the world of good!'

They walked down the alley and into the welcoming warmth of the tavern. The one-handed landlord bustled across to meet them.

'Sir John,' he greeted. 'Brother Athelstan.'

He ushered them to a table near the fire as Cranston bellowed out his order. Sir John slouched on the bench and beamed round the tavern.

'You are busy, Sir John?'

'I am still looking for Roger Droxford, who murdered his master in Cheapside. I have had news of him hiding in a tavern near La Reole so perhaps I may call there on my journey home. But, Brother, let us forget murder. The Lady Maude has invited you to dinner tomorrow at three o'clock in the afternoon. You and the Lady Benedicta.'

Athelstan blushed as Cranston grinned devilishly.

'Don't worry, she'll come. I have been to her house, had a cup of claret, and given her a kiss on your behalf.'

'Sir John, you mock me.'

'"Sir John, you mock me,"' Cranston mimicked. 'Come, Brother, there's no sin in liking one of God's creation. You'll come?' He added, 'I have a present for you.'

Athelstan nodded whilst Cranston wondered if the astrolabe he had bought would really delight this strange star-searching friar. The landlord brought their goblets and two dishes of hot spiced mutton.

'So, Sir John, everything is tidied away. Sir Ralph's murderer has been caught; Doctor Vincentius has left; my cemetery is safe; tomorrow is Christmas, and all is well.'

Cranston slurped from his cup and smacked his lips.

'Aye, Brother, but spring will bring its own basket of troubles. The Red Slayer will strike again. Man will always kill his brother.' He sighed. 'And Lady Maude must be looked after, she and the child must be kept safe.' Sir John lowered his head and glared at Athelstan. 'The child will be a boy,' he announced flatly. 'And I shall call him Francis, the name of your dead brother.'

Athelstan caught his breath and put down the wine goblet.

'Sir John, that is most thoughtful. It's very kind.'

'He will become a knight,' Cranston continued expansively. 'A Justice of the Peace, a man of law.' He paused. 'Do you think he will look like me, Brother?'

Athelstan grinned. 'For the first few months he will, Sir John.'

Cranston caught the humour in Athelstan's voice. 'What do you mean, monk?' he asked dangerously.

'Well, Sir John, of course he will look like you. He'll be bald, red-faced, drink a lot, burp and fart, bellow and be full of hot air!'

The rest of the people in the tavern stopped what they were doing and gazed in astonishment as Sir John Cranston, the King's Coroner in the City, leaned back against the wall and roared with laughter till the tears streamed down his face.

Athelstan grinned till he thought of dealing with two Cranstons. Then the friar closed his eyes. 'Oh, Lord,' he whispered, 'what happens if it's twins?'